TIMESWEPT

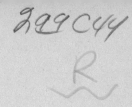

"**Intelligent characters, superb historical detailing, and sweet romance...***Time-Spun Rapture* **is an absorbing read!**"
—*Romantic Times*

SWEET DESIRE

"You're a damnable woman," Thomas smilingly chastised Astrid in the morning. "Seems my every encounter with thee results in fresh bruises."

"Poor baby," Astrid cooed, kissing his shoulder, which now bore the small bluish imprints of her teeth.

"God's blood!" he exclaimed, stretching back to look. "'Twas my battered arms I spoke of. I hadn't e'en noticed this freshed wound. 'Tis good I heal hastily." He kissed her nose.

"I'm sorry," she said with a pout. "I was only checking to see if you were real."

"And what did you discover?"

She laughed. "You're real and you taste good."

Other *Leisure* and *Love Spell* Books by
Thomasina Ring:
DREAMCATCHER
TIME-SPUN TREASURE

THOMASINA RING

To my mother, Olive Ring Klapp, a truly beautiful heroine who nurtured and encouraged my belief in wonder and magic; and to the memory of my father, Thomas Hilary Ring, always and forever my shining inspiration and guiding star.

Book Margins, Inc.

A BMI Edition

Published by special arrangement with Dorchester Publishing Co., Inc.

Printed in the United States of America.

Digest format printed and distributed exclusively for Book Margins, Inc., Ivyland, PA.

Prologue

In Richmond, Virginia, on April 30, 1989, the Sunday edition of *The Richmond Herald* carried a front-page story that set breakfast tables buzzing from Windsor Farms to Westover Hills.

LOCAL WOMAN MISSING

HOPEWELL, Va.—A four-county search is under way for a missing Richmond woman. Astrid Van Fleet, 27, an actress and part-time model, disappeared sometime Friday night in the Presquile National Wildlife Refuge near here. Her fiance, Derek Woodward, also from Richmond, reported her mysterious disappearance to local authorities Saturday morning.

Woodward, 28, son of Richmond industrialist Joseph Patterson Woodward III, told police he and Van Fleet had spent the night on rugged Turkey Island, a section of the Refuge. When he awoke, the woman and her sleeping bag were missing. Alarmed when unable to find her, Woodward rowed to shore and drove to Hopewell for assistance.

A police search of the island turned up no clues.

"It's as though she vanished into thin air," Sgt. Bob Perry of the Chesterfield County sheriff's office told reporters. "Her sandals and clothing were found at the site, but there's no trace of the woman or her sleeping bag." Perry said they found no signs of a struggle on the island.

Because the incident occurred on Federal property, the FBI has entered the investigation. Police departments of Hopewell and surrounding counties are cooperating. Dragging operations in the James River channel separating the island from the mainland began Saturday afternoon.

Van Fleet recently completed a critically acclaimed performance with the Henrico Players in Shakespeare's *Midsummer Night's Dream*. She has had numerous roles in dinner theater musicals and summer stock dramas in the Richmond area and has appeared in local fashion shows.

Three years ago, Van Fleet was selected Sweet-Scented Tobacco Queen at the Tidewater Tobacco Festival. She rents an apartment in the Fan District and has no known relatives in the area. Her parents, former Richmond residents John and Denise Van Fleet, were killed in a private plane accident in Florida last year. She has no brothers or sisters.

Van Fleet is said to be a strong swimmer who could have crossed the narrow channel unaided. Investigators, however, appear to discredit the theory she staged her own disappearance.

"It's hard to see where she could have gone or why," a puzzled Perry said. "As far as we know, she had no clothing and no transportation available out of the Refuge."

Acquaintances of the woman also expressed disbelief Van Fleet would have left the island alone.

"Astrid had no reason to do such a foolish thing," Richmond actress Joy Wilson, a friend of the missing woman, told reporters. "She was on top of the world at our cast party Friday night after the play's final performance."

Although trespassing on the Federal preserve is illegal, no charges have been filed. Woodward, described by friends as distraught, has been requested by police to stay available for further questioning. He and his family refused to speak with reporters.

According to police, Van Fleet is five feet, six inches tall, weighs approximately 115 pounds, has shoulder-length blonde hair and blue eyes.

"We hope the public can help us," Sgt. Perry said. He requested anyone with information or possible leads to contact the FBI or local authorities.

On page 23 of *The Herald*'s same edition, squeezed between large-type ads trumpeting a furniture sale and bargain videotape rentals, a shorter article received minimal attention.

DIG HITS SNAG

HOPEWELL, Va.—A disappointed team of archaeologists hit an unexpected snag yesterday in their exploratory dig at the 17th-century settlement of Bermuda Hundred.

Headed by noted resident archaeologist John Bothwick Sterns, the team has been working in an area identified as a "rubbish ditch," where settlers are believed to have dumped their garbage.

"We've found veritable treasures in the ditch during the past weeks," Sterns said, pointing with enthusiasm to rows of carefully tagged pottery shards, bent pieces of metal, and bone slivers. "It's been the stuff of dreams for us," Sterns added, admitting that "perhaps only a crusty old archaeologist could find dreams in the dust."

Until yesterday, Sterns' team was confident the ditch had been undisturbed since around 1700.

Yesterday they uncovered a 20th-century zipper.

"That blasts our 'undisturbed' theory to

high heaven," Sterns said. He explained that archaeologists date their finds according to *terminus post quem*, meaning the artifact judged most recent dictates the date of the last use of the find.

"There's no explaining why the zipper was on that strata," Sterns said with a shrug. "It's got us boggled."

According to Sterns, his team will continue its work until their funds run dry. He remains optimistic that the ditch, despite yesterday's puzzling find, is yielding valuable clues to domestic life in the settlement during the last quarter of the 17th-century.

"Of course, if we run across some Styrofoam cups, we'll have to go back to the drawing board," he said with good humor.

Chapter One

Astrid scooted down deeper into her sleeping bag. Blasted sunlight, she thought.

What time had she finally fallen asleep? Two? Three? Whatever, she knew she wasn't ready to face that sun yet—nor Derek, either, for that matter.

She was furious with herself. Why in hell hadn't she had the guts last night to break off this stupid engagement? Screwing up her face, she thumbed the heavy diamond ring in sluggish circles around her finger.

A pity to have to give that up, but the big problem was Derek—and he came along with the ring. Astrid knew she couldn't ignore the hard truth any longer. She'd reached the point where she couldn't stand the guy.

Oh, sure, she'd been captivated at first by the

Woodward charm, but she'd discovered along the way nothing else was behind it.

Not a damn thing.

Her mouth tasted sour and she wrinkled her nose. Face it, sister, you're not ready to settle down. She knew she enjoyed her freedom far too much to trap herself into a marriage to anybody, let alone Derek.

Oh, well, she thought, I'll make the break today. Our show's over as much as *Midsummer*. The curtain's down, and the magic's gone. She lifted an eyebrow. Guess she'd have to call last night one more for the road.

She tried to console herself. No one could act with any sense after all that champagne. Lord knows, the cast was giddy enough after the play's successful run. When Derek brought over those two cases of bubbly everyone took off like firecrackers.

Astrid's head throbbed, reminding her that champagne caused a whale of a lot of trouble per ounce.

And it sure had led her down the primrose path last night. How else could she explain going along with Derek's wild idea to camp out in a place like this? She squirmed restlessly, remembering it was brambles, not primroses, that had greeted them on the dark, silent island.

But it was neither dark nor silent any longer. A cacophony of bird noise pierced through her downy cocoon. Was all nature conspiring against her this morning? Even her body wasn't cooperating. Perspiration dribbled in ticklish streams over her bare skin.

Tentatively, Astrid stuck her head out for a breath of air, squeezing her eyes shut to avoid the shafts of sunlight.

What was that heavenly smell? The wind's off the river, she figured, pushing away those awful fumes from Hopewell's chemical plants.

She smiled. The fresh air was a needed tonic! She might bounce back to life after all.

Astrid opened her eyes. Tall trees towered over her, and tiny geometric patterns of a bright, crystalline blue glimmered through their leaves. She grimaced again as a dull ache pounded at her temples.

She turned to face Derek.

Now where the hell had he gone?

She frowned at the empty ground and underbrush beside her. It's just like him to sneak off and hide behind a tree.

"Okay, you clown! Come back here, and bring me my clothes, for God's sake." Her angry voice reverberated against the creeper-entwined trees. A swishing flutter high above was the only response. Startled, she jerked her head toward the sound and saw a flock of large black birds beating their wings and soaring away.

Astrid slid back into the dark green sleeping bag.

Better keep quiet, she warned herself. We're trespassers on this damned island. Illegal as hell. All we need is some game warden—or whoever watches over this Godforsaken place—to discover us. Derek had probably wandered off to take a leak, but why would he take his sleeping bag and her clothes with him?

But then, when did Derek ever do anything she could understand?

She wondered what kind of sentences they gave for trespassing on a wildlife refuge.

Wildlife! She shuddered. How wild? She must have been wild herself to go along with this latest insanity of Derek's.

A soft nudge punched the side of her sleeping bag.

Momentary terror faded into begrudging relief. He's back, she cheered silently. At last she could get dressed and return to civilization.

"It's about time!" she sputtered, coming up for air. "Where in hell have you . . ."

The scream froze in her throat. An icy pair of tiny black eyes loomed over her.

Snake!

Paralyzed, she watched the grotesque head aim for her face.

"No!" Her scream exploded, and she scurried down inside the bag. Terrified, she cringed in the darkness, knowing full well her thin shield was no barrier against ripping fangs.

Instead, there was a metallic *whoosh*! followed by a heavy silence.

Astrid held her breath, straining to hear something other than the deafening thump of her heartbeat.

A sturdier nudge shoved her hip. Instinctively, she slid away.

"The moccasin's killed. Who might you be?"

The voice was deep, resonant and unfamiliar. The game warden? He'd probably saved her life. Now, she supposed, he would arrest her.

She peeked through the top of the bag. Two heavy brown leather boots stood planted beside her, odd boots, flaring in wide cuffs below the knees. And then came white stockings and tan knickers. Crazy kind of uniform!

And that sword. Rapierlike, it was held by a huge, tanned hand topped by a ballooning white sleeve.

The tall stranger was a menacing shadow over her, blocking the eastern sun. Moving her eyes up with apprehension, she could see he wore something that looked like a vest over his open-necked shirt. Two wide straps crisscrossed his large chest. His face was dark, the features hidden by the wide brim of his hat.

"Are you deaf, woman? I asked who you might be."

"Astrid Van Fleet," she answered quickly. She realized her voice was midway between croak and squeak. Offer only name, rank, and serial number, she reminded herself.

She felt her courage returning. After all, how serious could trespassing be? Eviction and a fine, maybe? No big deal.

"Peculiar name," he said. "How came you here?"

"Me? I . . . I don't remember." Good ploy. Stall for time until Derek gets back and gets us out of this pickle.

And what the hell does this guy mean by "peculiar name?" What's so goddamned peculiar about it?

The man bent to touch the sleeping bag with his free hand. He still held the sword in his right hand.

"That's a devilish bondage entrapping thee, woman. Who did this to thee?"

Bondage? Doesn't this creep know a sleeping bag when he sees one? Are the Feds hiring certified nuts now?

She had a twinge of fear. Maybe he wasn't a game warden, after all. He could be a crazy weirdo. Where in hell is that Derek Woodward?

Fighting rising panic, Astrid tried to think fast. She was naked, vulnerable and absolutely defenseless.

Defenseless? Maybe not. You're an actress, she reminded herself. It's worth a try.

She moaned and bobbed her head back and forth. "I'm badly hurt," she groaned. "Get help. I think my legs are broken. Perhaps my arms, too. Please . . . get help."

With a heartrending sigh, Astrid pretended to pass out.

She felt a large cool hand press against her forehead but commanded herself to stay still. The hand pulled away, and she heard a low grunt.

"God's blood," he mumbled. From the rustling sounds, she sensed he was standing up. Twigs crunched beneath boots. Thank God, she thought, he's leaving. His steps grew fainter.

Silence.

He's gone!

She sneaked one eye open to be sure. The man was about ten feet away, and he had paused for some reason. His back was turned toward her.

Watching the man and fervently wishing he'd get the hell away, she was struck again by his odd appearance. Those boots, the stockings and knickers. That funny hat and the long rifle strapped across his back. The silly sword.

He was dressed like something out of an old story or a period movie.

That's it! It was a costume. This is no off-the-wall nut. He's a lousy actor!

Astrid almost laughed out loud. So that's what's going on—one of Derek's tired pranks. He's gone and hired this guy to scare me out of my wits. It's like something he'd do.

Granted, the snake was a bit much, but I wouldn't put it past him.

Relieved, but madder than an aroused hornet, she watched the man turn around. His arms akimbo, his stupidly garbed legs spread, he seemed to be trying to decide what to do next.

She felt a wave of sympathy for him. He thinks I'm mortally wounded, poor soul. There's no way Derek could be paying him enough for a scene like this.

Astrid lifted her head and shouted over to him.

"The joke's over, mister. I'm okay, so don't get all worked up."

She yelled to the silent trees around her. "Derek! Come out, you bastard! I know you're back there somewhere. Enough's enough!"

The man rushed over to Astrid, thrust his sword at the lower end of one of the crisscrossed leather straps, and knelt beside her.

"Delirious, are you, poor woman?" he asked.

"No! I'm perfectly okay, I told you. Look, just go on to your next gig. This act's over—exposed—kaput!"

She shouted back to the trees. "Derek, where in hell are you?"

"I understand you not," the man said, pushing her down with his hands. "But it's help you need, and help we'll find." He reached for the bag's zipper.

Startled, Astrid clutched her inside zipper to keep it closed at all costs.

"What's this?" he asked, bending over to study the metal beneath his fingers. "'Tis a devilish iron device locking you in!"

He stood and grabbed his sword, pulling it out in one swift motion.

"No!"

Astrid's scream split the air as the long, sharp point plunged toward her.

Chapter Two

Thomas Arrington tore his blade through the strange restraint around the hysterical woman.

Deftly, he maneuvered the sharp point away from the woman herself, taking care to attack only the binding. The soft explosion of white feathers was his first surprise. The unclad body of the terrified female beneath him was even more unsettling.

Embarrassed, he stepped back, averting his face. "Forgive me, milady!" he exclaimed. "I wanted only to free you from your bondage." He flailed against the rising cloud of feathers, not daring to look down at the unfortunate wench lying like a shorn lamb at his feet.

The woman frantically pulled shreds of the silky stuff around her and sat up quickly.

"Dear God," she said, "what's going on? Who *are* you?"

Still not looking at her, he replaced his sword in his baldric, removed his hat and ran his fingers through loose black hair that had fallen over his forehead.

"The name is Thomas Arrington," he said. "From Eagle's Crest, across the river at Curles." He cleared his throat and glanced back at the woman. He was relieved to see she had covered herself, but he still felt concern.

The wench needs assistance. She appears to be the victim of an abduction, perchance unspeakably abused, bound and abandoned to die like an animal in the wilderness.

But by whom? And who is she? Her speech is passing strange. Where might she hail from? How best can I transport her to Edward's house where she can receive proper care?

His thoughts and questions whirled in circles, each centered by the momentary vision of the bare ripeness he had seen. He wanted to wipe that vision from his mind or alter it to quiet the earthly impact it had had upon him.

She's far too bony, he told himself. Signs of being half-starved—scurvy, mayhap. She's soiled and unkempt. Her hair is so pale and wild, covered now with feathers like a savage.

But the flesh he had seen, 'twas smooth as alabaster. Her breasts were firm and round with peaks like dewy strawberries.

Good wife Sarah, he pled to himself, 'tis been ten months since fate tore you from me. Forgive your stricken husband for casting his eyes on the nakedness of this frail woman and having such lust-filled thoughts. Too long I've been without thee, dear Sarah.

Fright emanated from the woman's large eyes. The look in those eyes propelled his thoughts back to her helpless plight. He must assure her he meant no harm, that he wished to get her to his brother's house where his mother and Ann could care for her.

Thomas kicked aside the severed snake and sat on a stump opposite the frightened woman. He laid down his hat and pretended to relax, stretching his long legs out before him.

"I mean thee no harm, lady," he began. He hoped quiet tones would reassure her. "My brother's home is nigh, and there his wife and my mother wait to clothe thee and make thee well. I could carry thee, for the brush would tear at your unshod feet."

The woman did not appear to understand. Whimpering, she clutched the tattered green stuff more tightly about her.

"Perchance we could get thee back to your family," he continued. "Have you memory as to how you came here? Name the rogues who abused you so, and I and my men will hunt them down and bring them to justice."

"I—I remember nothing," she said in a tremulous whisper, her eyes darting wildly as she slid back against a tree.

"You remembered your name," he said. "Van Fleet, is it? Astrid Van Fleet?"

"Yes. I—I think that's it."

Thomas picked up a broken twig from the

ground and studied it for a moment.

"Where might be your home, Astrid Van Fleet?" he asked.

"Richmond," she said.

"England?" He chuckled softly. "That's a far distance from here."

"Virginia. Richmond, Virginia," she said.

"The county out on the Northern Neck?"

"No, the state capital. Richmond."

He frowned. "Jamestown's our capital. I know no 'state' here."

She was quiet, eyeing him warily. He met her look, his face mirroring her expression. A glitter from her finger distracted him. The large diamond caught a sunbeam and scattered an arc of rainbows.

With a quick movement, the woman shoved her hand beneath the silky cloth.

Who is she? Thomas asked himself again. That jewel is not one that would belong to a tavern wench. Is she a pirate's woman? The wife or mistress of a gentleman? Van Fleet is not an English name. A Hollander? How came she here?

Suddenly the woman gasped. "Over there!" she said in an excited whisper. "I saw him. He's behind those trees!"

Thomas jumped to his feet and pulled out his sword. "Where?" he asked, keeping his voice low.

"There!" She pointed behind him. Thomas leaped over the stump and ran back into the forest.

* * *

Astrid watched him disappear. Her heart pounding, she gathered the flapping remnants of the sleeping bag around her and fled barefoot in the opposite direction.

It worked! she congratulated herself. I'm rid of that damn crazy man. Panic seized her. But I've got to hurry! She ran toward the channel, wincing as the underbrush cut into her feet.

Her thoughts raced faster than her legs. *Run.* Find the channel. Swim with the rotten nylon between my teeth if I have to. There has to be help over there. The man's insane. Get away!

Briers ripped her legs. Where's the water? We were only yards from the channel. Where in hell is the water?

Astrid reached a clearing. She paused, breathing heavily. A tobacco field? Why would there be a tobacco field in a wildlife refuge?

Don't stop! she warned herself, racing ahead through blurring rows of green plants. Blood from her feet and legs splattered red-brown dots on the crusty soil.

"Woman!"

The voice hit her like a fierce blow. He's coming. *Run*! As she sped through the field, rapid, shallow breaths tore from her lungs.

Looking over her shoulder, she saw the man gaining ground. Her legs felt heavy, wooden. *Run*! She stumbled before picking up speed.

There! A house. *People*!

"Help me!" she yelled. She could hear his boots now, getting closer. Too close.

Struggling forward, she yanked the piece of

nylon from her body and waved it in the air.

"Help me!" she sobbed. One of the distant figures looked up. She heard a shout, saw an arm pointing in her direction. The group of people began to run toward her.

They're coming! Wrapping the cloth back around her she fell exhausted to her knees.

I'm saved. He can't harm me now.

The heavy hands clasping her bare shoulders felt like cruel vises. Despite her fatigue, Astrid reacted in an instant. She shot a karate chop backward into his right forearm.

With a grunt of surprise, the man relaxed his hold. Cat-like, she jumped to her feet. Twirling to face him, tears streaming down her dusty cheeks, she slammed the heel of her hand into his hard stomach and swiftly aimed her knee upward.

His defensive maneuver was like lightning. With one hand he locked both of her wrists. With the other he pushed down her knee before it could slam into its vulnerable target.

"Let go of me!" she spat. A victorious glint lit her wild eyes as she heard her rescuers approach. She turned her head toward them.

"Sir!" a young man at the front of the running group shouted. "Be there some trouble?"

Sir? Astrid stared with disbelief at the people. There were three men, with two women following close behind. All of them were wearing old costumes.

"Forsooth, Thomas," panted a plump woman in calico, a white cap perched on her graying hair. "Who might this be?"

"She's crazed," the man said, keeping his hand tightly around Astrid's wrists. His eyes never leaving her startled face, he bent to pick up the shredded sleeping bag from the ground and handed it to the woman who had spoken. "Cover her, Mother. She needs help. We must get her to the house."

Astrid felt the cloth fall over her. Heard the woman clucking in sympathy.

Beyond understanding, she looked up into the cold gray eyes of the man holding her captive. Gray, like granite. Or slate. Hard. Inpenetrable. God help me, she thought weakly. Her knees buckled, and her head fell backward.

Before the darkness enveloped her, she saw only those cold, gray eyes.

Thomas Arrington swept the limp woman up into his arms and began running toward the house. The knot of curious people scurried after him. A murmur of excitement like a swarm of disturbed bees swirled around their heads.

"Ann, get Jenny from the buttery and tell her to fetch water," the plump woman ordered. Her short legs moved like efficient scissors beneath her skirt. "Haste! And tell Dorothy to get the broth hot."

"Thomas!" she shouted ahead through cupped hands. "Place her on my bed."

Thomas heard his mother's words as he took long strides toward the door of the brick house. The unconscious woman in his arms was amazingly light. But what a bundle of fiery temper she had been! He felt still the marks of her surprising blows on his arm and middle. A weaker man would be felled by such a sally, he thought. Where might a lady learn such maneuvers? And that charging knee was no lady's tactic.

Lady or not, she was in deep trouble. A furrow darkened his strong forehead. Additional trouble we need not in these days of turmoil, but there's naught we can do for the nonce but shelter the poor woman.

Woman. The smooth curve of her hip beneath his hand sent a distracting tingle up his arm. All too well he remembered the ripeness of that too-slender body, the patch of short golden curls between the narrow, white thighs. Even now a firm round breast lay exposed, its soft tip rising toward the brushing motion of his sleeve.

Thomas reined in his stampede of unruly thoughts, ashamed of the swelling surge pressing against his leather breeches. With an angry flick of his hand he tossed a ragged edge of the strange cloth over the lush mound.

Reaching the door, he composed himself before turning toward the gawking men close at his heels.

"Back to the fields!" he shouted with irritation. "The women alone will take charge of this. Hie!"

Obediently, their faces flushed from excitement, the men turned and slowly began walking away. One, with a full black beard, cast a final curious glance at the near naked woman folded within Master Thomas's arms.

"Hie, you laggards!" Thomas bellowed, spurring the three men into a trot toward the fields.

'Tis improper for the workers to see the lady unclad thus, he fumed to himself, aware of a sudden protective feeling for his helpless burden.

The little woman in calico approached the shade of the overhang where Thomas stood holding the stranger. Breathing rapidly from the exertion of her run, she reached for the door.

"I'll open for thee, Thomas," she said between pants, straightening her white cap with fluttering fingers. Wispy strands of soft gray had fallen loose from her knotted hair and clung in damp coils to her flushed cheeks. "Bring her into the parlor."

Thomas followed his mother into the house's breezy coolness and to a large room off the hall. Carefully, he laid the woman atop the bed's dimity coverlet.

Scowling down at the pallid tear-stained face, he saw no signs of life. No movement behind the closed eyelids, their long dark lashes sweeping contrasts against the colorless cheeks. No beating beneath the sprigs of yellow hair cleaving to her temples.

"Damnation!" he exclaimed. "Fetch a looking glass, Mother. We must see if she has breath!"

"There's breath, Thomas," the little woman assured him. "Her chest rises and falls." Busily, she threw a quilt over the stranger, arranging it beneath her chin.

"Ann and I will see to her. She and Jenny are bringing water."

Knowing his mother had dismissed him, Thomas looked down once more at the motionless stranger. Against the colorful patchwork quilt, her face seemed as white as the feathers clinging to her wild hair. He reached down to brush a golden strand from her forehead.

"She's been abused, Mother," he said. "I found her abandoned and in bondage out on the point and had to release her with my sword. She gives her name as Astrid Van Fleet, but the fright has emptied her mind of aught else."

"A Hollander?" his mother asked, a catch of disbelief in her voice. "How came a Hollander woman to be bound on our point?" She watched quizzically as her son reached down to remove a feather from the stranger's rumpled hair.

"I know not," he answered with a perplexed sigh. "Nor does she appear to." He frowned at the limp feather in his hand. "Perchance she'll remember more when she awakes."

Ann bustled into the room carrying an armful of clean linens and a bowl and pitcher. The young servant Jenny followed with a wooden tub of water.

Thomas walked over to the door and paused, looking back as the three women began filling the bowl from the pitcher and unfolding the linens.

"You'll find she's wearing a large diamond ring," he said. "We must assume she is someone of great importance and care for her accordingly."

"We shall care for her as a fellow being who needs us, Thomas," his mother responded with determination. "It matters not who she is."

Before he stooped to leave through the low

door, he saw his mother place a wet cloth over the woman's eyes.

Thomas walked to the large room across the hall, went over to the darkened fireplace and absently picked up a long clay pipe.

No, it matters not, he thought, packing the bowl with dried tobacco from a copper box on the rough-hewn mantle. What matters is that we rid ourselves of her at the earliest opportunity.

Using one of Edward's brass tampers, he packed down the tobacco, bent over to stick a long straw in the brazier and lifted the flame to his pipe. Sucking in the sweet smoke, he folded his tall frame down on a stool in the corner and exhaled a wisp of thin blue spirals. As he watched the smoke curl into the air, his dark brows pulled together in troubled thought.

Attention focused on this house was the last thing the family needed in these troubled times. And news of that woman being here would surely spread. His gray eyes clouded. Edward had impulsively marched south with Bacon to quell the Indians, and he knew Bacon had no commission from the governor.

Cries of rebellion were ringing through the colony. Aye, Governor Berkeley himself had labeled Bacon and his men rebels.

Thomas shook his head. Arringtons aren't rebels. We're law-abiding planters and respected as such throughout Virginia.

But brother Edward is a hothead! Listen to me he wouldn't when I told him his place was here with his wife and child and mother.

"You can watch over them, Thomas," he had

said. "My place is with Nathaniel and the others. Wrongs need be righted, and the governor does naught but sit on his fat hands. The Indians must be quieted, commission or no. Dear God, Thomas, you know better than most the savagery of some of the tribes. Your Sarah and little Betty were felled by the heathen Doegs up in Stafford County less than a year ago."

Deep lines of sadness etched Thomas's eyes as the dark clouds of memory rolled over him. He clenched the pipe between his teeth. *Aye, too well I know the raw wounds of sorrow. Would only that I had ne'er allowed them to venture into the frontier without me. Her ill mother needed tending, Sarah had insisted. The Douglas home was established and safe, everyone assured me.* Thomas breathed a sigh of agony. *Oh, dear God, if only Thee had willed my heart pierced by those arrows instead of theirs.*

He shook his head. *But Edward and Bacon and the others are wrong. Foolhardy skirmishes with the Indians can ne'er bring back Sarah and Betty. Naught can return them to me. Worries enough we have these troubled days without picking a fight with the savages, let alone with Governor Berkeley. Drought made tobacco prices so low we scarcely make enough to pay our taxes—and, aye, they were growing beyond reason.*

Looking down, he plucked a feather off the front of his buff waistcoat. *And now this wild, undisciplined mystery woman appears as though she's fallen from the sky, bound up in silk and feathers and clamped together with an* intricate device like one wrought by Satan himself.

Thomas stood and studied the bowl of his pipe. Its fire was dead, and he laid it on the brick hearth. Resting his elbow on the mantle, he twirled the tiny feather between his fingers. Downy, like the underside of a goose, he thought. A dear price they get for feathers of this quality. Peculiar to wrap an abandoned woman thus.

He frowned, weary with the questions that multiplied even as he thought.

I'm a man for action, not for thought, he told himself. Perchance there are clues back on the point—tracks or signs of a boat putting in. Feathers or not, she didn't fall from the sky! I'll take Jeremy with me and scour the area.

He moved toward the door. Casting a glance into the parlor he saw the women ministering to the quiet figure on the bed.

As he left the house, he muttered a silent prayer. Recover woman. We need get thee to someone who can find where you belong. We need be rid of thee—and soon.

Chapter Three

Dark cool wetness covered Astrid's eyes. She listened to the drone of voices around her, struggling to sift sense from the strange cadences.

Her consciousness had returned slowly like a gradual creeping up through heavy fog. At first her throat and limbs had refused to work. Now, she was purposely keeping them quiet. She needed time to think, time to sort through what was happening to her and understand—if such a thing was possible. Most of all, she needed time to plan a way out of this mess.

Let them think I'm still unconscious, she decided. Don't move until movement can help. Listen to them. Find out who they are and what they plan to do with me.

They seem to be taking good care of me for

the time being. They've put me on something as fluffy as a cloud and are tending to my sore legs. But who on earth are they?

Listen, Astrid, listen!

Are they speaking English? They have to be. How else could I pick out so many words?

But it must be a kind of dialect. It's English, but with lots of crazy old-fashioned words like the dialogue in *Midsummer*. Work on those vowels, Astrid, and you can understand.

Understand? Their words, maybe. But how does one understand a nightmare? An island's no longer an island. You're chased by a wild man. Then a group of costumed people come up and call him "sir," obviously on his side but also treating you well.

Have I run into some way-out sect? Stay quiet. Find a way to escape. Listen.

"She's a Hollander, methinks. Thomas says her name's Astrid Van Fleet. She remembers naught else." *A woman's voice.*

"Never have I seen hair so light. 'Tis like the tassels on summer maize. I've heard Hollanders have such hair." *Another woman. That's two.*

"How came she here like this without clothing?" *Yet another. That makes three.*

"She was bound, Thomas said. He set her free with his sword." *Number one again.*

"The peculiar green stuff on the floor yon. 'Twas that part of the binding?" *That's number two speaking.*

"I know not, Ann. Faugh! Be gentle there, child. You mustn't rub on those torn legs so. Here, let me show you. Pat thusly, and keep the linens fresh with water." *She called number two "Ann." Ahh . . . that feels better!*

"I'll put clouts on her feet. They're sorely blooded." *Oooh, that's glorious! Clouts must be wet bandages.*

"Good, Jenny. Ann, replace that clout over her eyes."

"Aye, Mother Arrington."

The one in charge must be the crazy man's mother. Mother Arrington. Number three's name is Jenny. Okay. Only three of them. Thank God that man isn't here.

"What dost thou think of the ring on her finger, Mother Arrington?"

Derek's diamond! Don't let anything happen to that, for heaven's sake! I've got to give it back to him. It's an heirloom.

"I've seen none with such a large stone, even on the Lady Berkeley. Worth a king's ransom, I wager."

Astrid was alarmed. She wanted to cover up the ring but dared not move yet, not until she'd learned a bit more. She wasn't ready to face them before she could plan a way to get the hell out.

Fighting her impulses, she remained limp and silent.

"Methinks Thomas speaks the truth. She must be someone of great importance. Dutch royalty, perchance?"

"A pity she's come to this then." The mother sighed. "Not even a lowly tavern wench should be treated thus."

"All those feathers in her hair, Mizzus

Arrington. Do you reckon Indians had her?''

"The heathens would have prized such a scalp, Jenny. No, I think 'twasn't Indians. 'Tis not their way.''

Indians? Are they all insane?

"Pirates, then?'' the woman named Ann asked excitedly.

"No pirates e'er ventured this far up river, and it seems unlikely they'd get past the armed ships at Jamestown.''

There's Jamestown being mentioned again. Pirates? Armed ships? Good lord, what next?

"Dutch ships aren't allowed in the waters either, Mother Arrington. Not since the Acts. How could a Hollander woman be in these parts?''

"There be a few Dutchmen in Jamestown and Kecoughtan so I hear, Ann. Tile makers, mostly. But 'tis a certainty none of their women would have such a jewel on her finger.''

Well, Astrid thought, they're as puzzled about me as I am about them. Maybe—just maybe—I can work that to my advantage.

"Didst Thomas say she has no memory?''

"Aye. But we must pray her memory awakes with her eyes.''

A warm hand brushed across Astrid's forehead. "We should stop all the prattle now and await her stirring. Jenny, take away the water, girl, and see how Dorothy progresses with the broth. Ann and I will keep vigil here. There's naught else we can do for her for the nonce.''

Astrid heard feet shuffling. Jenny must be leaving. The hefty sighs indicated Mother

Arrington and Ann were settling down until she stirred.

Astrid's mind went over what she'd heard. These people behaved and talked as though they were living in the past. She crinkled her brows beneath the wet cloth and suppressed the gasp leaping from her throat.

The past! Have I fallen through some time warp, for God's sake?

Nonsense. Such things don't happen outside of the *Twilight Zone*, she assured herself. They're the ones out of kilter with the rest of the world. You're all right, Astrid. Just hang in there!

Her thoughts raced, grasping for something to get a handle on.

So, she asked herself, other than that absurd stuff about Indians, pirates, Jamestown and armed ships, what have they told me?

They think I'm a Hollander. Dutch, I guess. They believe I've been kidnapped or something and that I don't remember anything.

A faint smile curled around her dry lips. That's it! They've handed me my script. I'll play along with their cockeyed assumptions. I don't believe these simple people are out to hurt me. I'll get my strength back, get some clothes, and find a way out.

Her plan made beautiful sense to her. She only had to play another role for a while. She was used to slipping into different characters, and this one seemed easy enough.

Confident now, Astrid pretended to wake up. With a groan, she shifted her stiff limbs.

"She wakes!"

The cloth was lifted from her face. Astrid fluttered her lids open. The sweet round face above her blurred into focus, the tender light shimmering from warm hazel eyes assuring her she had been right to think she was safe.

"Be frightened no longer, my child," the woman purred. She took Astrid's hand and patted it soothingly. "You've found a haven at last."

Astrid smiled weakly and closed her eyes again. "I thank you," she whispered through parched lips.

"Ann, go fetch a cup of fresh water for our guest. She thirsts. And tell Dorothy to make haste with the broth. Only the good Lord knows how long 'tis been since she's had nourishment."

"Yes, water," Astrid mumbled. Not much talent required so far, she thought, and I'm thirsty as hell.

"There, there," the woman crooned. "We'll have thee hale and hearty betimes."

Astrid surrendered herself to the woman's amiable care. She was finding her part easy to play. After all, she *had* been through somewhat of an ordeal.

She opened her eyes again, staring up into the kind face.

"Where . . . where am I?"

"At the house of Edward Arrington on the south side of the James River. In Bermuda Hundred."

"Ber . . . Bermuda Hundred?" She'd heard of it, but hadn't it disappeared long ago? She remembered seeing a historical marker near the spot Derek had put their boat in the channel.

No, that's impossible. These people must have chosen the old name along with their back-to-basics life style.

But what had happened to the island and the channel? She knew that channel had been cut through back in the 1930s. It wasn't there this morning. She had run through a tobacco field.

Astrid shuddered, and the attentive woman patted her forehead with calming strokes.

"Shhh. Fret not, little one. Yes, Bermuda Hundred. And in Virginia we are. Have you no memory how you came here?"

"No." She shook her head, frantically trying to clear it of the dark thoughts spreading like tendrils of horror.

Am I the one who's insane? How could this be happening to me? Can it be I've been swept through some black hole and fallen back into another era?

Despair hit her. If such a thing could happen, I really am an alien and truly without memory, for no memory of mine can help me now.

"My youngest son Thomas found thee when he was hunting this morning," the woman said. "You gave him your name. Remember you that?"

"Astrid. Astrid Van Fleet."

"Aye, so he told me. That's a Hollander name, methinks. Dutch."

Astrid nodded weakly. She tried to quiet her silly thoughts. Time travel? That's impossible!

But the evidence had been piling up since the

moment she had awakened this morning—the sweet, clean air, the colonial costumes on these people and their archaic speech.

No, they were just part of some kooky sect. Weren't they?

Her mind wouldn't stop. But what about the other things like the tobacco field where a channel was supposed to be?

She struggled to remember the night before. Was there anything unusual? The champagne fog had clouded everything, confusing the sequence of events after she and Derek had gotten to the island.

The ground had been rocky and hard, she remembered, and had bothered her. Sometime during the night she had moved her bag a few feet from Derek over to a softer, mossy spot.

And she had seen a shooting star. When was that? Not during Derek's feeble attempts at making love, that's certain. It was later, after she had moved and right before she'd finally fallen asleep.

Can a mossy spot and a shooting star explain the unexplainable? She fought the whole idea. Surely she could still escape.

But could she? She'd been on a seesaw of misconceptions since the arrival of that strange man this morning. Up and down. Up and . . . now?

Down with a thud.

In spite of the warm face above her, Astrid felt terrifyingly alone.

She was afraid she'd been given a role she couldn't pull off. A permanent role? Lord, don't let it be that. The role of her life? She had to face it. Her survival depended on how she handled it.

The woman fluffed the quilt up under Astrid's chin. "I'll ask thee no more for the nonce. With rest and nourishment, perchance you'll remember more. For now, think only on mending thyself."

She reached behind her. "Would'st like a bolster?" She held up a long, covered pillow. Astrid nodded. The woman cupped her hand under the matted blonde head and slid the soft support beneath.

Her eyes elevated now, Astrid could see the room was clean—Spartan, actually—and about 24 feet deep. Unscreened, uncurtained casement windows stood open on both ends, letting in a refreshing cross draft.

It was some kind of a multipurpose room, apparently. A second bed—a lower, smaller one—stood over in the far corner. And there were a number of chests, a pine table, a tea cart, several wooden chairs with cane seats, and a long wooden couchlike piece with bright calico cushions perched in its corners. The floor was wide pine planking with small handwoven rugs in muted designs scattered here and there. The walls were whitewashed over rough plastering and held no pictures or decoration. Sturdy exposed cypress beams ran across the ceiling. A large, open, brick fireplace was on the wall behind her.

All in all, it was a primitive room, but bright, airy and comfortable.

Only Astrid didn't feel comfortable at all.

"Mother bade me come with the water, Grandmama!" A dark-haired girl danced into the room, her large green eyes glowing with excitement. "She's ladling the broth now and follows." She stole a glance in Astrid's direction and curtsied hurriedly. Her flushed cheeks matched the color of her smocklike dress.

"That's good, Lizzie," the woman said as she took a stoneware cup from the girl's hands.

"Here, my dear." She held the cup to Astrid's lips. Too weak to help herself, she let the woman tend to her like a newly weaned child. The water was cold and fresh.

After a few sips, Astrid motioned she had had enough. The woman set the cup on a chest beside the bed. "You'll need more anon, but 'tis best if we go slow," she said.

"Thank you." Astrid tried to smile. Her lips curled only slightly, but the terror in her eyes softened.

"Your English is good for a Hollander," the woman said, brushing straggly waves of yellow hair away from Astrid's pale cheeks. "Do you understand me well enough?"

"I understand some of what you say," she said slowly, trying to capture the speech patterns. The vowel sounds eluded her, but she hoped they'd chalk that up to a foreign accent. She'd have to listen carefully to pick up the different vocabulary and not say too much. Their thinking she was Dutch would be an advantage—unless, God forbid, they found a real Dutchman to come talk to her.

"That's good you ken some English. I'll try to

speak slowly for thee." The woman's face was wreathed in a crinkle of smiles. "I am called Elizabeth Arrington, the mother of Thomas, who rescued you, and Edward, whose house this is." She wrapped her arm around the dark-haired girl's shoulder. "This is my granddaughter, Lizzie, daughter of Edward and Ann. Edward is away for the nonce, but Ann will be in soon with the broth."

"Mrs. Arrington," Astrid acknowledged, managing a stronger smile. She nodded toward the wide-eyed girl. "Lizzie."

"Here's broth at last." Ann ran through the door balancing a blue and white bowl. "Fie! I thought 'twould ne'er come to a boil. That Dorothy's a sluggard. She ne'er gets the fire hot enough."

Seeing Astrid propped up and eyeing her curiously, she paused, then bustled over, her long skirt a beige whirl, and placed the steaming bowl in Mrs. Arrington's waiting hands.

"And this is Ann," the older woman said warmly.

"Good morrow," Ann said, bowing her head self-consciously. She was a handsome woman, with black hair like her daughter's, but swept up and knotted back severely under a white cap. Her youthful face was punctuated with large green eyes, also like Lizzie's though lacking the dancing light. She wore a crisp white blouse with a full spread collar and sleeves that cuffed below the elbows. A lightweight brown vest curved in a row of tiny buttons over her buxom chest, cinched in tightly at her not-so-slender waist, then flared over her full hips in a peplum.

Like her mother-in-law, Ann wore a white apron and a belt with three small tasseled pockets that dangled low down the side of her skirt.

It was an attractive costume, but way too heavy for a hot day. Astrid suspected she had layers of petticoats underneath.

Would she have to wear clothing like that? That might take some getting used to.

She greeted Ann with a nod and tentative smile. She thought best to resort to pantomime as much as possible.

Mrs. Arrington dipped a wooden spoon into the hot broth and blew away the steam before holding it to Astrid's lips. "'Tis nourishment for you," she coaxed. "'Pon my soul, you must be half-starved."

Astrid tested the soup. It was thick and tasty. Chicken, she guessed, with a tantalizing trace of herbs. She accepted another spoonful and welcomed the warm boost of energy. Lord knows, she told herself, I need all the help I can find to face this crazy world I've apparently fallen into.

Mrs. Arrington shooed Ann and Lizzie from the room "to go assist with the midday meal" and lovingly urged Astrid to continue "supping" the hot spoonfuls until the bowl was almost empty.

"No more," Astrid sighed at last, feeling fairly content considering the circumstances.

The sight of the tall figure standing outside the doorway destroyed Astrid's fledgling sense of well-being, and she tensed backward, pulling the patchwork quilt up around her neck.

It's him!

Mrs. Arrington patted the top of her head. "'Tis only Thomas, my child. He'll do thee no harm."

The man stooped to enter the low doorway and walked over to the bed. Astrid cringed, uttering a small cry of protest as he stared down at her.

"She's awake, I see," he said, addressing his mother but not taking his eyes off Astrid's frozen face.

"Aye, and she's had some water and broth. She's sensible, Thomas, and knows some English."

"But crazed, still. She cowers like a cornered rabbit."

There were those cold gray eyes again. How well Astrid remembered them! The incredibly long black lashes surrounding them she hadn't remembered. Such luxuriant fringing should melt ice, she thought irrationally. In his case, it only seemed to lower the temperature of the silvery cubes beneath. She shivered.

"'Tis thee, Thomas. You're a man, and you frighten her." Mrs. Arrington soothed Astrid's tense brow. "She seemed not crazed with the women."

Thomas grunted his exasperation and turned away from the bed.

"We must be rid of her, Mother. Get her clothed, and I'll take her over to Colonel Hill's house. He's a councilor. Let him find where she

41

belongs." Long bronzed fingers pushed through the black waves falling against his loose collar. "There's naught out at the point to show us how she came to be there. No sign of a ship putting in. Naught!" He turned again to face his mother.

"Eyes enough are on this house with Edward's foolishness. She must be gone."

Astrid stiffened. The man's square jaws on his clean-shaven face were set and determined. His low black brows bristled with disapproval. She tore her eyes from his uncompromising features and looked pleadingly at the soft warm face of his mother.

"She must stay, Thomas. 'Till the morrow at least. She has not the strength to cross the river today." Mrs. Arrington's voice, though calm, was as strong and uncompromising as her son's expression.

"If you choose, you may report her presence to Colonel Hill," she continued. Her hazel eyes looked across into his icy silver ones. "'Tis not like you to act thus, Thomas. You—the bravest of my sons, the family's soaring eagle—you have ne'er heretofore turned from challenge or duty. This helpless woman is both of those. Leave us now."

"Damnation, Mother, can you not see the danger she brings to us?"

"Arringtons have ne'er shirked from danger. Methinks we'll not do otherwise this day."

"Very well, but I like it not," he said, heading for the door. "On the morrow, then." His voice lowered with resignation. "Tend to her well, for tomorrow she must go."

As he was leaving, he spotted the shredded sleeping bag on the floor. A part of the zipper still clung to the material. He picked it up and closely examined the glistening metal.

"Here!" he said excitedly, rushing over to the bed. He held the remnant close to Astrid's startled eyes.

"The iron binding is marked *Talon*. Dost that not jar your memory?"

"N-no," Astrid gasped, shaking her head. This could be funny as hell, she thought crazily, if this man didn't scare me witless.

Frustrated, he pulled the cloth away from her. "Talon," he muttered to himself. "The claw of a bird of prey. It could be the mark of a pirate."

Astrid watched him walk out of the room clutching his remarkable find. She squirmed beneath the quilt. This was theater of the absurd for sure, she realized, and pitfalls galore could be waiting for her out there on a stage where the other players could run the gamut from pirates to Indians. Not to mention that dark impatient man who wants me out of his sight immediately and sees me as a danger for some reason.

How can I protect myself when I have no earthly idea what's going on? The horror of her predicament hit hard. How can I be clever and survive when I don't know a damn thing? I've been plopped like a fully grown newborn into the middle of a world that I can't even begin to understand.

The woman beside her might help. Astrid reached over for Mrs. Arrington's arm and dug her fingers into the calico.

"I-I'm frightened, Mrs. Arrington. I remember nothing—naught," she corrected herself. She continued slowly, measuring her words carefully. "Can you tell me the day?"

"'Tis Saturday, child. The second day of May."

Astrid frowned. Saturday was right, but the date's all wrong. The play had closed last night, Friday, on April 28th.

And what year was it, dear God? She was afraid to ask.

"Your son," she said, "he does not want me here."

"Faugh! Forget what Thomas spoke. He's not himself these days. He has had a tragic loss."

"A loss?"

"His wife and child were slain by Indians near a year ago."

"Indians? How terrible!" My God, no wonder the man's so gloomy. Indians! Astrid felt a sense of panic. "Was their home attacked?"

"Nay. They were up in the frontier in Stafford County, where Sarah was nursing her ill mother. The whole plantation was laid low so we heard —family and servants as well, many of them Thomas's." Mrs. Arrington shook her head. "'Twere a black day."

"I'm sorry." Astrid tried to digest the woman's awful words. She wrinkled her brows. Did Mrs. Arrington call Stafford County 'frontier'? Dear heaven, how far back have I come?

"He said 'eyes are on this house' and something about 'Edward's foolishness'." Astrid knew she was prying, but she needed to find out all she could.

The woman's hazel eyes shaded, and her small round mouth tightened around the edges. "That's naught to do with thee," she said, "and naught for you to worry with." She rose from her chair, announcing with an efficient clap of her hands that the conversation was over.

"You'll want a bath now, methinks. I'll have a tub brought in, and I'll find clean clothes for thee. Ann's may do, but you're such a slender reed we'll have to alter a mite, I vow." She looked down at Astrid with a smile. "Before I go, woulds't like help with the chamber pot?"

"Chamber pot?"

With a chuckle, the plump woman reached down and pulled out an apple-green earthenware bowl with a flat rim and an oval handle. Astrid's stomach knotted, and her cheeks flushed.

"No help," she protested. "I can manage alone, I believe."

The woman nodded. "Very well. I'll place it on the stool here to make it easier for thee." With a final reassuring pat on Astrid's shoulder, she turned to leave.

"I'll close the door, for you'll want privacy, methinks," she said. "Ring the small bell on the table yon if you need assistance." With a parting smile, she left Astrid alone, closing the heavy pine door behind her.

Astrid studied the black metal hinges on the rough, lopsided door. Primitive, she thought. Everything's so goddamned primitive!

She looked over at the squat pot on the low stool and wrinkled up her nose. Oh, well, she sighed, throwing off the quilt and working her sore legs over the side of the bed. When nature calls . . .

As she limped toward the ugly, taunting object, she had a wry thought.

Astrid, you've come a long way, baby!

Chapter Four

"Fie! The bodice needs tightening as well. Here, lass, let me have at it with the needle."

Astrid unfastened the long row of buttons on the ill-fitting beige vest and handed it to Mrs. Arrington.

"You're naught but skin and bones," the woman tutted, pulling needle and thread from one of her dangling pockets. "Methinks the rogues who had thee kept thee starved."

Astrid watched the woman squint at the back seams of the garment and sit down heavily in a cane-bottomed chair to begin her alterations. If these people knew about the regimen of sweaty exercises and skimpy meals she'd suffered through to keep that skin and bones look, they'd be shocked as hell, she thought with grim amusement.

She was standing in the middle of the room, burdened already with two layers of long petticoats, a thin camisole shift with sleeves that ruffled at the wrists, and a stiff white blouse similar to the one Ann was wearing. It cuffed below her elbows, and the camisole's ruffles stuck way out—a layered look the women had assured her was proper and highly fashionable.

Astrid despaired, knowing too well about hot, humid Virginia summers. If pirates and Indians and God-forbid-what-else didn't do her in, the clothing alone might do the trick.

There were no underpants, and she hadn't dared ask for them. Maybe they haven't been invented yet, she thought. There were no stockings, either, thank heavens. She was glad for at least a touch of freedom.

With Jenny's help, she had bathed and washed her hair in a big wooden tub. The bar of soap had smelled of bayberry and barely made suds, but it had cleaned well enough.

Now, refreshed and smelling like a Christmas candle, Astrid waited for the top layers of her costume. She felt useless watching the assured efficiency of the other two women.

She envied them. They were at home and knew what they were doing. She was the one without tools to cope. They, on the other hand, seemed to have an inexhaustible supply of useful equipment in those strange little hanging pockets. They also had a decided advantage with the language and customs of their world.

And it was their world. It sure as hell wasn't hers.

Astrid was tired of her nonstop quandary. A few times she had thought of the fun she'd have telling this weird story to her friends back in Richmond, only to be pulled up short when she realized she might never get the chance.

Through the whimsy of some unknown fate, she'd been whisked unceremoniously out of the 20th century. Certainly, all present evidence was pointing in that direction.

Was she going to be whisked back as whimsically? A sliver of hope brought a sparkle to her eyes. Or—and the sparkle fizzled at the thought—with her rotten luck, would she wake up in the Stone Age next time?

"Now. 'Tis ready for thee, methinks." Mrs. Arrington's pleasant voice interrupted Astrid's rambling thoughts. Like an obedient child, she pushed her double-sleeved arms into the bodice the woman held up for her.

"And the skirt's ready, too," Ann said, breaking a slender strand of thread with her teeth and fluffing out the dark, hefty cloth.

Buttoned into the garments, Astrid turned around for the women's approval.

"Fie, fie, fie! Her ankles show, Ann. She's such a tall one." Mrs. Arrington knelt on the floor, tugging the skirt down. Scowling, she pushed herself back up with a puff of exertion.

"It will have to do for today, I suppose," she fretted. "The hem's not deep enough to lengthen. But we must find something better for her when she goes to Colonel Hill's on the morrow."

"My sky-blue taffeta will be the one for that, methinks," Ann said, sounding not too pleased.

"It will match her eyes and is more fitting for a lady."

"Aye. We'll sew on it this evening."

It was decided then. Thomas Arrington was going to have his way. She was being taken somewhere else "to find out where she belongs."

Astrid knew she could save them a lot of trouble by telling what she believed was the awesome truth, but she didn't dare. She well could be committed to some horrific colonial version of bedlam.

"Who is Colonel Hill?" she asked.

"Colonel Edward Hill. He lives across the river at Shirley and is a grand, important man who will see to thee properly," Mrs. Arrington said.

Shirley! She'd taken a tour of that elegant mansion once. Her stock was going up in this world.

Astrid tied back her still-damp hair with a brown ribbon Ann had pulled out of a small chest. Completing her ensemble was a pair of wooden clogs belonging to Jenny, because "alas, these be the only shoes in the house to fit."

And so, other than the unacceptable exposure of two well-turned ankles, she almost looked as if she belonged in her new surroundings.

She wondered if she'd ever feel she belonged any place again.

The Arrington family had their midday meal outside on a rustic plank table under the shade of a tall cottonwood tree. Astrid was welcomed as an honored guest.

Thomas wasn't part of the luncheon group, she noted with relief. *Probably across the river reporting me*, she guessed, *and covering his ass. Well, let him! He'll be doing me a favor when he takes me over to Shirley*, she thought snidely. *After all, Dutch royalty would be accustomed to more luxurious accommodations.*

But would the Hills be as kind to her as these simpler folk? Not even all of the Arringtons had received her with open arms. Grim Thomas certainly hadn't. Would she find a similar cold reception elsewhere?

"Now eat, my pretty," Mrs. Arrington said jovially as she placed a brimming plate in front of her. "You need plumping out."

Astrid's tight stomach rebelled when she saw the pile of food before her—fried chicken, corn, pickled fruit, greens, a large hunk of flat grainy bread. A pewter tankard, its sides invitingly beaded with moisture, stood beside her plate. It held a brownish liquid. Iced tea, she hoped, as she raised it to her lips.

Beer! After the initial surprise, she discovered it was a delicious, light brew, not frosty, but laced with the pleasant coolness of a running spring or a dark cellar.

"Thomas brings us our small beer," Mrs. Arrington said, pleased with Astrid's look of approval. "Makes it himself, he does, at Eagle's Crest. The best in Virginia, we tell him."

"'Tis good." Astrid nodded, proud of herself

for the *'tis.* Conscious of the older woman's worried scrutiny, she reluctantly bit into a crusty piece of chicken. That and the corn, at least, were safe finger foods. No forks were on the table, only spoons and knives. She'd have to observe how the others ate their greens and fruit. She felt she had so much to learn—and too much to eat. She knew she'd have to make a dent in the stuff to placate Mrs. Arrington.

"Do they eat chicken in Holland?" Lizzie asked from across the table. She, too, had a tankard beside her plate.

"I'm not sure, Lizzie," Astrid responded truthfully with a smile. "But I somehow knew it was chicken—and called by that name."

The Arrington women chuckled good-naturedly.

"Do you know pone?" the girl asked, her green eyes twinkling as she lifted her hunk of bread.

"Pone? Do you call all bread 'pone'?"

Lizzie giggled. "No. Bread is bread. Pone is pone. 'Tis made from cornmeal, and I like it best of all."

"The butter is in the tub yon," Mrs. Arrington told Astrid, nodding her head toward a small earthenware bowl in the center of the table. "Fresh churned and sweet, if the cow has stayed away from the field onions."

Everyone laughed as Astrid helped herself to the butter.

At the congenial table, she learned the brandied fruit was "apricocks," that her plate also contained mustard greens (recommended to be doused with cider vinegar from the "cruse"), and spring corn ("not so sweet and fat as our summer corn"). Watching the others, she mastered the art of pushing greens and fruit with the knife onto her spoon.

Astrid was amazed to see how much she was eating of the surprisingly tasty food. Mrs. Arrington would be pleased. At this rate, she thought, I'll plump out in no time at all. She declined the offer of bread pudding for dessert, protesting, "No thank you. I'm about to pop."

They didn't question her spontaneous remark, but she reminded herself she'd better watch what she said.

"May I help clean up?" she asked. Good manners dictated as much, though she didn't have a clue how they washed their dishes.

"Dorothy and Jenny will tend to it," Mrs. Arrington said with a smile. "Wouldst like a nap now?" she asked. "Ann and I usually snooze a bit after the midday meal."

Astrid shook her head and placed the linen napkin beside her plate. "I'd prefer to walk around some, if you don't mind," she said. "Perhaps . . . perchance Lizzie could join me?"

The exuberant girl would be a perfect companion, she thought. Away from her mother and grandmother, she'd be free to chatter as much as she wished, and Astrid knew she needed to do some serious probing.

With dire warnings not to venture into the woods, the two women agreed to her proposal and sauntered back toward the house.

Astrid and Lizzie, walking side by side, set off

in the opposite direction. The girl's loose black hair bounced around the shoulders of her short-sleeved pink smock as she began pointing out spots of interest on the Arrington land.

"That old wooden building there is the tobacco barn where they hang the leaf," she explained. "Those two clapboard houses yon are for the servants. Dorothy and Jenny have one all to themselves now that the other two women got themselves wedded." Her rosebud lips pouted in exasperation. "The women servants ne'er finish out their time, it seems, and it makes my mother furious."

"Their time?" Astrid inquired, carefully stepping around a flock of chickens.

"My father paid their passage on the boats from England. In return, they're s'posed to work five years for us. The pretty ones forever find husbands long before then. Father ne'er protests, but Mother fusses. Says she hardly gets 'em trained 'fore suitors are at the doorstep." Lizzie giggled. "Says he should transport only ugly, pox-scarred maidens in the future."

"Your father's away now, your grandmother told me."

Lizzie skipped ahead jubilantly, clapping her hands. "He's off to war against the heathen Indians," she said. "He marched south yesterday with Colonel Bacon and scores of others. My father's to be a hero, I'm sure of it."

Bacon! Astrid caught her breath. Bacon's Rebellion! That's what I'm in the middle of? It was covered in her history classes, but she couldn't remember one blasted thing about it.

When was it? Sometime in the 17th century, she thought. Damn, she had hoped she'd be up into the 18th at least with Washington, Jefferson and the Revolution—any era she knew a little something about.

Lizzie continued bubbling about a big gathering last week at a nearby place called Jordan's Point where the men had chosen Bacon as their commander and had signed their names to an oath in "a round robin" so that the ring leaders couldn't be identified.

But Astrid barely heard her. The 17th century! Good God, I've fallen back more than three hundred years.

"And here's the ditch where we dump things we have no further use for." Lizzie's voice broke through Astrid's numbed mind. "The latrine ditch is over yon." The girl's button nose wrinkled in revulsion. "But let's get no closer. 'Tis odorous." She reversed direction in a pink twirl. "We best turn back, for the woods are yon."

Before joining Lizzie, Astrid looked down into the rubbish ditch. Inside lay broken pieces of pottery, an animal's skull and some rusty knives. On top of the jumbled heap was a shredded piece of dark green cloth with a broken zipper attached.

She stared down at the last pitiful remnant of her old world as tears blurred her eyes. Could she, with everything so topsy-turvy, call that world so far in the future her past?

Quickly wiping away the tears, she turned

away to follow the girl back toward the house.

"That little brick building in the rear with the smoke coming out of the chimney is our new summer kitchen," Lizzie continued. "Keeps the big house so much cooler," she bragged happily. She seemed oblivious to Astrid's wan expression.

Chickens scurried about their feet. In the distance, Astrid could see cows and sheep lazily dozing in the deep shade of a big clump of trees. A trio of pigs wandered freely close to the woods. The only fence she saw was a small post-and-rail affair that enclosed a rectangle next to the house.

"That's our kitchen garden," Lizzie explained. "Only some salad and mustard greens ready for the picking now. And a few herbs. But soon, we'll have onions, beans, and peas—almost everything. I love the summertime!"

Jenny's clogs clumped uncomfortably under Astrid's feet, and she had trouble keeping up with Lizzie's sprightly pace.

"Could we sit a while?" she asked, pointing to a weathered bench under a spreading sycamore down near the river.

"If you'd like." Lizzie nodded in agreement and skipped toward the tree.

Astrid followed slowly, limping slightly. When she reached the bench, she removed the clumsy shoes and wiggled her sore toes.

"You're accustomed to silk slippers, I'll wager," Lizzie said.

"That's possible," Astrid replied with a shrug.

"But you must remember my feet took a beating this morning."

"The rogues beat thee?" the girl asked excitedly.

Astrid chuckled. "I remember no rogues, Lizzie—nor silk slippers either, for that matter. I meant my feet were injured somehow." Looking down, she was relieved to see her scratches were superficial. She doubted that antiseptics had arrived on the scene yet.

With a sigh, she leaned back against the tree's peeling bark. "Tell me things, Lizzie," she said.

"Things?" The girl's green eyes grew wide.

Astrid felt the tears swelling again in her own eyes.

"Things," she repeated, a soft plea in her voice. She fought back the tears and stared ahead at the river.

The James was so familiar with its expanse of silver ripples and its lush tree-covered banks. But it was different now, too. Odd-looking sailboats busily plyed its waters. She had learned in school how the James and other tidewater rivers had been a lifeline for early Virginians—their main connection with the outside world and with each other. She knew the James had suddenly become more important to her, too. She'd never really given the river much thought. It simply had always been there.

She looked at the wooden wharf jutting out from the Arrington's land. It was big enough for large boats, but only a single-masted sailboat bobbed there now. Across the river, where she figured Shirley should be, was a bigger wharf. Moored there was a huge two-masted ship flying a Union Jack.

She felt a sudden chill.

Lizzie grabbed her cold hands. "Poor lady," she whispered. "It must be frightful to lose all memory. Would you like me to talk about anything? 'Tis that what you meant?"

Astrid nodded and smiled weakly down at the girl's clouded face.

"It would help, Lizzie. I feel as if I know nothing. Tell me your memories."

The girl looked thoughtful. "I'm but three and ten and have but a child's memories. I doubt you would find them interesting." Her pretty face brightened. "But I can tell thee family stories I've been told."

Astrid encouraged her with a stronger smile. "Please do," she said.

"I'll tell Grandmama's story first. 'Tis most exciting."

Astrid soon became absorbed in Mrs. Arrington's saga. How, as a girl of 16, daughter of wealthy, important Howards, she had defied her family and eloped with a handsome indentured servant, Edward Arrington. The angry Howards had relented enough to give Edward his freedom but had disinherited Elizabeth.

"That mattered not," Lizzie said proudly. "For Grandpapa was not only the most handsome man in the colony, he was intelligent and hard working as well. And ere long he himself had great parcels of land and growing wealth." She bounced on the bench beside Astrid. "Isn't that a beautiful love story?" she asked.

Astrid nodded.

Lizzie's lower lip puffed in a rosy pout. "'Tis strange, tho'. Grandmama scolds when I get moony-eyed over Jeremy."

"Jeremy?"

The girl's eyes danced. "Jeremy," she repeated, making the name sound like Adonis. "Jeremy Robins. He's one of our indentured men. Came over two years ago when he was but four and ten and is the smartest, sweetest lad in all of Virginia. He'll be freed and given five acres of land in eight years."

Astrid pushed back some unruly raven locks from the girl's cheek. "I think your grandmother scolds because you're but three and ten, Lizzie, not because Jeremy's indentured. You have time —lots of time." She felt like a 17th century Ann Landers.

Lizzie looked up at her worshipfully. "You understand, methinks." She out-beamed the brilliant sun. "I like thee, Lady Van Fleet. I hope you find your memory."

"Me too," Astrid sighed. "But please call me Astrid. Lady Van Fleet sounds so formal."

"But what if you really be royalty? I could ne'er call a princess or countess or duchess Astrid," the girl protested.

"You have my permission, Lizzie. Even if we do find out I'm a countess or something," she said with a laugh. "Now, tell me more about your family."

"Well, Grandmama and Grandpapa settled over at Curles, on the land where Uncle Thomas lives now—tho' his house be much grander than theirs." She raised four stubby fingers. "They had four children. My father, Edward Junior, is the oldest. Then came Robert—he lives over in Gloucester by the York with Aunt Judith and my four cousins. Uncle Thomas and Aunt Margaret, the twins, are the youngest. Aunt Margaret and Uncle James live up at the Falls now. She and Uncle Thomas were born after Grandpapa was slayed by the Indians in the great massacre of 1644."

"Your grandfather was killed? How terrible." Astrid did some quick calculations. Thomas looked to be in his early thirties so it must be the 1670s now.

"'Twas terrible, I'm told," Lizzie said sadly. "He had been out with his men in the fields and was returning to his cabin and family. They set upon him with axes. Slayed all t'other men, too. Scalped them all." Her small shoulders shuddered.

"How did your grandmother and her children survive?" Astrid asked, horrified yet again by a tale of colonial terror.

Lizzie smiled. "That's the exciting part," she said. "Grandmama bolted the cabin door, hid her two wee sons in the root cellar, pulled a great gun from the wall, and with the help of a servant named Joseph shot ten raving heathens! The remainder scurried off into the woods." She shook her head. "And she with Uncle Thomas and Aunt Margaret growing in her belly, too."

Astrid tried to imagine that sweet, mild woman holding off a mob of Indians. She looked down at Lizzie in wonder. "That's indeed an exciting story," she said. "I'm sorry about your grandfather, but I know you're proud your grandmother is so strong."

"All Arringtons are strong," Lizzie said proudly. "I'll be strong, too, some day."

"I believe you already are," Astrid said, giving the girl a quick hug. A movement near the wharf caught her eye. Turning toward the river, she saw a small boat with a full gray sail.

"Someone's coming," she whispered.

"'Tis Uncle Thomas and Jeremy," Lizzie said, enthusiastically jumping to her feet to wave a greeting. A slender, sandy-haired boy returned her wave, then hustled to help the solemn dark man bring in the boat. Thomas Arrington didn't look toward them.

"Jeremy worships Uncle Thomas," the girl said, sitting back down beside Astrid. "I hope he doesn't buy his 'denture from Father, tho'. He does that sometimes and ever sets them free. He's a stubborn man, Uncle Thomas is. Refuses to hold people, even when they don't mind and expect to serve their time. Pays all his workers wages every month. 'Tis not the way to get ahead, tho' Uncle Thomas does that as well as any man."

"You'd prefer Jeremy to work out his time here until he's four and twenty?" Astrid teased with a smile. So Thomas Arrington's an early-day man of principle, she thought.

"Well . . . until I'm ten and six, at least," Lizzie smiled back.

Thomas Arrington's face was glowering as

61

usual, Astrid noted, as he stepped from the boat. He tossed back a terse order to Jeremy to tie up the boat and headed toward the house.

Seeing Astrid and Lizzie on the bench, he paused a moment and took a step in their direction. Apparently changing his mind, he turned toward the house. His glower remained constant.

As Astrid started to ask the girl if her uncle's mood was always so bleak, the sound of an approaching horse's hooves caught her attention. She, Lizzie, and Thomas simultaneously turned toward the clatter. The rider, a paunchy little man, dressed much like Thomas in an open buff vest, tan knickers, leather boots and wide-brimmed hat, greeted the younger man with a wave, pulled up his horse and dismounted. Unlike Thomas, his shirt had a row of ruffles at the wrists, and he wore a ludicrous bouffant brown wig. The two men began talking quietly.

"That's Mr. Henry Isham," Lizzie whispered, "one of our Bermuda Hundred neighbors. He might have news about Father."

The low voices of the men were muffled by the rustling of the sycamore leaves and the lapping of the water against the wharf. Astrid tried to pick up what they were saying.

"Mr. Isham's daughter Mary is the most sought-after maiden around." Lizzie chattered on, spoiling any chance Astrid might have to eavesdrop. She stopped straining to hear the men and directed her attention to the girl beside her.

"She's pretty enough, I guess," Lizzie added somewhat petulantly, "but her father's wealth helps, too." She snickered behind her little hand. "The bees swarm around the honey hive, but methinks William Randolph of Swift Creek has snared the queen."

Well, she was getting an earful of local gossip if nothing else.

"I wager she's not nearly so pretty as you, Lizzie Arrington," Astrid said with a laugh. "You'll knock 'em dead one of these days yourself."

"Knock 'em dead?" The green eyes looked bewildered.

"I mean the bees will be swarming at your father's door before too long. Just wait and see." She ruffled the girl's soft black hair with a loving gesture, warning herself again that she'd better watch her language.

When Astrid's more understandable words registered, Lizzie trilled a happy laugh. Together, the two turned their attention to the wharf where Jeremy struggled with the boat's rope.

Thomas heard his niece's gay laughter behind him and wondered at the camaraderie that seemed to have sprung up between the child and that annoying Hollander woman. But something else was annoying him even more at the moment—Henry Isham's words.

"We need your support, Thomas," the older man said. "The Arrington name carries weight in the colony. Edward signed on with enthusiasm. Indeed, he surprised us by marching south with Nathaniel and the others on the foray against the heathen."

Thomas's jaws tightened. "So he did," he said. "And left his house and family when the fields need him most."

"He has men enough here to tend to that. What he does now with Bacon protects all our fields—and our families as well." Isham removed his hat and punched a pudgy finger up under his wig, setting it slightly askew. "Damnation! These things grow hot in the summertime."

Thomas lifted a scoffing brow. "Fashion, Henry. 'Tis vanity as ill-placed here in the colonies as that peruke is on your muddled head."

Isham chuckled and adjusted the heavy wig. "You be right, I s'pose. Mayhap I should box the thing until winter." He grew more serious, wiping the perspiration from his face.

"We want you with us, Thomas. Can you not see we're honorable men, all of us—not rabble, as the governor accuses. Along with Bacon, himself a councilor, there be William Byrd from the Falls, your neighbor James Crews, your own brother and myself. Your comrades and very kin, Thomas. We're not rebels, you know that. 'Tis that we see what must be done. And pray we do that Governor Berkeley soon sees we are right."

"The governor has already authorized forts, Henry."

"Forts. Faugh! Nothing but little mousetraps. What good be small armed garrisons scattered hither and yon against roving heathen? Every plantation on the frontier sits open to their savagery. News arrives each day of attacks on our people."

Isham replaced his hat and looked searchingly into Thomas's face. "Your wife and child were victims last year, Thomas, and e'en now your beloved sister Margaret is up at the Falls. Can you not see the—"

"Aye." Thomas's gray eyes darkened. "I plan to leave for the Falls on Monday to persuade Margaret and James to return home until the danger subsides."

Isham nodded. "A good idea I believe, son." He mounted his horse. "Think on what I've told thee. We need your name and reputation on our side. The governor will pay heed to such as you."

A great commotion down by the wharf drew the two men's attention. Three men from the fields had run to the water and were pulling something out. Thomas squinted toward the scene. It was the lad, soaked like a drowned rat and lying still!

"Jeremy!" Lizzie screamed. She and the yellow-haired stranger were running toward the group.

"God's blood!" Thomas cried, rushing to join them. Henry Isham dismounted quickly, his short legs pumping in a futile attempt to catch up with the taller man.

As Thomas approached, he saw the Hollander woman shove away the men and fall across the lad's body.

She was straddling the boy and pushing on his chest! She pinched his nose, and like a shameless deranged wench covered his open blue mouth with her own. She was pushing again, repeating that vulgar kiss.

Thomas tore through the mesmerized clutch of men gathered around the gross obscenity.

"Stop, you strumpet!" he shouted, pulling her hair back with a yank to get her wanton mouth off that of the dead lad's.

"Leave me alone!" she shrieked, her eyes flashing. Panting, she resumed her rhythmical pumping of the thin chest, mumbling ciphers, ". . . eight . . . nine . . . ten . . . eleven . . . twelve Then back she fell with her lips over the boy's.

Thomas grabbed her arm and pulled her away with a jerk. She flailed against him in a crazed frenzy, screaming that she must get back to the boy. He pushed her aside angrily. She fell backward on the sandy soil, her bare legs kicking under the whirling roll of skirt and petticoats.

"Get thee gone, woman!" Thomas bellowed. "He's drowned. You're naught but a wanton wench."

"Look, Master Thomas!" exclaimed the black-bearded man on his right. "The lad breathes!"

Thomas looked down at the wheyfaced Jeremy. The boy moaned. His lips were turning pink, and his eyelids quivered.

The Hollander woman quickly bent over Jeremy, circled her hand around his wrist and looked up at Thomas with triumph gleaming in her eyes.

"No thanks to you," she said bitterly. "He will be all right now, I believe." She stood and went over to console a sobbing Lizzie.

"Are you a witch, woman?" Thomas asked, his

voice deeply troubled. "What dids't do to him? He was dead."

The field hands began to murmur among themselves, nodding their heads and looking with awe at the golden-haired, barefooted stranger who had brought Jeremy back to life.

Henry Isham stood transfixed behind Thomas. "Who is that woman, Thomas?" he asked.

"I know not," Thomas said, staring hard into the wild blue eyes where the earlier defiance struggled with growing fright.

Dorothy and Jenny ran from the house and started tending to the drenched boy who was sitting up and asking in a squeaky voice what had happened.

The black-bearded man scooped Jeremy up in his arms, and the group of servants, talking excitedly, followed them back to the clapboard cottages.

Thomas and Isham stood facing the woman and the weeping girl. Lizzie moved closer within the circle of Astrid's arm.

"Who are you?" Thomas asked in a husky whisper.

Astrid shook her head. Her face was pale. Her light hair fluttered loose from the ribbon and whipped about her head. Her bodice and skirt were dark with splotches of water.

Lizzie raised her eyes and looked at her uncle.

"She's a Hollander countess methinks, with the name of Astrid Van Fleet," she said, her voice firm and sure. She embraced the woman whose heaving breasts strained against the soiled beige bodice.

Thomasina Ring

"She has wonderful powers, Uncle Thomas. She breathed life into Jeremy."

Thomas was confused. His troubled eyes bore into those of the stranger's, trying to penetrate the woman's awesome secrets.

"God's blood!" he muttered under his breath, turning away.

Chapter Five

Astrid was alone in the Arringtons' large room across from the parlor, staring out an open casement. The river and sky were leaden gray in the growing dusk, and the trees stood like dark sentinels, their leaves a black filigree against the twilight sky. Fireflies dotted myriad pinpoints of light on the shadowy backdrop.

She sighed deeply. Her own internal dusk held no glowing pinpoints.

Now I've really done it, she told herself, but I couldn't have stopped myself from using CPR on that boy—even if I'd remembered these people wouldn't know what the hell I was doing.

Was she going to be marked as a witch? My God, she wondered, what do they do with witches? She knew they were burned at the stake up in Massachusetts—but in Virginia? She felt a sudden chill despite the muggy air and her multiple layers of clothing.

Lizzie, bless her heart, simply said she had wonderful powers, and the girl had glued herself to Astrid through the evening meal with puppy dog devotion. At least she had one ally in her new 17th century world.

Maybe two, she thought with a smile. Jeremy Robins had appeared at the door after dinner holding an armful of wildflowers. With winning shyness, he had thanked her "for giving me back my life's breath when I lost me footing and fell like a dolt into the river."

As tall as Astrid, but seemingly all arms and legs, Jeremy had shuffled awkwardly as he plunged the flowers into her hands. Smiling her appreciation for the colorful, if scraggly, bouquet, she felt a deep warmth for the boy. Though she hadn't dared, she'd wanted to give his wild shock of sandy hair a maternal smoothing.

She liked his youthful, unformed face—the upturned nose sprinkled with freckles and the soft jawline with its hint of peach fuzz. His eyes, particularly, had struck her—a deep green flecked with amber. They were sharp, wise eyes for such an innocent setting and told her Jeremy Robins hadn't had an easy life. He was old in experience if not in years, and she felt sure he would be her friend.

Big deal, she thought. Lizzie and Jeremy. So far she had the grand total of two children on her side.

What about all the others? Astrid fingered a limp daisy in Jeremy's bouquet. Mrs. Arrington had remained pleasant but had been a tad stand-offish. Was she suspicious of those recently revealed, so-called powers?

Certainly, Ann had been overly nervous and had avoided meeting her eyes. She had hovered over Lizzie, pulling her away from Astrid as soon as she could. "The child must have her Saturday night bath and time for praying before bedtime," she had said.

The praying part was emphasized—to counterattack a witch's influence, no doubt.

Astrid shivered again. She wouldn't see Lizzie until morning. Ann had announced firmly that her daughter would be sleeping upstairs with her "so that our guest may have Lizzie's bed in the room with Mother Arrington."

And what about Thomas? His disapproval was palpable now. He had scowled at her throughout dinner, announcing he would "sleep here this night so I may sail the lady across early on the morrow."

She knew he was hanging around to protect the family from her.

What on God's earth had he thought she was doing to the drowning boy? "Wanton wench," he had called her. "Strumpet!" She cringed, wondering how she'd ever adapt to a naive world where an effective lifesaving technique was considered vile lust—or, maybe even worse, witchcraft.

Anger bubbled in her breast. He almost had pulled her away before she had saved the boy.

Be patient, she told herself, pushing down her anger. You'll be elsewhere tomorrow. Surely the

Hills are more sophisticated. This witch business will be forgotten, glossed over and ignored, hopefully, once she was in the right hands.

Astrid grabbed onto this shred of hope and moved away from the window. Holding her bouquet close to her bodice, she walked slowly across to the parlor, her assigned bedroom for the night.

Mrs. Arrington sat by a flickering candle, sewing on the blue dress Astrid would be wearing the next day.

"'Tis nearly finished, milady," she said, her tone reserved and with an edge of coolness. "I've turned back your feather bed yon." Without looking up, she nodded toward the small bed in the corner. "There be a nightshift for thee across the bolster."

"Thank you, Mrs. Arrington. You've been very kind."

Astrid felt lonely and miserably misunderstood.

She placed Jeremy's wilting flowers on a chest beside Lizzie's bed and silently began undressing. Having no idea what to do with her daytime clothing, she piled them at the foot of the mattress and slid the white nightgown over her body. Like everything else in this damnable place it didn't fit her—too short for their tastes and way too long for hers. Ruffled sleeves clamped her wrists, and the lacy collar brushed high under her chin.

This gown's a perfect symbol for my lousy state of affairs, she thought bitterly. Unnecessary, unwanted, and a complete misfit.

"I'll put your clothing away anon," Mrs. Arrington said. "There's water in the pitcher and a bowl if you wish to wash."

"Thank you." Astrid didn't turn around. No "thee," "child," nor "pretty one" any longer, she noticed. She felt a terrible loss.

And all because she'd saved a life. Damn it! Enough separated her from these people without this extra burden.

She splashed water on her face and dried with a small linen cloth. Suddenly, through the window before her, she saw the thin streak of a shooting star.

With a surge of hope, Astrid screwed up her face. I'm ready, she whispered silently. Take me back, she pleaded, now—this very moment!

Nothing happened. Even before she unclenched her eyes, she knew she hadn't budged. She was still in the dimly lit room redolent with beeswax candles and still shrouded in the dreadful nightgown that threatened to choke her. Rebelliously, she loosened the ribbon under her chin.

With a heavy heart, she moved to the bed and sat on the edge of the plump mattress. She clasped her hands in her lap and bowed her head.

Across the room, Mrs. Arrington took a final stitch in the glistening blue dress and stood up with a sigh.

"You'll look a proper lady for the Hills, methinks," she said.

"I'm sorry to be such a bother," Astrid said, her voice trembling through the lump in her throat. "Someday I hope I can repay your kindness."

"Faugh! 'Tis only what we'd do for any stranger in distress." With a swish of cloth, the little woman removed her pink calico dress and layers of petticoats and slipped into a nightgown identical to the one Astrid was wearing. Astrid couldn't help but notice that on Mrs. Arrington it looked perfectly all right.

With dispatch, the woman put away the daytime clothing. Astrid was too tired to care what she was doing with the blasted things. She'd learned enough for one day, anyway.

After a quick wash-up using another bowl and pitcher nearer her own bed, Mrs. Arrington snuffed out the candles and padded over to the open window next to Astrid.

"There are folk who fear the night air," she said. "Be you one of those?"

"No, I think not," Astrid replied, hoping fervently the Arringtons didn't count themselves among those folk.

"Good," the woman said, a touch of her former accessibility returning. "With fustian nightshifts and feather beds, I find the evening breezes welcome indeed. 'Twas ever thus with my family, and we've withstood ague better than those who persist in shutting them out."

She heard Mrs. Arrington move across the room and climb into her bed. After a brisk "Goodnight, milady," the little woman grew quiet. Within minutes, her soft breath fell into the deep, regular pattern of untroubled, innocent sleep.

Astrid lay back on the warm, enveloping mattress and stared up at the dark beams against the ghostly moonlit ceiling. No untroubled innocence at this end of the room, she thought, her heart racing.

And no sleep either. She wished she'd mastered the art of meditation. What was it she had read? A mantra? Repeat in your mind over and over a special sound. Om?

She closed her eyes and tried it. Om . . . Om . . . Om . . .

Clomp!

Her eyes flew open. What was that? Something on the other side of the wall.

No. Silence now. Only night sounds from outside—frogs, insects, an occasional bird.

Her lids clamped tightly. Om . . . Om. Keep trying, Astrid, you need rest for tomorrow. Om . . . Om . . .

Thud!

Again! Someone's out in the hall. Giving up on her silent chanting, she sat up, pressing her ear against the rough plaster.

Footsteps. A rustling sound. A squishy squeak. They're sitting on something.

The cot. She'd seen it next to the wall in the hallway, parallel to her bed.

Who would be sleeping out there?

Thomas Arrington, of course—the Great Protector! She grimaced. Protector for the others but not for her.

Against her.

Astrid strained to hear—a low sigh, silence, then a light whisper of a snore. He's asleep!

The whole family seemed to doze off in seconds, and she envied them.

Hopelessly awake, she frowned up at the beams.

She had to get up, had to move. She needed to go outside to look at the sky and the river, do anything to get herself calmed down, to put herself back into some semblance of order.

Carefully, she moved off the feather mattress and tiptoed to the closed door. Holding her breath, she pulled it open slightly, praying the heavy hinges wouldn't creak and give her away. Thank God, they were quiet. She didn't tempt them further, but slipped through the narrow opening into the hall.

The front door stood invitingly open. With her skin prickling, she glanced over at the shadowy figure on the cot, still asleep.

No, he was moving!

Astrid leaned up against the wall and pressed her hands against the cold plaster.

A throaty sigh came from the cot. She didn't move as a wave of nausea rose from the pit of her stomach. What would he do with her if he found her roaming around like this?

Wait—he's quiet again. He's only shifted his position. That rhythmic soft snoring means he's still asleep.

Relieved, she moved toward the open door. A floor board's squeak paralyzed her. She stopped, not daring to breathe.

No, he hadn't heard.

Quickly, Astrid fled through the door and ran barefoot across the dewy soil toward the sycamore tree and the old bench. Under the deep leafy shadows she sat down. She was hidden from the house, she hoped, hating the full white nightgown that glowed in the bright moonlight. She longed to be invisible.

The pounding of her heart began to subside. She knew she'd been wise to get out of that restricting house. The night air felt refreshingly cool. The river lay like a diamond-studded black mirror, and stars pricked the sky. They were twinkling and bright, more than she'd ever seen.

They're ageless, she mused. What's a piddling 300 years to them? They measure their time in millenniums.

With this thought, Astrid felt incredibly small, her own plight insignificant. Her new perspective provided a boost of courage. She was going to survive, damn it. She'd take on the whole cockeyed 17th century if she had to.

She decided she'd just hang on to her advantages. After all, she knew more than these people. She might have to keep most of it to herself, of course, but she knew things they'd never know—how the country would develop, for example, and the coming revolutions. There would be the one for independence first, and then the industrial one. She knew about the technological advances ahead, like steam power, combustible engines, split atoms, microchips and computers. There would be electricity to drown out the stars, skyscrapers to reach for the heavens and airplanes to soar through them. And spacecraft to go beyond, to the moon and past the farthest stars.

There's so much ahead!

Her heart sank.

And so little here.

They already knew about wheels and fire, and that pretty well wrapped up what she could recreate from her former world. Electricity? Telephone? Television? Even the steam engine? She had no earthly idea how any of them worked.

Was she really any better off than the Arringtons?

A big tear rolled down her cheek. I'm so damned stupid my disadvantages outweigh any advantages I possibly could have.

The tears streamed.

You know CPR, a little voice whispered inside her. And a helluva lot of good that does me, she whimpered. At best, I'm a witch. At worst, I'm some sort of necrophiliac who lusts after dead boys.

Her face was soaked, and the front of her loosely tied nightgown grew wet.

Damn it all! I'm glad I saved that sweet Jeremy's life, no matter the consequences.

Lord, she wished she could tell these poor simple people how to concoct smallpox vaccine, penicillin, the whole shebang.

Astrid didn't hear the footsteps behind her.

There's the witch! Thomas Arrington moved silently toward the sycamore. 'Tis nigh midnight, and she sits alone in the moonlight. Is she conjuring? Communicating with the devil? Her hair shimmers like spun gold. She looks so small, so alone. Her shoulders tremble. God's blood! She weeps.

A sharp pang twisted his heart. He couldn't understand what he was feeling. He wanted to wrap his arms around her, comfort her and protect her.

Was he under a spell? He stopped for a moment, ordering his senses to resist her powers.

Hold thyself, Thomas. The woman's naught but trouble. In the name of God, fall not under her sorcery.

The eerie howl of a wolf wailed from out on the point. The woman leapt to her feet, a tiny cry of fear escaping from her throat before she slapped a hand across her mouth.

"'Tis only a wolf, milady. He calls for his mate and has no interest in harming thee."

She twirled to face him, her eyes filled with terror.

"You!" she gasped. She stepped back and nervously tied the open neckline of her tear-stained nightshift.

"I meant not to frighten you," he said apologetically. "I could not sleep and came out for some night air. It sometimes helps." He was madly conscious of her full breasts pushing against the clinging fabric. The remembered curves of her slender body were impressed clearly into his brain.

What web of witchery is she weaving about me? he wondered. Here in the moon's glow she looks more angel than devil.

He tore his eyes away from her. You must concentrate on the water beyond, he commanded himself. Look on the sandy soil beneath your unshod feet, on the tree, on the sky. Look at anything other than this bothersome woman whose rare beauty is magnified beyond reason in this magical light.

"Wolves! My God, what's next?" the woman cried. She slumped down on the bench. Her contorted face fell into her open hands, and her slight body heaved with great sobs.

"I can't stand it. I just can't stand it anymore!" The broken sobs wrenched from her throat. The golden hair flowed like lustrous silk around her quaking shoulders.

Her tears broke through Thomas's wobbly defenses, and he ran to the bench. As he sat beside her he encircled his arms around her, drawing her close. This is no witch, he told himself. She's but a poor child in heartbroken distress. I must calm her before she wakes the entire household.

"There, there," he mumbled into the soft, sweet hair. "Too much has happened to thee this day. Cease your weeping, my sweeting."

Sweeting! What in God's name am I saying? He ignored his question and pulled her face onto his bare chest. Her hot tears bathed his flesh. He held her tighter, gently rocking her to and fro to soothe her.

"No harm will come to thee, I pledge it," he whispered into her ear. Her scent was roses and columbine. The satiny skin of her back burned through her nightshift and into his softly kneading fingers.

"I pledge it," he repeated huskily, acutely

aware of her nearness and the wonderful feel of her. He admitted to himself only one overriding emotion—pity. She's but frightened and horribly distraught. He could not let her suffer thus alone. He must make her know she isn't alone.

Somewhere in her misery, Astrid heard Thomas's whispered pledge. The strength of his hard chest beneath her face was a wonderful rock she could lean upon. The muscular arms holding her were warding off the unknown and the terrifying knowns. The low encouraging whispers in her ear told her she was safe at last. She pressed closer to him, digging her fingers into his wide, bare shoulders.

She wanted to stay like this forever, to climb inside him if she could, to keep his strength wrapped around her.

Gradually, her sobs quieted. Finally, in this crazy world, she had found a spot of comfort. Astrid didn't move, contently locked up against him in the dark warmth. I'll think later, she thought fuzzily. For the moment, let me stay right here, safe and protected.

But she couldn't! This was Thomas Arrington, and he hated her!

Didn't he?

She felt weak. Drained from her emotional outburst, she remained in his arms. Stay still, she commanded herself. Don't break the spell. You're not ready for reality yet.

His heart thumped against her ear. She inhaled his strength, trying to absorb it. She needed it so, and he had quantities to spare.

Thomas's hand brushed her damp hair away

from her cheek. "Better now?" he asked, his voice so soft she barely heard it.

"Yes," she said with a weak nod. Time to pull away, she told herself. But her body wouldn't move.

"Thank you," Astrid whispered, keeping her sopping cheek pressed tightly against his chest. "Maybe—perchance I can sleep now."

Thomas moved first. Gently, with his hands on her shoulders, he lifted her away from him.

"Aye. We both should sleep." His silvery eyes had lost their coldness. They searched her face in the moonlight, reached her own eyes and fastened there. For long moments she was impaled by them. What messages were they sending her? She saw bewilderment and concern. Worry was definitely there, along with a heavy sprinkling of confusion. She suspected her eyes reflected the same emotions in that same order.

"I know not what you are, Astrid Van Fleet. Countess? Witch? Nor know I from whence you came." His voice was deep. His eyes never left hers. "But you must be strong henceforth and give not in to the fright you must feel with no memory in a strange land. Do you hear me?"

She nodded, hooked by those hypnotic eyes. Her hands kept their feverish grip on his shoulders.

"My pledge to thee was earnest," he continued. "No harm will come to thee while I have breath. On the morrow I shall take thee to people who will help thee. Do you understand?"

Again she nodded. His eyes were the color of the James on a hazy summer day—silvery gray and filled with warm light.

"If you have problems there, I shall come to thee," he said, "but I expect there'll be none from here on. The Hills will find where you belong. And, once back with your family, where'er they be, your fright shall soon leave and your memory shall return."

Astrid looked down and reluctantly removed her hands from his sinewy strength and folded them in her lap.

"I think not," she said quietly, "but I thank thee for your strength and pledge. I shall remember them both . . . always."

With a sigh, Thomas rose from the bench and reached for her hand, pulling her up.

"Hie thee to your bed now, milady. Dawn is nigh and sleep is necessary for the strength you must find within yourself."

After a final look of gratitude, she ran back to the house.

Climbing onto the softness of Lizzie's small bed, she clasped the bolster to her beating chest.

Thank you, Thomas Arrington, she breathed into the plump pillow. Perhaps I have considered you unjustly.

Not realizing she was smiling, she fell into an exhausted, dreamless sleep.

Thomas sat for a long while on the bench beneath the sycamore. He'd made his pledge to a helpless, weeping woman. But was the Hollander truly helpless? Fiery and tempestuous she was, and blessed with strange powers.

Powers over him? He sat wondering, watching

the light of the waning moon play on the waters of the James.

She troubled him. There was something so different about her—her speech, her strange manner, that unbridled wildness he had witnessed more than once.

The sky was growing light in the east, and the mourning doves unleashed their plaintive, five-note call. He remembered the Hollander's haunting scent and the heat of her skin through the fustian nightshift.

He shook his head violently. Think not on your own base needs, Thomas, he scolded himself. This woman is not of your kind.

She's so unlike us, he thought. Is she like her own people? A strange folk, Hollanders, if that be so.

Chapter Six

Aye, she is a flower of beauty, Thomas thought as he helped the Hollander into the small sloop.

The blue taffeta—he recognized it as Ann's favorite dress—had never graced his sister-in-law as it did this yellow-haired maiden. The ecru modesty piece properly covered the disturbing curves of her breasts, and she was stockinged at last and wore blue slippers gallooned with gold thread. Her hair—silken beams of light rivaling the eastern sun—was twisted high on her head in a fashion he had never seen. A plump, intricate knot it was, with a blue ribbon woven through it.

Small and demure she looked to him as she settled into the narrow side seat of the gently rocking boat and waved her farewells to the dressed-up family members on the wharf. Off to church they were heading in a short while. The lad Jeremy and Richard, Edward's black-bearded servant, would be sailing them to Varina Parish in the larger sloop.

After hoisting his single sail, Thomas took his place in the back of the boat and cast off, expertly handling the small tiller. He kept his eyes on the Hollander woman who was pale. She was staring toward the far bank and didn't speak.

He was relieved she didn't turn her wide sky-blue eyes in his direction, since further conversation with the woman he wanted not.

Thomas's face was hard and set. Already he had said too much, weakened by her flood of tears last night. But a pledge he had made, and he didn't take his pledges lightly. Only pray she will not be needing me, he thought, as he checked the wind, deftly catching the westward zephyrs in his sail.

For sure, Councilor Hill shall care for her properly and have her returned to those she knows.

Blessed with the favorable wind, the sloop cut through the water smoothly. Their journey would be short. Soon he would be free of her.

And, God willing, I may never have to see her again.

The silk slippers pinched Astrid's feet, and she wiggled her toes reaching for space that wasn't there. The impractical shoes were Ann's, purchased to match her best dress, and both Arrington women had insisted she wear them, "small tho' they be." They had said the clogs were servant's footwear and would never do. She remembered those things hadn't been so comfortable either, and at least the slippers were softer. Maybe they'd stretch a bit.

Today, Astrid had a few extra layers to contend with. Underdrawers had been provided—scratchy, baggy muslin things that tied with a flimsy string at the waist. Her stockings were white silk, held up with a confining straplike device. She wore two petticoats—a plain one they called "tabby" and over it a more elegant one of ecru lace. In the style of the day it was clearly on display under the tacked-up folds of the taffeta skirt. Her chemise was garnished with additional lace that ruffled over the low neckline of the long-waisted bodice and peeked out beneath its loose elbow-length sleeves.

The prim modesty piece had been added at the last moment to her chemise's neckline ruffle to cover the "pit of the bosom."

None of it was to Astrid's taste, of course. Her Richmond wardrobe had been tailored understatement with an emphasis on comfort.

Mrs. Arrington had warned her to keep her arms close by her sides "lest a careless movement uncovers your elbow." Good lord, Astrid thought, the whole Arrington household including the servants had seen her in the all-together less than 24 hours before. Now the wrath of God was expected to descend upon her if she only exposed an elbow.

Adding to Astrid's discomfort, a stiff panel called a stomacher pinched into her diaphragm.

It's obvious they don't allow slouching as well as elbows and bosom pits, she surmised as she straightened her shoulders to relieve the pressure. Nor heavy eating, either, though food was the last thing on her mind right now.

She was worried about the Hills. Lizzie had warned her they were "haughty, pompous people." She wondered why Thomas would willingly put her into the hands of people like that.

Thomas was back to his normal, scowling self, she noticed. So much for pledges, she thought bitterly. What was the bombshell he had dropped at the breakfast table? He's leaving tomorrow for the Falls—wherever that is—to pick up his twin sister. Going away! Now how the hell could I call for him if I need him? I'll find my own strength, damn it. There's really no one I can depend on but myself anyway.

Astrid began to feel queasy and wished she hadn't indulged in the herbal tea and pone at breakfast. It was all she'd take, despite Mrs. Arrington's pressing her to join the others in the heartier fare of fresh eggs and side meat. Lord knows, the stomacher and rocking boat were playing havoc with the little bit of food she'd eaten.

She kept her eyes on Shirley's wharf and thought it strange that she couldn't see the grand mansion yet. Before (in her earlier life or was it her later life?) it had stood proudly exposed on its bank overlooking the James. But now it was hidden from view, somewhere deep in that copse of trees above the wharf, she figured.

As Thomas led her from the docked sloop up

the weedy embankment, Astrid realized it wasn't just the trees that were different. She could see the house now. Was this an earlier Shirley? Though bigger than the Arringtons' home, it was the same simple one-and-a-half story design with a brick facing of English bond and a cypress roof. Two huge chimneys were on either side. A confusion of weathered outbuildings were scattered here and there, and chickens, cows and pigs roamed around the land.

This was definitely not the Shirley she'd had in mind. Oh, well, she sighed, my rotten luck holds.

"They have guests, perchance," Thomas said, pointing back to the dock and the large brigantine flying the Union Jack.

They were the first words he had spoken to her all morning. Astrid stopped her climb and looked back with a frown at the ominous-looking vessel.

"English?" she asked.

Thomas grinned. "We're all English in Virginia," he said.

It was the nearest thing to a smile she had seen on his ruggedly handsome face. He should try it more often, she thought. It was a vast improvement.

"Perchance not me, tho'?" Her thin brown brows arched her carefully worded question.

"Perchance. We'll find that out in time," he said, turning back toward the house.

Astrid followed, feeling like a poor relation in spite of her Arrington finery. Courage, girl, she reminded herself. Remember the Dickens and Bronte heroines. Think about Jane Eyre. That put-upon lady was shifted around from pillar to post and survived.

She watched the muscles of Thomas's strong back ripple against the white shirt as he moved ahead of her. He's a gorgeous hunk of a man, she thought, a little mad at herself for noticing. He'd stand out in any era.

Down, girl! He doesn't care a twit for you. He's made that blatantly clear from the beginning. That odd encounter in the moonlight last night was out of character, I'm sure, only misguided chivalry brought on by the nearly full moon and my stupid tears.

Still, he had calmed her down, and his arms had felt exceptionally good.

Thomas began knocking on the big oak door of the house. Astrid straightened her shoulders and lifted her chin. She pulled up behind him, choosing to assume a subdued stance of prim propriety in his long, lean shadow. She decided she'd aim for the Jane Eyre look.

When the door opened they were invited in by a tall, rotund black woman wearing a brown calico dress and white apron.

Greeting "Master Thomas" warmly, she eyed Astrid with curiosity and rolled away in a substantial wave of brown cloth to fetch the colonel.

Astrid stood quietly beside Thomas in the cool hall, keeping her hands folded demurely in front of her billowing skirt. On my apron, she thought with mild amusement, looking down at the square wisp of ecru lace decorating her skirt. The entire female population here wears aprons, it seems, even on their Sunday finery. That should keep our minds on our proper role in society, should stomachers, petticoats and modesty pieces fail.

Her cynicism gave way to apprehension as a man walked briskly into the hall, an aura of harumphs hovering around his bewigged head. He shook hands with Thomas and greeted Astrid with a click of the red heels on his black buckled shoes. His heavily garbed head bowed tersely.

Colonel Hill, Astrid presumed.

He looked as if he had stepped out of a musty old portrait. Ruffles and braids frivolously dotted his otherwise somber outfit. His beady brown eyes were overpowered by the black curly wig and his bulbous, purple-veined nose. His weak, lipless mouth seemed more prone to snarls than smiles.

Lizzie had described him perfectly— pompous and haughty to a fault. Astrid hated him on sight.

Thomas held his wide hat in his hands and apologized for the unexpected call. He briefed Colonel Hill on the purpose of their visit, which surprised Astrid. She'd assumed he had already reported her.

Without looking at her, the older, shorter man cupped Thomas's elbow and began leading him into his library "for more details on this troubling matter."

Astrid bristled at being excluded. She stood stiffly, waiting for some cue as to what she should do in their absence.

Thomas extricated his arm from the Colonel's grasp and walked back to her.

"You may sit on the settle yon while we talk," he said, sounding almost as kind as his mother as he guided her to a cushioned pine bench near the library's door. She thanked him, fluttering her long, dark lashes downward. She hoped she looked properly helpless and harmless to the colonel.

After the two men left her and closed the elaborate walnut paneled door behind them, Astrid made a face and stuck out her tongue. Then she concentrated on their muffled voices, struggling to hear what they were saying.

Only occasional words penetrated through the heavy door. "Damnation, Thomas! . . . Hollander? . . . The governor, grief enough he has." Thomas's deeper voice was calmer and more decisive. "Bound and abandoned . . . must find where she belongs . . . royalty, perchance." The colonel again garbled gruffly reaching for a roar. Then Thomas said, ". . . must help her."

It seemed forever. She sat tensely on the bench, feeling like an accused criminal waiting for a verdict. A bulky old clock in the corner of the hall ticked the minutes away slowly.

At last, the door opened. The acrid-sweet smell of smoke followed the men out of the room. Smoking the peace pipe together, she thought angrily. Deciding on my future over their precious Virginia leaf, and neither of them once considering that I should have some say-so.

"It's decided, Lady Van Fleet," the colonel said, walking over to her and bowing his wig-swollen head. "You shall be our guest at Shirley until the morrow when we'll take thee to Green

Spring for further action."

Green Spring? Action? She didn't like the sound of it.

"Green Spring is Governor Berkeley's home, milady," Thomas explained softly, searching her colorless face with his heavily lashed, silvery eyes. "'Tis down near the fork of the Chickahominy. The governor's not home, Colonel Hill tells me. He's marched north to head off Bacon and his men before they cause more troubles with the Indians. But the Lady Frances is there to care for thee, and the colonel assures me the governor's men shall search for your true home."

"The governor's marched north?" she asked. Hadn't Lizzie told her that Bacon and his men had gone south?

A warning glint from Thomas's eyes stopped her from pursuing the question. She looked down at her clenched hands. Derek's diamond glittered tauntingly. An odd sort of passport, she thought. One sparkling jewel had promoted her to royalty status and was opening doors for her. Good thing she hadn't returned it Friday night as she had planned. God knows, without it, by now she might have been tied to a burning stake.

What else had Thomas said? "The Lady Frances is there to care for thee." Good. I only have to spend one day in this gloomy place, and then it's on to bigger and better things. Green Spring sounds a little brighter.

"Whatever you wish, Colonel Hill," she said politely, keeping her eyes down. "I mean no bother, but without memory 'tis very frightening." She looked up into the colonel's rheumy eyes and flickered her lashes in a piquant, pitiful plea. Lay it on, girl, she instructed herself. Try for a perfect mix of helpless female and royal hauteur. That'll keep them off balance and help you in this macho world of chauvinistic cavaliers.

"I leave thee now, milady," Thomas said. He seemed to sense his words had upset her and reached for her hand. "You be in better hands now, methinks," he said.

Astrid didn't think so and grabbed his long fingers. An electric tingle ran up her arms as he answered with a reassuring squeeze.

With sudden clarity, she knew she preferred to stay in his hands. She wanted to be back at Bermuda Hundred under the sheltering wings of his mother, in the cheerful bubble of Lizzie's presence, away from this depressing house and its stern master. She wanted to hide again inside Thomas's arms.

Yes, she'd admit it to herself now. She sorely needed this man's wonderful strength.

As if he could read her thoughts, Thomas patted her trembling fingers. "Be strong, milady," he said soothingly.

She stared up into his shadowy face, her large blue eyes pleading.

"Strength," he whispered and turned away.

Astrid bit her lip, fighting back tears. She would have folded, but the stomacher stiffened painfully into her middle.

It reminded her to straighten up, put on a brave front and trust her own strength. The tears dried before they formed, and her chin lifted. Taking a deep breath, she watched Thomas pluck his hat from a rack, shake hands again with the dastardly colonel and start for the door.

Silhouetted against the outside sunlight, he looked back at her. As he placed the hat on his head, Astrid remembered the first time she had seen him. So he looked now—bigger than life, the outline of his muscular arms highlighted against the wide sleeves of his open-collared shirt, his long sinewy legs taut under the tight leather knickers, his cuffed jackboots standing tall over his spread feet.

His clothing no longer looked at all silly.

In a surprising move, Thomas tossed her a jaunty salute. She smiled. Was he smiling, too? The light behind him kept her from knowing for sure.

And then he was gone. Oh God, I hate to see him leave.

Colonel Hill began bustling about, calling for someone named Marcy, running back to a narrow stairway at the end of the dark hall, stopping, turning toward her, twirling around again. His doughy face was red. Astrid wondered if he would drop from apoplexy on the spot. His attention was aimless, or at least aimed everywhere but at her. She sat on the bench, feeling miserable.

The black woman who had met them at the door rushed into the room. "Marcy, take the lady to her room and see that she's comfortable."

Astrid rose from the bench, took a sturdy

breath and moved to follow in the woman's ample wake.

Colonel Hill harumphed a couple of times, his usual preliminary to speech. "We'll have our midday meal when my wife Elizabeth returns from church," he said. "There's another guest here—Lord Percival Dunwoody, a visitor from England. Please feel welcome at my humble house."

That was it—short and to the point, hospitality without warmth. And the colonel lies glibly as well, she believed. Humble house, ha! The pompous ass thinks he's king of the hill. He should see the home his descendants will build on this land, then he truly could call this place humble.

Astrid said nothing but nodded, keeping her eyes down while he spoke. When she looked up, it was to follow Marcy. She didn't trust herself to meet the colonel's cruel eyes again. She easily could blurt out some of her choice 20th century vocabulary, and she knew that would never do.

Her room upstairs was relatively commodious. Two little green-leaded casements pierced the dormers on one wall. Though only half-windows, Marcy opened them for her, letting in a welcome breath of river air. The small openings looked out on the James. With a wistful eye, Astrid singled out a tiny gray sail making its short journey across to Bermuda Hundred.

Goodbye, Thomas Arrington, she whispered. I'll bet you're pleased as punch to be rid of me.

Feeling alone, despite Marcy's spacious presence, she looked around the room and saw better quality furniture than the Arringtons', and more of it. Too much for the space, actually. The whole thing impressed her as pretentious, much like its owner. A full-length wavy mirror in a dark wooden oval frame stood in one corner. A "great looking glass" it was called. Lizzie had told her about them. They were considered especially grand.

The large bed was pine with four pencil posts pointing toward the cross-beamed ceiling. Its fluffy high mattress indicated she would be sleeping on feathers again tonight. She had learned that was considered first-class. Humbler folk slept on flock mattresses stuffed with scraps of cloth, milkweed, or cattail-fluff, whatever that was. The bed was covered with something that looked like an oriental rug, and she fingered it with curiosity.

"Turkeywork," Marcy said without Astrid's asking. "Fine stuff, like all the Hills' belongings."

"Fine," Astrid agreed to be on the safe side. But much finer on the floor, she thought, which is exactly where I'll toss it tonight. Damned if I'll sleep under a heavy rug in this heat.

"Has you mo' clothes for me to hang, lady?" the black woman asked with a smile.

"No, I have no more with me." But more than enough on me to dress ten women, she thought wryly.

Marcy stood by an ornately carved chest and shuffled her wide clogs. Looking ill-at-ease, the woman started to speak but stopped herself.

Astrid watched her cautiously. She tried to look extremely royal and make her think we nobles always travel light. She kept her chin tilted upward, challenging the dark woman to have her say.

"Lady . . ." The woman looked toward the ceiling, the whites of her eyes growing large as she rolled them upward. Then she lowered them and shuffled again. "'Tis that we servants has heard of the wonderful thing you did yestiday, savin' that Jeremy Robins. I gonna see you has clothes for sleeping and anything else yo' pretty li'l heart desires."

Astrid was stunned. The word had spread, then, among the servants at any rate. Do the Hills know? As new fear flooded through her, two large black reassuring hands grabbed her own. Astrid's fear receded. With her wan face full of questions, she looked deeply into the liquid warm ebony of Marcy's eyes.

"De master and mistress don' know 'bout it, lady," Marcy said. "Jus' us po' servants. We calls you 'Countess,' we do. And we loves you fo' breathing life back into dat fine boy. Has no fear. We he'p you, alls we can!"

"Thank you, Marcy. I needed that." Astrid dropped her hands and went over to a padded chaise in the corner. She sank into its downy softness, removed her tight slippers and wiggled her sore toes.

"When's lunch?" she asked, feeling relaxed for the first time all day.

"Lunch, Countess?"

"The midday meal, Marcy. I don't want to go downstairs until I must."

The large woman chuckled throatily. "Don't

blames you. De master, he not a pleasant sort most of the time. De mistress, neither. But don' you tells 'em I said dat."

Astrid giggled and raised her hand to her lacy breast. "Your honest words stop here, I promise."

"They eats midday later on Sundays 'cause of the church meeting, prob'ly 'bout two hours from now."

"Then I'll rest here until then. Please call me when I'm expected, if you will." Astrid leaned back against the cushions. "Thank you, Marcy." She twinkled a conspiratorial smile toward the happy mahogany face. "For everything."

"Yes'm." The servant left the room in a blur of brown and white.

Astrid snuggled back into the cool, crisp fabric over the feather-filled pillows.

Well, I've got two children and possibly every servant in Virginia on my side now, she thought. That's getting to be quite an army.

She smiled. Move over, Mister Bacon! The countess and her troops are just getting organized!

Chapter Seven

"Ho, my pretty! Hold up and I'll stroll with thee."

Astrid paused on the narrow path in Shirley's garden and turned to see Lord Percival Dunwoody trotting to catch up with her. He's a regular court dandy, she thought, watching the Hill's other guest swagger closer. His elegant plush coat and pantaloons and richly embroidered waistcoat were probably the latest fashion in misty, cold London. Here under Virginia's cloudless sky and brilliant sun, she suspected he was developing a riotous case of heat rash.

She had to admire his cool composure though, as he pulled up alongside her and placed his delicate fingers under her lace-covered elbow.

"You put the heliotrope and periwinkle to

shame, my lovely," he said with a sweeping bow. "Mayhap we could find a green glade to hide thee from their jealous eyes so they might lift their heads once again."

Astrid smiled. " 'Tis not my presence that wilts them so, Lord Dunwoody, but the absence of timely rain, I vow." She was pleased with her turn of phrase. She was catching on quickly.

He squeezed her elbow and chortled. "Aye, my beauty, e'en the rain clouds hesitate to visit this wilderness outpost, and I understand their reluctance well." His sensuous lips beneath the clipped russet mustache spread in a dazzling smile that suffused his finely sculptured face but skittered around his pale green eyes, which were a shade too crafty to absorb the sparkle.

Taking a measure of those eyes, Astrid put herself on alert. My Lord may speak prettily of weather, but methinks he's got seduction on his mind, she warned herself. Keep your guard up, sister!

"The truth is, my lovely lady, 'til you appeared at the board this midday, my abiding impression of Virginia was 'tis an unseemly place peopled only with the unseemly. With but a whisper of blue taffeta you've caused me to alter that negative impression."

Astrid lowered her eyes. She wondered if he would interpret the color of her sun-kissed cheeks as a proper blush. No way did she want to antagonize this young gallant with his certifiable status as a man of connections.

On the other hand, his flowery come-on annoyed her. He was definitely on the make. Keeping him at arm's length while taking advantage of his lofty position was going to require careful strategy.

But, as usual in this strange world, she didn't have a glimmering as to how to play the game. For the time being she opted to remain silent, hoping some brilliant ideas would come to her.

Lord Dunwoody steered her from the garden path toward a weathered bench under a sprawling oak tree overlooking the James.

The cool shade was welcome after the strong sun. Astrid's ample layers beneath the blue dress were damp with unladylike perspiration. As she sat primly on the bench, she was glad for the whiff of breeze off the river. Instinct told her that wet patches under the arms of the taffeta would be quite unseemly to her companion. Maybe something could be said for the protection of cotton layers, as well as for staying out of the hot afternoon sun. No wonder every lady in the vicinity retired to her cool room after those heavy lunches. She had foolishly wanted to get some exercise.

Lord Dunwoody walked toward the edge of the shaded circle and bent to pluck a branch from a small plant. Sniffing its stem, he came back slowly to the bench.

Astrid watched him, sizing him up. She'd have called him foppish, but then, all the gentlemen she'd seen so far—with the exception of Thomas Arrington—looked a trifle sissy with their wigs, ruffles, ribbons and fancy shoes.

Granted, Lord Dunwoody outdid them all in that respect—a mark, perhaps, of his coming only recently from England and being privy to the king's circle, as she'd learned at lunch.

He was a riot of color—burgundy, blue and silver—and sported an array of silk ribbons that dangled about his lacy ruffled wrists and streamed from bow-knots at the gathered sides of his pantaloons like the ends of birthday party snappers. A puffy wig spilled curls about his shoulders and was the same russet color as his mustache.

The clothing overwhelmed any quick judgments she could make about him, but she tried.

He wasn't tall—only about five-nine, she guessed—but his bearing was good. He moved gracefully, almost like a dancer, and he was poised beyond his years, which she estimated to be in the mid-to-late twenties.

"Sassafras," he said, placing the aromatic twig beneath her nose. "Grows like weeds in this savage country, but 'tis highly prized by the folk in England and thought to be an effective physic for many ills. I shall take back a portmanteau filled with it as gifts for my friends."

"That's very kind of you, Lord Dunwoody." She couldn't think of anything more intelligent to say. Her knowledge of sassafras like everything else was limited.

He sat down beside her, slyly arranging himself so that his beribboned knee pressed against her full skirt. She sidled away just a hair's-breadth.

"You may call me Percy, my sweet," he said, still dazzling. "I sense we're two of a kind, thrust upon these alien shores. You, like I, are accustomed to a far grander life and could ne'er become part of this uncivilized land."

When his soft hand circled hers, Astrid felt a sour bubble of repulsion. Sliding his small prey toward him, Lord Percy maintained a decisive pressure with his knuckles so that she felt them brush suggestively through the layers of cloth over her leg. At the end of its short journey, her hand lay trapped against the warm fabric of his plush pantaloons. The tip of his index finger drew oval patterns around her large diamond.

"Aye, 'tis a grander life you've known," he said wistfully, his green eyes concentrating on the impressive stone.

"Perchance," Astrid said, pulling her hand away under the pretense of shooing a bothersome gnat. "I have no memory, as you were told at the midday board."

"A pity, that." His hand ventured to retrieve hers, but she kept her fingers busily out of his reach, adjusting the ribbon in her upswept hair, checking the lay of the modesty piece, pressing unseen wrinkles from her skirt. Undaunted, he placed his arm across the back of the bench and fondled her right shoulder.

"But 'tis the future that matters, my Teutonic beauty," he said with a wink of his unsmiling eyes. "I'll see to that meself."

Astrid cleared her throat nervously. "Yes, Lord Percy, I would welcome your assistance in finding my family and homeland," she hedged. She strongly objected to the possessive motions of his fingers on her shoulder, but thought best to ignore them at the moment.

He smiled, pressing his leg dangerously close to her hip. "The king's court would be graced by such as you, my lovely. If the buffoons at Green Spring can find naught about thee, I'll carry thee back to London. His majesty would welcome such a fair-haired jewel in his palace, and I'd stay close by to fill thy needs."

You're a bit too close now, buster, she wanted to shout, but remained silent. London? The king's court? Was that to be her destiny?

Astrid knew they were going to come up with zilch in their search from Green Spring, but she'd just have to let this drama play itself out. Better perhaps a courtesan in a glamorous setting than a witch among the provincials.

Still caressing her shoulder with his right hand, Lord Percy leaned toward her. With lightly dancing fingers, he provocatively outlined the swell of her breasts beneath the modesty piece. Astrid shuddered.

"A prize of a mistress you'd be, my love," he whispered huskily. "Think on it. Cooperate not with those at Green Spring, and I'll find thee a perfect place where we can make memories for thee in abundance." His full lips pressed against her heated cheeks. The stiff bristles of his mustache sent warning prickles into her sensitive skin.

A lump of nausea swelled up in Astrid's throat. She desperately wanted to leap away from his cloying embrace but restrained herself. Instead, she giggled daintily, slowly wormed herself out of his arms and stood up with a tender sigh.

"You paint a lovely picture, my lord," she said, not daring to look back at him, "but my past may preclude its happening. S'pose as is suspected we find I am indeed Dutch royalty? Their king might battle with England for me."

"Ha! The Orange monarchy stands fangless in that stupid republic," he scoffed. "And the Dutch navy sulks in the shadow of our superior English force since the Treaty of Westminster. You, my flower of loveliness, may be well worth a war, but methinks the Hollanders have no stomach for further battle with us."

Astrid frowned out at the glittering James and chastized herself for paying too little attention in her history classes. Did the Dutch have a republic already at this early time? Fat lot of good it did her, then, to be thought part of a royalty without power.

Lord Percy pounced on her silence. "See how it benefits thee to disappear within our own court? A much improved and merrier life for you, my golden-haired goddess." His voice oozed with lust.

Her mind raced. Should she grab for the tarnished brass ring he was offering her?

The warm light from the silvery river reminded her of something. What was it? A pair of eyes, impaling hers in the moonlight—eyes with pledges of help that couldn't be fulfilled, she reminded herself. She pushed away the memory.

Use common sense, Astrid. You're on a giddy carousel, and that ring the lord is dangling before you, tarnished though it may be, is about the brightest thing available at the moment. She turned around and looked into Lord Percy's stony eyes.

"How would you suggest I not cooperate at Green Spring?" she asked.

"Give them no information, e'en if you should remember aught."

"They'll find naught," she agreed with a sigh.

Astrid prepared herself for dinner with a sense of dread. The Hills were a gloomy pair, and their dark, heavily furnished dining room was even gloomier. Now that dusk had fallen, she knew the atmosphere around their table would be depressingly gothic.

Earlier, Marcy had brought her a tub of water and a bar of lavender soap and had supplied her with a stack of fresh undergarments. She was stuck with wearing Ann's blue taffeta outfit again, but she removed the stiff stomacher. It wasn't needed to cinch in her slender waist, and she'd remember to hold her shoulders up. She always had.

When Astrid finished dressing, she spotted a jar of scented potpourri on a tall chest and scattered a pinch of the dried flower petals down her bodice. Looking at her wavy reflection in the candlelit mirror, she made a hasty decision to forego the modesty piece. She reasoned a bit of exposure would be acceptable at Shirley's dinner table. At any rate, she knew she'd be cooler, and it might even look as if she'd properly changed for dinner.

She only hoped Lord Percy wouldn't drool too much.

Marcy brushed Astrid's long hair until it sparkled, clucking approvingly at "de head full of sunbeams de countess has."

Wondering if she might be living too dangerously, Astrid decided against arranging her hair back into the topknot. She bowed to the propriety of her new era by tying the sides back with the blue ribbon.

"Now youse the prettiest vision dis ol' house has ever seen," Marcy exclaimed.

"Thank you, Marcy," she said with a tiny smile. "But what this vision needs right now is courage to face another meal down there."

Marcy's hefty laugh rolled across the room. "Countess, I 'spects you got courage 'nuff to face more dan meals. Just don' let dat English lord turn yo' pretty little head, tho'. I don' laks dat man, nosirree!"

"He won't turn my head, Marcy." She giggled. "Nor any other part of me, if I have my way."

She wished she felt as sure of that as she sounded.

Steeling herself, she left the smiling black woman and started down the dark steps.

"That's terrible, terrible!" Mrs. Hill was saying with a frantic shake of her head as Astrid entered the dining room.

For a moment, she thought the woman was reacting to her low-cut dress and unknotted hair, but she was turned away from Astrid and

109

couldn't have seen her.

Colonel Hill had his arm around his wife's bent shoulders, attempting to console her.

Astrid stood in the doorway, reluctant to interrupt the troubled couple. She had an odd premonition that whatever was concerning them would concern her, too.

Cold perspiration beaded her palms, and she clasped them together. Holding her breath, she remained still in the flickering shadows near the door. Mrs. Hill's sobs frightened her.

What on earth had happened?

Like a colorful bantam rooster in green brocade and flapping red and black ribbons, Lord Percival Dunwoody swept into the somber room.

"Ho, there! Have you some canary to brighten our evening, Colonel Hill?"

With a final consoling pat on his wife's back, the colonel harumphed and turned toward his guests.

"Aye, of course we have canary, Lord Percy." He lifted a silver bell and tinkled it nervously.

"You must pardon my wife's sorrow for the nonce. We've received disturbing news from the frontier at the Falls. Yet another innocent family of our acquaintance has been savagely murdered by Indians!"

Astrid gasped. "What is their name?" Surely not . . .

"Watkins—James and Margaret Watkins. She was one of the Arringtons."

"Thomas's sister?" Her trembling voice was only a whisper.

The colonel nodded. "I fear 'tis true, milady. That family has had the sorrows of Job heaped upon them of late."

Immense sorrow encircled Astrid's heart. That gentle family . . . how they must be suffering. Tears pricked her lashes. She closed her eyes tightly, wringing her chilled hands together.

"How horrible," she mumbled weakly. She leaned back against the paneled wainscotting for support.

"But surely to be expected in this wild country," Lord Percy whispered back in her direction as he walked briskly to the sideboard where a black servant poured wine into slender crystal glasses. "Here, now, my good colonel and lovely ladies. Let's drown out this heavy mood with the solace of fine wine."

He lifted two glasses, handed one to the colonel and waited with smiling impatience as Mrs. Hill dabbed her eyes with a lacy handkerchief before accepting the offered wine. The woman kept her head bowed, a stricken look on her thin, pale face.

"And for you, my Hollander princess," the lord said gaily as he approached Astrid with two additional glasses. She pressed against the wall looking at him with disbelief. How could he be so callous and unfeeling? A wave of hatred for the man rolled over her.

"Take it, my lovely," he said under his breath, placing a small glass in her trembling hand. "What matters it to thee that Virginia peasants were felled by Indians?"

She shook her head. "The Arringtons were

kind to me. I feel sorrow for them." A tear slithered down her cheek. She kept her eyes on the liquid in the fragile glass in her hand.

Another harumph gurgled from across the room.

"Lord Dunwoody speaks sensibly, goodwife Elizabeth and Lady Van Fleet," Colonel Hill said. "There's naught we can do to bring back the murdered ones. News travels slowly from the frontier. Those poor souls departed this cruel world more than a week ago." He harumphed again. "Of course, our sympathy goes to our neighbors Arrington in this latest loss, but for the nonce, the young lord's good suggestion needs be obeyed." He raised his glass. "Here's to happier days."

"Hear! Hear!" Lord Percy crowed, lifting his glass to his sensual lips. Colonel Hill and his taciturn wife followed suit. Astrid stared at them, gripping her glass closely to her chest.

"To happier days, my fair lady," the smooth voice beside her insisted, signaling her manners were remiss.

Automatically, she sipped the sweet wine. It burned as it slid down her tight throat. Taking a deep breath, she closed her eyes, upturned the glass, and drained it with rapid swallows. She prayed for a quick numbing of her horror-filled brain.

"That's better," Lord Percy crooned. "I'll refill it for thee." With his reptilian eyes caressing the curves of her half-covered bosom, he lifted the glass from her shaking hand and walked back to the sideboard.

Astrid's thoughts whirled in a confusion of anxiety, chagrin and sorrow—anxiety over her future, chagrin she'd left off the modesty piece to further entice that cocksure rascal, and aching, piercing sorrow for the Arringtons. Sorrow, especially, for Thomas. She wished she could return to them. She wanted to comfort them in some way, to comfort him as he had her last night.

Get a hold on yourself, girl! She pushed away from the wall and walked toward the seat Colonel Hill was indicating was her assigned place for dinner. What comfort could you possibly be for anyone here, alien that you are? You're absolutely useless.

She sat down at the large table laden with silver goblets, crystal, blue china plates and creamy linens. Still no forks in sight. The spoon-knife routine again, she thought dejectedly. Maybe when she got established in this society she could design a fork and make a name for herself.

That's the rapidly gulped wine speaking, she tutted inwardly. She was far from established anywhere.

She sat to Colonel Hill's left, across from the disgusting English lord. Mrs. Hill, keeping her swollen, simpering face under rigid control, sat opposite her husband at the foot of the table.

Astrid had learned at the midday meal that the couple's three young children were visiting relatives down in Surry County near Jamestown. "My wife has not been well," the colonel had explained, "and has not the strength to have the wee rowdies underfoot for the nonce."

Astrid had noted a puffiness around Mrs. Hill's middle and suspected the worn woman was pregnant with yet another wee rowdy. Watching her accept a third glass of the strong canary, she wanted to warn her about the dangers of alcohol to expectant mothers, but kept silent.

Let the pitiful woman find relief where she can, Astrid told herself. Besides, this is obviously neither the time nor place to offer a 20th-century health tip.

A cadre of black and white servants brought in enough dishes to feed an army. With no appetite, Astrid dutifully picked at her food and listened half-heartedly to the conversation between Lord Percy and the colonel. Mrs. Hill, too, remained silent, keeping her eyes down and eating little.

"I hear word of troubles among some of your people, Colonel," Lord Percy said. "I understand they mean to search out the marauding Indians in defiance of Sir William's specific orders not to do so."

"Faugh! 'Tis but fiddle-faddle," Colonel Hill responded, spearing a hunk of meat with his knife and stuffing it into his already full mouth. He chewed noisily and washed it all down with a hearty gulp of claret from the silver goblet. "There be only some disgruntled ragtag farmers led by a handful of so-called gentlemen fire-brands," he added.

"That ne'er-do-well Nathaniel Bacon commands them, I'm told." Lord Percy laughed disdainfully. "Trouble enough he caused his father back home in England with his profligate ways. The old man feared Nathaniel would run through his inheritance before e'en he'd inherited it and wisely shipped him over here where he might learn thriftier ways."

The colonel motioned one of the attending servants to open another bottle of claret and to refill the goblets around the table. He looked thoughtful.

"Young Bacon found early favor in Virginia. He has an older cousin of the same name here, as you may know, and an honored man he is in the colony," he said. "The senior Nathaniel's influence paid rich rewards for his young cousin." His chuckle was hollow. "Why, Governor Berkeley appointed him to his council before his boots were dry from his voyage."

"Ha! And the young Bacon's wife be a cousin to Sir William Berkeley to add more influence." Lord Percy's next words were aimed directly toward Astrid. "I see connections are an asset in Virginia, just as they be in England."

She took a sip of claret and looked down at her plate.

"Aye," Colonel Hill responded. "But I vow the young Nathaniel has o'er stepped himself this time and has aroused the wrath of his honor the Governor. E'en now the good man's out to stop the empty rebel, and mark my words, he'll bring him to his knees as well as the other malcontents."

Not by marching north he won't, Astrid thought light-headedly, finding herself secretly rooting for Bacon and his men. She wasn't sure why, she couldn't remember how any of this turned out, but she decided she'd side with any faction opposing the likes of Colonel Hill and his cronies.

"Who be the other firebrand leaders you spoke of?" Lord Percy asked, twirling his goblet in his hand.

"Old Henry Isham of Bermuda Hundred. James Crews nearby at Curles. Those trouble-makers Lawrence and Drummond down in Jamestown. Maybe young William Byrd from up at the Falls." The colonel colored each name on his list with a touch of venom. "And I hear Edward Arrington brashly signed on and has joined Bacon in the unauthorized foray."

"Arrington?" Lord Percy inquired. "Related to the Arringtons of the recent tragedy?"

Astrid looked up with interest.

"Aye. The eldest son."

"Was not the tall fellow in rough clothing who brought over our charming Hollander this morning also an Arrington?" The sly green eyes probed Astrid's face. She remained expression-less and turned her attention to the food on her plate, but she made only a stab at eating. She kept her ears open, listening intently.

"That be Thomas," the colonel responded. "Thanks be to God that he's far too level-headed to get involved in such foolery. And tho' Thomas dons the outer clothing of common men, he's a passing uncommon man himself. Large hold-ings he has, and industrious he is. In Virginia, we consider him a true gentleman."

Mrs. Hill sobbed again. "And so I pray he remains," she said, breaking her silence. "I worry this latest loss may unsettle him."

"Nonsense, Elizabeth," Colonel Hill grumbled. "Stronger stuff he is than most men. We can count on Thomas Arrington to keep his balance, despite this last mighty blow that's befallen him."

It was late before Astrid could pull herself away from her dinner companions and escape to her room upstairs. As she closed the large door behind her, she saw there was no lock. She frowned. Damned if I'll let that bantam rooster drop in for a midnight visit, she fumed, quietly slipping a heavy chair across the floor and propping it under the unbolted latch.

With the entry secured to her satisfaction, she looked about the room. Now, like the rest of the house, it was shadowy and gloomy. Candles lit for her hours ago by Marcy burned low by her bed, beside the wash basin and over on the window sill.

Astrid was exhausted. The heavy business of being constantly on stage without either a script or clear direction was getting to her. At least for a few blessed hours she had a brief intermission.

She removed her clothing and draped the myriad pieces carefully across the chaise. She didn't want them to wrinkle, for she'd have to wear the whole superfluous mess again tomorrow.

Tomorrow. She didn't want to think about it. What new traumas were waiting for her down at Green Spring? And what about that obnoxious Lord Percy? Was she half-committed now to an unwanted liaison with the greasy scoundrel?

God help me, I'll fight that, she swore. His mistress, indeed. That'll be the day!

Better not worry about any of this now, she decided. I need these private moments to charge my batteries.

Quickly, Astrid splashed her face with the cold water in the ornate bowl on her washstand and patted herself dry with a soft cloth. She longed for a toothbrush. She'd have to find out soon what they did for dental care—or devise something if they hadn't thought of it yet.

She tossed some potpourri in a cup of water and rinsed her mouth. Maybe, she thought with faint hope, rose petals fight cavities.

As she had pledged earlier, she dumped the turkeywork rug off her bed into a crumpled heap on the floor. Marcy had laid a sheer linen nightgown across her pillow. Thank you, Marcy, but no thank you, she thought impishly. Tonight I sleep in the buff. She flung the flimsy garment across the room.

After blowing out the candles beside her bed and basin, Astrid walked over to the window and snuffed out the final one. The full moon brushed her skin with a pale glow. Below, the river twinkled back its captured light.

The beauty of the sweetly scented night captivated her. Enchanted, she propped her elbows on the sill and cupped her chin with her hands. Breathing deeply, she inhaled the essence of the warm Virginia darkness. Her eyes misted as they scanned the star-filled sky.

The magical river lay beneath. Dark, still clumps of trees guarded its banks, spreading black feathers on this side and solemn dense clusters on the far side.

The far side. Bermuda Hundred! The horror of the evening's news swept back over her. Those sweet Arringtons, how they must be suffering.

And Thomas. What of Thomas? Is he there close by his mother? Or is he back at Eagle's Crest, alone with his sorrow?

Poor, dear broken man, Astrid whispered to the dark, distant bank. If only I could help thee.

Not even noticing the odd vocabulary of her thoughts, she covered her face with her hands and wept.

She didn't hear the door scraping open behind her as it slowly pushed the protective chair forward.

Chapter Eight

"Where be you, my pretty?" Lord Percy's drunken whisper hissed through the door. Astrid slid back into the shadows and held her breath.

Warily, she watched him move into the room and walk unsteadily toward the empty bed. The moonbeams streaming through the casements lit him like a spotlight. Barefooted, he wore a silly looking white nightshirt that hung loosely around his calves. His wigless head was capped with short russet curls. The expression on his flushed face was a threatening blend of lust and smugness.

Astrid cringed in the darkness.

As he reached the bed, Lord Percy patted the mattress. "Hiding from me, are you now?" He sounded damnably sure of himself.

With a snicker, he looked about the room.

"Playing yet another game with me, my coy mistress?"

Astrid felt panic rising in her throat. Once again she was naked as a jaybird at a bad moment. Spotting her nightgown on the floor just beyond the casement, she longed to retrieve it for at least a shred of protection. But she didn't dare move.

"Aha! Is that lovely shadow yon my waiting beauty?" he asked, looking over at the chaise where she had piled her clothing.

As he started to lunge toward what he thought was his willing prey, his foot caught under the clump of rug that Astrid had thrown from the bed. With a grunt of surprise, he sprawled forward onto the floor.

Taking advantage of this blessed distraction, Astrid crouched under the moonlit casement and swiftly grabbed her discarded nightgown. Wishing Marcy had left her something sturdier, she threw on the thin garment and cowered against the shadowy wall. Her racing heartbeat pounded so loud in her ears she was certain he could hear it.

"Damnation!" he swore. "What in Satan's name was that?" He sat up, rubbing his bare legs. He looked back at the lump of rug.

"So that's where you be, my clever toy?" he said. Throwing his arms around the awkward bundle, he rolled over on top and playfully embraced it. "A pity to smother such loveliness," he cooed into the thick weave. "I'll uncover thee and we can play a far better game!"

Astrid wasn't amused. She knew she had only

seconds to escape. That empty rug wasn't going to give him the pleasure he was seeking, and she'd be damned if she'd oblige him either. She ran for the half-open door.

"No, you don't, milady!" Lord Percy leapt from the floor like a toad in heat. Grabbing Astrid away from the door, which still had the useless chair propped against its latch, he clasped her wrists tightly with his hands and pinned her arms over her head against the wall.

"Let go of me, you bastard!" she cried, praying someone would hear and come to her rescue.

"I like my damsels fiery," he crooned, his lascivious sneer sickening her. His breath, fetid with wine, blew hot waves across her face before his full lips invaded hers.

She struggled wildly as his bristly mustache, hard teeth, and stabbing tongue mounted a combined assault against her reluctant mouth. Her screams were muffled by his battering attack. His body pressed hers firmly against the wall.

"Aye, you be a spirited wench," he mumbled wetly, pushing even closer before stifling her frenzied protests again with his insistent mouth. Still clamping her wrists above her head with his hands, he crushed his ribs into her breasts. He began a rough undulating motion across them—a heavy, aggressive caress that spread shock waves of pain through Astrid.

She was frantic. He was far stronger than he looked. He had caught her unaware and bound her now in a restraining grip she couldn't fight. Full of loathing and disgust, she shook her head furiously, desperately trying to avoid his repulsive kisses.

But her violent movements were like a bellows to his blazing ardor.

Horrified, Astrid felt a hot pulsing hardness rising insidiously against her stomach.

That does it, you skunk! With a sudden surge of strength, she shoved her elbows into his shoulders and rapidly thrust her knee upward.

Lord Percy folded forward with a groan of agony.

Free from him, Astrid crazily tore her nails down his rigid cheeks and began pummeling her fists against his bent shoulders.

"Get out of here, you bastard!" she sobbed. "Get away from me!"

Lord Percy fell to his knees and rolled over sideways. He lay stiffly curled on the floor.

"Countess! You need he'p?" Marcy pushed through the door and ran into the room. Her big eyes stared at the fallen lord, and she looked back with disbelief at Astrid, who was sobbing uncontrollably.

Marcy wrapped her arms around the hysterical woman and held her close to her ample bosom. "What on earth happened, my chile?" she asked.

"I think I've killed him, Marcy," Astrid whimpered between sobs. "He was trying to . . . trying to attack me!"

Lord Percy groaned from the floor.

"He ain't dead, Countess, but I think you pulled in the rascal's sails a mite," the servant said with a deep chuckle. She gave Astrid a comforting squeeze. "I better take him to his room where he belongs."

Paralyzed, Astrid watched Marcy help Lord Percy to his feet. He was a miserable sight. Blood dribbled from the gashes on his cheeks and he looked small and weak in his disheveled nightshirt. He remained curved over like the question marks that filled his pale green eyes. He aimed those eyes upward at Astrid.

"God damn your blood," he hissed. "I'll . . . . I'll ruin you!"

Astrid shivered. As Marcy led him out of the room, she saw his face distorted with pain and hatred. He leaned against the large black woman and shuffled like a broken old man through the door.

"You made an enemy now fo' sure, Countess," Marcy said when she returned to Astrid's room a short while later. "But dat man he no good friend to have neither. Don' you worry none. He ain't gonna hurt thee. Us servants see to dat."

"I hope you're right, Marcy." Astrid shook her head. "I've certainly started out on the wrong foot though."

"Wrong foot, Countess?" the servant asked. "What you mean?"

Astrid sat on the edge of the big feather bed and sighed. "Nothing, really. I'm so upset I don't even know what I'm saying."

"Youse a mighty brave lady, I'll say dat." She walked over to Astrid and took her hands. "I don't know what you did to dat man, but I know he deserved it ev'ry bit."

Astrid began to tremble again. "I'm not sure what I did either. I was so frightened." She looked up at Marcy, her face full of fear.

"What will they do to me, Marcy? The Hills . . . surely they haven't slept through this uproar."

"Dey sleep downstairs on t'other side of the house, and dey sleep mighty sound. Dey don' know nothin'." She smiled down at Astrid. "And dey won't neither. Dat bad lord ain't gonna tell 'em he tried to harm their lady guest, you can rest easy on dat."

"I'm afraid, Marcy," Astrid repeated.

Marcy soothed the tousled blonde hair. "Now you jus' turn over and lay yo' pretty head up on dat bolster and close yo' eyes," she said. "I gonna rub yo' back and hum a song 'til yo' fear flies away."

Astrid did as she was told. She lay on her stomach on the fluffy mattress. Marcy's hand ran gently across her back, and the dark woman began to hum a soft tune. Gradually, the tight spring of tension within Astrid uncoiled.

She closed her eyes. Lulled by the tender motions of Marcy's fingers and the dusky sweet sounds of an ancient tribal melody, she gradually drifted off into a warm cradle of sleep.

The large brigantine *The Fearless* looked forbidding to Astrid as she boarded it early the next morning. The name of the vessel was a mockery to her—she was so filled with fear her knees shook. Luckily, they were well hidden beneath the blue taffety skirt, and she somehow maintained a calm, self-assured facade.

Not so, the sulking Lord Percy. The Hills had looked inquisitive when he appeared at the breakfast table. His ashen face, punctuated by the thin, jagged scratches on his cheeks, had obviously aroused their curiosity, but their seventeenth-century manners kept them silent.

They seemed to accept his lame excuse about "thrashing about during a nightmare's visit," but Mrs. Hill had expressed concern over the state of his health and offered him some "fever-root to purge thee, for the colony is rife with ague."

Lord Percy had declined, mumbling something about a "black choler" that descended upon him occasionally and adding he had already drunk a "physic" in his room.

A little hair-of-the-dog, Astrid suspected.

Nevertheless, he looked like hell. And Astrid couldn't be sure if it was manners or lack of perception that had prevented the Hills from commenting on the blatant scowls he kept casting in her direction.

She had come close to losing her composure when she learned she'd be traveling alone with Lord Percy and his crew on the voyage to Green Spring. Marcy came to her rescue, though, with a plea to accompany them "so I might visit my po' ailing cousin, she in the Lady Berkeley's service."

When the Hills agreed to her request, Astrid had breathed a sigh of relief. Good old Marcy, who probably was lying through her pearly teeth about the cousin, had saved the day.

As the odd trio of lost Hollander, black servant and pale English Lord boarded the vessel, Colonel and Mrs. Hill stood on Shirley's bank. Astrid detected a more relaxed expression on their bland faces. The departing visitors had apparently been an unaccustomed strain on their tenuous hospitality, and they looked as though they might break into an uncharacteristic burst of glee when the ship's sails were hoisted.

A group of servants clustered in the background. Their warmth toward Astrid had not gone unnoticed by her, and her few smiles of the morning had been reserved for them in private moments away from the Hills' eyes.

Though they were fully respectful of Lord Percy on the surface, the help the workers had offered him had been uneven at best. One lanky youth had tripped clumsily on the gangplank, losing his hold on a fancy family-crested portmanteau that plunged with a heavy splash into the river. This mishap brought Colonel Hill's wrath down upon the servant and an ensuing sputtering of apologies to Lord Percy.

Astrid had secretly winked at the shirtless lad as he walked by her with his head bowed. Only she and Marcy caught the knowing half-smile he tossed in passing.

As *The Fearless* set sail, Astrid chose to stand on the starboard side of the deck as far as possible from Lord Percy, who perched gloomily on a capstan on the port side. His soaked luggage, retrieved for him by one of the sailors, dripped puddles near his feet. Astrid wondered if his prized sassafras might be steeping a premature tea inside.

But she warned herself not to let her guard down just because a few servants had given the rogue a hard time. He was still plainly a danger to her.

She also was troubled by the letter that Colonel Hill had given Lord Percy to deliver to the Lady Frances in the governor's absence. Protocol evidently didn't allow Astrid to deliver the letter herself.

The large white envelope with a red wax seal emblazoned on its flap sat tauntingly on Lord Percy's lap. She longed to know what the colonel had written and was bitterly opposed to its having been entrusted to the English popinjay.

With Marcy standing close by her side, Astrid crossed her arms on the railing and watched the Hills, their servants and Shirley slowly disappear from view behind the ship's stern as it pulled away from shore and turned south in a large arc. The river's strong breezes furled the sails and whipped Astrid's loose hair about her face.

As the boat made its turn, she looked over at the point jutting out from the Arringtons' land. There it was—the site of her strange arrival. My God, was it only two days ago? It seemed, literally, like centuries.

Astrid wished she could sneak back over, search for that mossy spot, and sit and wait for another shooting star. She was damned tired of trying to cope in this stupid era.

"Dat rascal Lord he done hid dat letter under

129

his vest, Countess," Marcy whispered, interrupting Astrid's thoughts. "I don' trust dat man!"

"Watch him best you can, Marcy," Astrid said without turning around. She felt a new uneasiness. "I don't know what that letter says, but even Colonel Hill's words will be safer for me than anything Lord Percy might get into his crazy head to tell Lady Berkeley about me."

Marcy pushed away from the railing. "I gonna mosey over t'other side and keep my eye on him during the voyage," she said in a low voice. "You jus' stay over here as far as you can 'way from us."

Humming the same haunting tune she had used as a lullaby the night before, Marcy slowly sauntered across the deck.

The era might be stupid, but that woman's worth her hefty weight in gold, Astrid thought.

Looking out at the silvery water, she wondered what that crafty devil Percy had up his sleeve. She knew what he had in his vest. And there were nothing but venomous snakes in his head and heart—plus a slightly sore one in his fancy pants, she thought, stifling a sneer.

A small gray sail crossing over toward Bermuda Hundred caught her eye. All thoughts of Lord Percy's devilment and her own sorry plight vanished, and her heart flip-flopped in a funny little somersault.

Thomas Arrington! She could see him clearly. He was sitting ramrod straight, holding the boat's tiller steadily and staring ahead toward the Arringtons' wharf.

His face in profile was strongly set, like a

marble sculpture, but she felt she could see a ripple of tautness along his rugged jaw. In a surprising move, he turned his head toward her. His shaded eyes were too faraway for her to read their expression. She sensed they were hurt and deeply stricken, and she ached for him.

Astrid didn't know what to do. She wanted somehow to communicate to Thomas that she knew about the death of his twin sister, that she was feeling deep sympathy for him, and that she was willing to relieve him of his pledge to help her, even though she could really use him at the moment.

What signal could possibly transmit all that? Feeling hopelessly inadequate, she stared at him and remained frozen at the rail.

And then Thomas waved to her. She felt tears filling her eyes. He, the bobbing little boat and the bright water blurred together for a moment. Astrid blinked back the tears and waved back.

He turned his face and looked back toward the Arringtons' wharf.

The Fearless completed its wide arc and began its slow journey through the bends of the James toward Green Spring.

Astrid looked at the riverbank moving past her. That brief encounter with Thomas Arrington had lifted her spirits. But why on earth? Nothing makes sense any more. Maybe it's because he's the one who had given her those guiding words: "You must be strong from now on, milady. You must find the strength within yourself."

She glanced over at Marcy, who was idly

standing close to Lord Percy.

As she looked back toward the river and its west bank, she whispered, "I'll be strong, Thomas Arrington."

Thomas docked his boat at Edward's wharf. Before walking up to the house, he watched the brigantine grow small in the distance. The Hollander was on her way back to her own people. She, at least, might find happiness again. He wished her well.

For a brief moment, her golden hair and bright blue dress had floated across the murky blackness of his thoughts, reminding him with a stab that the earth still held color.

None for him, though. Ne'er again. The darkness enshrouding him was colorless, and heavy and dense enough to snuff even the sun's radiance. Astrid vanished quickly from his thoughts.

His heart lay like lead in his chest. It was as if it had stopped beating yesterday when the dusty rider from the Falls imparted his terrible message, and it had been unwilling since to pick up its old rhythms.

Dear Margaret, you also are now torn from me. You, my beloved sister, blood of my blood, flesh of my flesh. We always were two like one. My soul already had crumpled like a sail from its mast at the loss of Sarah and Betty. Now, with you gone too, I am truly alone.

He'd be alone until his dying day, he knew with grim certainty as he started toward Edward's house on this Monday morning.

The distant thunder of hooves reached his

ears, and he stopped, looking southward.

Jeremy Robins came running from the woods.

"'Tis the guv'ner and hundreds of men, Master Thomas!" the lad shouted. He ran up to Thomas, flushed and out of breath.

"He's enlisting all who'll join him to stop Colonel Bacon and t'others. I told him you were in mourning and all, but he's determined to talk with you and is heading this way." Jeremy's words tumbled out in a rush. "Master Thomas, the fool's marching north! Didn't Colonel Bacon and Master Edward and t'others go sou . . ."

"Take a breath, lad, and cease for a moment," Thomas interrupted with a frown. "And show proper respect for our governor henceforth. A fool he's not, my lad."

"But . . ." Jeremy looked flustered.

"We know naught about the direction Colonel Bacon and his men went, remember that well."

"Yes sir." The boy nodded and lowered his eyes.

"Now run in and tell Mrs. Arrington we're expecting guests. She'll want to offer them fresh water from the well."

As Jeremy ran toward the house, Thomas sighed wearily and braced himself for the encounter with Governor Berkeley.

Knowing full well what to expect, he dreaded the meeting. The governor would be unctious with his gentlemanly condolences, mouthing empty words Thomas didn't want to hear, and then he would follow with prying questions about Edward's whereabouts. He undoubtedly would grow vexed and bad-tempered when

Thomas fended off his inquiries and told him nothing.

Which Thomas knew he must and would do. Though he had disapproved of Edward's folly, he was now convinced the Indians' heinous actions must be stopped.

Perchance Bacon's foray will turn the tide, he prayed.

Let the ranting governor go on his wrongheaded march north. Thomas knew he would tell him naught today. Later, when the governor returned to Green Spring, he would call upon him to plea for more sensible actions. For now . . .

The thud of horses' hooves grew louder. A throng of mounted men, led by the fat, scarlet-cloaked Governor Berkeley, broke into the clearing.

Thomas stood his ground and watched them approach.

The governor removed his plumed hat with a practiced swirl. The small eyes in the rosy round face blinked with a studied effort to express concern.

"My heartfelt sorrow, Thomas," he began as if on cue. "I but heard the dreadful news."

Chapter Nine

Astrid's Journal

Green Spring—Late p.m., May 15, 1676

Now I suppose you could call me a thief. But you have to understand how desperate I am. I'm hoping Governor Berkeley won't miss the quill pen, ink pot, and few sheets of paper when he returns home. When I saw them on his desk this morning, I knew what I must do.

Let's face it, dear diary, I'm fighting for my sanity at this point, and you're going to be my weapon.

Maybe I'm foolish jotting down my thoughts like this. No one's going to see you but me, though. I've found a nifty hiding place—the old loose floorboard routine—with plenty of room for you and my purloined stationery supplies.

Thomasina Ring

I need you—desperately. There's no other possible confidante, so it's either using you this way or carrying on conversations with myself. And the odds are that mumbling out loud would get me into hot water far faster than this bit of secret writing.

I'll play those odds.

How do I begin? Two weeks ago tonight I was wrapping up a good run as Helen in *Midsummer Night's Dream*. It was 1989. I drank some champagne, joined a young man on a joy ride to a wild island and woke up the next morning in 1676!

Anyone else might have ended up with a simple hangover, a few regrets and a mosquito bite or two. Not me. *I* landed smack dab in the middle of a half-remembered rebellion 313 years before my time.

Good fortune, as you see, is not one of my strong suits.

The determination to survive, however, is.

And I've done fine so far, damn fine. The diamond ring helped, and my recent experience with Shakespearean dialogue hasn't hurt either. Maybe both were just dumb luck.

Okay. But how about my ability to cope and adapt? Now that's not happenstance, though I'll admit my coping talents are crumbling around the edges. Which, of course, is why I've come to you.

Let's talk about Green Spring. It's a fancy place, the grandest thing around, I suspect. Suffice it to say it's way bigger and more richly furnished than anything else I've encountered since my arrival. And the gardens are something out of a storybook.

Servants are everywhere to attend all my needs, except the primary one—my gnawing need to get back to the 20th century!

Oh—and a genuine bathroom would be a godsend.

All that aside, you could say I'm pretty comfortable under the circumstances.

The gentleman of the house isn't at home, so I haven't yet met Governor Berkeley. He's up looking for Bacon and his troops near a place called the Falls. I have a hunch that's near where Richmond will be someday.

The Lady Frances (Mrs. Berkeley) is an okay person, I suppose, if your standards for okay aren't too picky.

She has two driving interests—clothes and men—and the time, money and opportunity to indulge herself royally with both.

Between her fittings and flirtations, however, she seems to welcome my company. I believe she's starved for girl talk, and, lucky for me, she considers my ear a receptive one.

She's 40 if she's a day, but refuses to act that old—and amazingly, she pulls it off. Maybe it's true you are what you think you are. I see her as a prime example of the power of positive thinking.

In the absence of her husband, she's currently fooling around shamelessly with that scoundrel Lord Percy. It's so obvious it's almost laughable.

Though I should add that I find it hard to

laugh about anything having to do with Lord Percy. The man's hatred for me is downright frightening.

To think I used to consider Derek Woodward the epitome of a spoiled brat. Compared to Lord Percival Dunwoody, Derek was (is? will be?) a man of rare quality.

Rotten Percy was thwarted at the pass by Marcy when we landed at Green Spring. He had hidden Colonel Hill's letter under his vest and evidently had it in his twisted head to do me in. Marcy and I suspect he had planned to turn me over as a prisoner accused of spying and treachery.

"Does the governor's jail have room for yet another?" were his first words to the Lady Frances as we disembarked.

Marcy and I were close behind, waiting for an introduction. She had been helping me with a piece of gold thread that had dangled loose from my slippers. It had tripped me up on the gangplank, and I'd almost fallen into the Chickahominy.

When Marcy heard Lord Percy's words, she laughed heartily, straightened up to her full mammoth height and shouted right over his red wig so the Lady Frances would be sure to hear.

"Don't forget to give de Lady Berkeley dat letter from Master Hill you got in yo' vest pocket, Lord Dunwoody," she said.

Marcy has a special air about her. I think it's that combination of regal bearing and impressive size. And though I'm sure it's unusual for servants to speak up like that, she got away with it and saved the day for me again.

Lord Percy looked flustered, but he pulled out the letter and handed it over to the lady of the manor. And he covered himself well enough, though his face turned magenta, almost a perfect match with his ribbons.

He said something like, "How careless of me, milady. Of course, I should have presented this and the Lady Van Fleet before aught else. But your rare beauty overwhelmed me, and I considered the mere act of feasting my unworthy eyes upon the governor's fair lady should be cause enough to have his men fling me into a dark cell."

His flattery impressed Lady Frances. It was clear he had taken a giant step toward her boudoir with his smooth lies, and I'm sure that's where he's landed nightly since our arrival.

Colonel Hill's letter was straightforward, providing only the meager information Thomas Arrington had shared with him about me.

I understand the governor's men have made inquiries to the few Dutchmen down in Jamestown and have had no success. I'm still a mystery woman.

Green Spring—Afternoon, May 20, 1676

I saw Thomas Arrington yesterday, and I can't get him out of my mind.

He was in Jamestown. I'd gone down in the coach with Lady Frances who has invited me to accompany her on shopping excursions several times.

He was coming out of one of the small brick cottages on Back Street, across from the State House.

Thomas was grim-faced as usual but looked wonderful! Lady Frances fluttered her eyelashes until she nearly blinded herself, but he didn't pay her a bit of attention. Oh, he was polite enough, but he treated her the same way he did me, which was well-mannered and cool as all get out.

He seemed preoccupied by something.

Jeremy was with him and I almost hugged the boy, I was so glad to see him again. The feeling was mutual, I believe, but we restrained ourselves and only exchanged pleasantries. I told the youngster to give my greetings to Mrs. Arrington, Ann and Lizzie. He assured me "they're in good health and will be pleased to know the countess is likewise."

Running into Thomas and Jeremy made me realize how much I've missed being around durable, earthbound people like the Arringtons. Since Marcy left last week to return to the Hills, I've had no real allies nearby. The Berkeley's servants haven't given me any hints they think I'm some kind of heroine. They seem to be a cowed bunch.

I'm damnably lonely and worried about what's ahead for me. I'm also concerned about Thomas.

After he and Jeremy left us, Lady Frances told me he'd probably been visiting "that trouble-maker Richard Lawrence who is one of the instigators of this nasty Bacon business, for that house belongs to him."

If she's suspicious that Thomas himself is in on the so-called nasty business now, she didn't let on—not to me, anyway—but heaven only knows what she's said to others. And the governor is due back home any day now.

I hope Thomas isn't in any danger.

For sure, he could face some danger on another front.

Lady Frances heaved a wistful sigh as she watched him walk away from us yesterday. "Thomas Arrington is by far the loveliest morsel of manhood in Virginia," she said. "And, just think on it, he's free of ties since the slaying of his wife."

I could see the wheels whirling behind her bright brown eyes, conjuring up a way to finagle him into her busy bed.

I think she's barking up the wrong tree this time. May I add "I hope so"? Thomas Arrington strikes me as a man far too principled for such frivolous dalliances. Besides, I've got to believe in somebody around here.

And he is . . . well . . . far too special for the likes of Lady Frances.

Incidentally, they tell me that coach the lady and I ride to Jamestown is the only one in the colony. I don't think coaches will catch on for a long while. First of all, there are no roads, so a coach can only be used when it's dry like it is now. Also, the wooden wheels and lack of springs give a far from luxurious ride. It's damnably hard to maintain my ladylike cool while bouncing around inside, but the trip's only two miles or so.

Jamestown's a dusty, squalid, overcrowded little town, and it smells to high heaven. Lady Frances and I primly hold perfumed hankies to our noses as we parade down to the dock where ships laden with bolts of silk and other luxuries await us.

She's purchased all kinds of finery for me, so I'm dressed to the gills most of the time. "You must have clothing fitting for your rank," she tells me. Ann Arrington's blue taffeta is packed away and will be returned to her soon, I hope. "It is sorely out of fashion," Lady Frances says. "Not at all what the London ladies are wearing now."

Unfortunately, what they are wearing is similarly overdone.

Woe is me, dear diary. Writing to you is turning out to be as tiring as trying to sift through my daily thoughts. Maybe I'm doomed to end up insane.

But I don't have time for that right now, nor for continuing this conversation with you. The time for afternoon naps is over. (I've learned to stay indoors and rest after lunch.) The Lord Percy and good Lady Frances will be stirring about before long.

I suspect they've been doing more than stirring in that overstuffed bedroom of hers these past two hours.

It's vaguely amusing to see their flushed faces and glazed eyes every day at teatime.

Ah me, all that lustiness in this sweltering heat! How she stands him, I can't imagine.

As for her hankering after Thomas Arrington, that I can understand.

But enough! Down you go into your hiding place. I'll bring you back anon.

Green Spring—5 p.m., May 25, 1676

I'm terrified!

They're planning to send me to England on the first of June. I'm scheduled to sail with Lady Frances and Lord Percy.

The mere thought of it scares me out of my wits, and I'd probably find it fatal as well. Lord Percival Dunwoody definitely has me on his black list, and I'm sure he'll try to arrange a convenient accident at sea.

In three words, I'm not going.

And I think I've found a way to escape. Heaven only knows where I'll escape to, but I've got to get away.

A plan of sorts is falling into place, thanks to Jeremy Robins. Talk about bread cast upon the water. I saved his life, and now I think he's going to save mine.

Let me backtrack a bit, to get my own thoughts in order.

The governor returned a few days ago. He was in a rage because he'd discovered in his march through the colony that he was far from popular any more. The people are sick of his heavy-handed policies and let him know it.

They're also tired of his ineffective handling of

the Indian situation and are murmuring about his self-serving reluctance to do anything to interfere with his own lucrative beaver trades. Rumors are rampant that he's lost his senses in his old age.

He got wind of all of it and is in an explosive temper most of the time.

A lost Dutchwoman is low on his list of priorities. In fact, I'm only a minor nettle while the rest of it is stinging him like a swarm of killer bees.

Grumbling all the while, he's been taking action right and left to prevent an all-out rebellion. In an attempt to placate the colonists, he's called for a long overdue election of assemblymen and is, for the first time, allowing freemen as well as property holders to vote. Needless to say, women don't count.

He's also issued a pardon to all those who joined Bacon in the unauthorized foray—except for Bacon himself, that is. He swears he'll hang him.

It was a real blow to the governor when he found out the rebels had marched south. Though they haven't returned yet, rumors have it they've been victorious, and Bacon's become a real folk hero. This drives the governor up the wall.

In his flurry of rapid-fire decisions, he's arranged to send the Lady Frances to England "to be his emissary to King Charles in this unfortunate matter." Lord Percy was due to sail next Monday, so Governor Berkeley booked passage for the lady and, as an afterthought, saw a way to get me out of his hair at the same time.

Of course, he has no idea how chummy his wife and Percy are, or he might have thought twice before packing them off on the same ship. It would never occur to him that the good Lord Dunwoody would bed down his wife, let alone dump a Hollander countess into the ocean.

However, I've seen the bitterness and hatred in Percy's eyes when he looks at me, and I'm getting out!

When I ran into Jeremy today down in Jamestown, I saw a way.

He was alone, standing outside the Lawrence house. Thomas was probably inside, but I didn't see him.

With Lady Frances next to me, I had to be careful, so I watched my words.

"I'm sailing to England next week," I told him, "and, alas, I so wish to return Ann Arrington's dress. Coulds't you perchance come to Green Spring on the morrow and take it for her?"

Then I had a stroke of luck. Lady Frances spotted a passing gentleman acquaintance and, with fan fluttering, walked away from us to greet him.

Grabbing Jeremy's hand, I dropped all pretenses and let him see my desperation.

Quickly, I whispered that I must talk with him alone. He was to tell no one, but I had to escape. I needed him, and I had a plan.

All of it was true except the last bit, but I knew I'd have a plan in mind when we met again. I'd have to.

Lady Frances rejoined us then, and I put the

pretenses back on my face. It's what I've come to think of as my slightly superior, totally complacent countess look.

Jeremy was perfect. His cherubic expression never changed, but the amber highlights in his eyes sparkled, a reassuring sign he understood and would come through.

"Milady," he said to me after politely acknowledging Lady Frances's return, "I will come this evening instead, if that be convenient. Master Thomas wishes to leave for Eagle's Crest at dawn tomorrow."

"Come when you will, lad," Lady Frances interjected. She was bored with the conversation and wanted to move on. "The servants will bundle up the dress. Go to the rear door when you arrive, and they'll hand it to thee."

I protested, insisting I wished to give it to Jeremy personally. What else could I do? Fortunately, the Lady was distracted by a pair of gentlemen heading our way and ignored my breach of etiquette with a wave of her fan.

"Whatever," she said with disinterest. Pulling me along, she turned on her best smile and walked toward the men.

"I'll be there at nine, Countess," Jeremy called out to me.

Green Spring—Near midnight, May 25, 1676

Jeremy was right on time tonight. I met him at the garden door.

Getting away from the others was simple. As usual, they'd dipped deep into their cups before, during and after dinner. By 8:30, their conversation, which is boring enough when they're sober, had deteriorated into the ridiculous.

I feigned a headache and asked to be excused. None of them batted an eye. And Lady Frances had forgotten all about Jeremy's coming for Ann Arrington's dress.

I had counted on that. The subject hadn't come up again, and I packed the dress myself rather than have one of the servants do it. While I was at it, I included in the bundle one of the more fashionable ensembles Lady Frances bought for me. Lord knows, I won't be needing it much longer. There'll be no room for luggage when I make my break, and the green outfit will look smashing on Ann. It's a minor repayment for that family's kindness to me.

My plans for escape were far from complete when Jeremy arrived, but I had the basics down pat—money, timing and transportation.

Money is the first order of business, and the diamond will help me there. Timing's important, and I figure my best opportunity will be Friday night during the gala farewell ball they're having for Lady Frances and Lord Percy here at Green Spring. For transportation, it'll have to be a horse. I'm a novice at sailing, and that would be impossible at night anyway.

It all hinges on Jeremy, and I have faith the lad can do it.

We talked in the garden less than an hour, keeping our voices low. The sense of urgency made both of us sharp-witted, and our strategy fell into place quickly.

Jeremy never questioned the need for my escape. He seemed to accept that as a given. Knowing I was right about needing money, he reluctantly agreed to take the diamond ring and try to sell it. He'll get silver for it, he said, and buy me a strong horse. And he'll bring me dark, sturdy clothing that will make a good disguise, he promised.

Friday, at midnight, I'll meet him behind the stable. If my luck holds, the party will be at its highest pitch, and I'll be able to slip away unnoticed.

Jeremy argued vehemently that I couldn't go off alone, that he must go with me, but I held my ground. I won't risk his life, I told him, and besides, his place is with the Arringtons. "It's out of the question, Jeremy. Better that I drop the whole idea and sail to England."

He finally gave in, but he looked unhappy.

"Where will you go, milady?" he asked plaintively.

"North," I answered with a bravado I didn't feel.

Anywhere but England, Jeremy. I'll take my chances here in Virginia.

Chapter Ten

Thomas Arrington didn't like to waste time on idle fancies like a frivolous ball at Green Spring. Had it not been for Richard Lawrence's ardent persuasion, he never would have agreed to come.

He was still in mourning, and this invitation from Governor and Lady Berkeley was somewhat improper. He was not often on their social list. Why did it come now, with him, like the rest of the colony, reeling from inner turmoil?

"What matters why they invited you, Thomas?" Lawrence had insisted. "'Tis an opportunity for thee to have the governor's ear. He'll listen to none of us, for we're marked as Bacon's men. You, by grace of this invitation, may steer him from his distempered course that leads the colony down but one path—to full rebellion.

Go, Thomas, and prevail upon him the good sense of pardoning Bacon and giving him a commission upon his return. Naught else will save Virginia nor the governor's skin."

A mighty mission, Thomas thought with a sigh as he approached Green Spring. Bright torches encircled the large house, their gawdy fingers of flame beckoning the guests to enter. His horse slowed to a walk, as reluctant as its tall rider to get closer.

A stable boy ran awkwardly toward him. The youth wore an ill-fitting peruke and a ruffled shirt over stiff leather breeches. His new buckled shoes were already lightly dusted with powdery soil.

Foolish to dress a stable hand thus, Thomas thought as he dismounted and handed the reins over to the boy.

"He'll need some water when he cools down, Peter," he said with a warm smile. "And you look somewhat dry yourself, lad. Best you take a few sips of your own at the well."

"Aye, Master Thomas." The boy crinkled a toothy smile. "'Tis rain we need, sir, and 'tis damnably hot this May."

Thomas knew Peter Cook only slightly. A strapping lad from Devonshire, he was a friend of Jeremy's. The two youths had met on the boat to the colony and, when Jeremy was in town and the boys' duties allowed, they spent companionable hours in a tavern by Jamestown's wharf.

Thomas's brow furrowed. Jeremy had disappeared this noon while Thomas was visiting

Lawrence and hadn't returned before he had set out for Green Spring. 'Twasn't like the lad to go off without telling him. He'd assumed he was with Peter, but he saw now that Peter was occupied tonight.

Thomas paused before stepping up to Green Spring's entry and shouted back to the youth.

"Do you know where Jeremy might be this even, Peter?"

"Nay, sir," the boy said with a shake of his head. "'Tis been a fortnight or more since I seen 'im. Tell the rogue I miss his unseemly face."

Thomas turned and climbed the torchlit stairs. Laughter wafted on waves of spirited music through the open door. Hautboys and fiddles had struck up a lively schottische.

He pushed thoughts of Jeremy from his mind. The lad was not one for getting into trouble. There'd be a good explanation on the morrow.

Thomas tightened his jaws and steeled himself. For now, he needed to withstand this frivolity and to catch the governor's ear.

A servant met him with a bow and a smart clicking of heels and took his ostrich-plumed hat. It wasn't his. Lawrence had foisted it on him along with this damnable mission.

Removing his baldric and sword, Thomas hung them on a rack beside more decorative weapons of the other gentlemen guests. He walked into the grand hall where ladies in a rainbow of gowns whirled around their brightly dressed partners. The party was in full bloom.

Thomas, in his somber black waistcoat and

breeches, stood stiffly against the wall. He looked around for the governor, hoping he'd find him soon so he could put this evening behind him.

He saw the Hollander woman across the room. Happy enough she appeared now, he noted. She seemed at home in this make-believe world in her fancy pink ballgown that bared her shoulders and the pushed-up rounds of her bosom. Her fan was a teasing flutter as she chatted gaily with an obviously entranced gentleman.

Not coy that one, he thought, wondering why it should pang him to see her thus content. Had his own losses embittered him so that he couldn't bear to see others enjoy life?

Feeling a heavy sadness, he moved his eyes away from her and resumed his search for the governor.

To Astrid, Thomas had loomed suddenly and unexpectedly in the scramble of bright colors.

Why was *he* here? Surely Jeremy hadn't told him their plans! Was this going to ruin everything?

She kept up her idle conversation with Mr. Williams, putting her practiced facade in overdrive while her mind raced in panic.

Damn you, anyway, Thomas Arrington! Just stay out of my life. If you foul up my escape, I'll wring your neck.

"Why no, kind sir, I have no memory about the popularity of the minuet in my native country, but 'tis a lovely dance. Don't you agree?"

Flicker eyelashes. Smile sweetly. Lift the fan just so.

Has he stopped Jeremy from helping me? Please, God, don't let that happen! Maybe he doesn't know. It could be that he was invited. That's it. That's just what Lady Frances would do. She's mad for him.

Giggle with charm. Let your eyes twinkle. Keep calm.

"You're so amusing, Mr. Williams. Why of course I'll save the next minuet for you. Like you, I find the schottische far too lively. But would you excuse me for the nonce? I must go to the Lady Frances. She's beckoning for me."

Keep smiling, Astrid. Wend your way over to Thomas Arrington and see what he has to say for himself.

Where could Governor Berkeley be? Thomas had looked the room over and hadn't seen his host. Damnation! It would be an exceedingly tiresome evening. As he turned to step back into the foyer to inquire where he might find the governor, he felt a feathery touch on his shoulder.

"Welcome to Green Spring, Thomas," Astrid said brightly, lowering her fan demurely across her dimpled cheek. "I'm sure our hostess would have preferred to greet you first, but she's dancing the schottische with Lord Dunwoody and doesn't know you've arrived."

Thomas looked down at the Hollander and smiled despite himself. Her clear blue eyes sparkled up at him. A cloud of golden curls, interwoven with pink rosettes, haloed her head. The flesh of her shoulders were like the creamy petals of a soft camellia.

She was assured now, not the crazed, frightened rabbit he had found on the point. Royalty indeed she must be, he thought, a Hollander countess.

He reached for her hand and bowed over it, lightly brushing his lips over her lace-mitted fingers.

Astrid's knees tingled. It struck her as a weird reaction, especially when this man could be planning to mess up everything.

"My honor to see you again, milady," Thomas said. He released her hand and stepped back. "Grateful I am the governor and his lady have tended to you well."

"That they have," she said with a controlled smile. "And on Monday I'm to sail with Lady Frances to England."

"So Jeremy has told me."

Astrid bit the inside of her lip but continued smiling. What else had he told him?

"And Jeremy? Is he with you this evening?" she asked, her voice soft and kittenlike. The apprehension she felt inside was far less tame.

"No. He stayed in Jamestown to await my return."

Astrid studied Thomas's face. Was there more behind those words? Did he know? Don't tell me he's ordered Jeremy not to come.

Thomas chuckled. "Mayhap I should add I believe him to be in Jamestown. The lad vanished this noon, and I haven't seen him since.

I'm wondering now if he's found a comely lass to distract him."

Astrid relaxed. Thomas didn't know. Jeremy had vanished on purpose. He had a diamond to sell and a horse to buy. He'd be here at midnight. She could count on him.

"Such a distraction on Jeremy's part would distraught our Lizzie, I vow," she said with a broader smile. "How is the lovely child? And Ann and your mother?"

"All are well. Ann is grateful for the gift of the dress you sent her."

"But a token for my own gratefulness. The color is that of her eyes, and I trust it fits her."

"Of that I know nothing," he said. "I know only that she is saving it for Edward's return."

"And will that be soon?" Astrid asked. She regretted her stupid question immediately.

Thomas's silver-gray eyes hardened just enough to let her know she'd overstepped herself. Of course. He's on Bacon's side, and naturally he thinks I'm firmly in the governor's camp now.

The irony struck her. Thomas would be surprised if he knew the truth. Their rebellion was the least of her concerns at the moment.

"I know not when he's expected," he responded, an edge of tension in his voice. He turned away from Astrid slightly, and she sensed a veil had fallen between them. Strange it should bother her so. Thomas Arrington meant nothing to her. She had more important things on her mind.

His demeanor made her uncomfortable, and

she decided to give him the distance he apparently wanted.

"The room is warm, Thomas," she said. "If you'll but excuse me, I'll . . ."

"Mr. Arrington, how pleased I am you could come to my farewell party," trilled Lady Frances, swooping in beside them like a bird of prey. She has enough feathers on her dress to qualify as one, Astrid thought as she turned toward her hostess.

"I was just taking my leave of your guest, Lady Frances," she said sweetly, hoping her forced smile looked genuine.

Needless effort, she realized, as she nodded her farewell to Thomas and excused herself. Lady Frances's dark eyes were focused only on Thomas.

You're on your own now, Thomas Arrington, Astrid thought as she moved away from them. You'd better be made of sturdy cloth or she'll have you wrapped up in those vulture feathers before you know it.

"I had hoped to have a few moments alone with the governor, milady. Do you know where I might find him?" Astrid heard Thomas's question as she stepped into the foyer.

Now *that's* sturdy cloth, she told herself with surprising happiness. Better luck next time, Lady Frances.

Astrid glanced at the clock. 9:20. She'd meet Jeremy in less than three hours. A shudder of new apprehension threatened her outward calm.

God help me, she prayed.

* * *

With Lady Frances's assistance, Thomas found Governor Berkeley in his library. He was at his desk, scowling at a long sheet of paper. A dusty messenger stood quietly in the corner.

"Where's my favorite quill, my pet?" the governor asked his lady without noticing Thomas's presence. "I haven't seen it since my return, and this inferior one splotches more than it writes."

"Your manners are remiss, my dove," she cooed. "The grand hall is filled with our guests who await thee, and you sequester yourself here over colony fiddle-faddle." She rustled to his side and kissed the top of his peruke.

Thomas stood by the door and watched the woman fuss over the governor. Jeremy had spoken rightly when he had called the man a fool, he thought with disgust. *All hope for peace in Virginia lies within the power of that overdressed bucket of lard, while he sits and frets over a lost quill.*

Lady Frances looked toward Thomas briefly, then turned her attention back to her husband.

"Thomas Arrington stands yon waiting for you also, my love. He asks for but a moment of your time in privacy," she purred.

Governor Berkeley raised his head and squinted over his candle toward the doorway.

"Ah yes, Thomas," he said. "I'll be honored to give you some time. Let me but put my signature to this paper and dispatch the messenger. Then all will be well."

Thomas watched as the quill scratched across the bottom of the page. *Perchance,* he prayed, *that's the pardon and commission for Bacon and* our hopes already are answered.

"Hie now, John. Take this to the lawyer Sherwood and tell him I order it posted with haste throughout the colony." The governor handed the paper to the man and rose from his chair. Thomas moved to one side to allow the messenger to pass hurriedly through the door.

"You, my pet, must attend to our guests whilst I speak with Thomas," Governor Berkeley said, dismissing his wife with an affectionate pat on her shoulder. "Assure them I'll join their merriment soon." Lady Frances glided across the room and tossed Thomas a piquant smile before leaving and closing the door behind her.

Thomas's mind was forming words for the governor, and he paid the woman no heed.

The men shook hands, and Governor Berkeley offered Thomas a chair across from the large desk. The fat man sat back down with a heavy sigh, folded his fingers across his ample middle and looked up at the tall Virginian.

"What's on your mind, Thomas?"

"The need for a pardon and commission for Councilor Bacon, your honor. May I hope that was the subject of the document you have dispatched?"

"Indeed you may not have such hope!" the governor roared, an unhealthy purple coloring his puffed face. "Ha! A pardon and commission to legitimize that rebel? Not while I have breath! And, mind you, Nathaniel Bacon is a councilor no longer. God rot him! 'Twas an errant day on which I brought the scoundrel into my circle!"

Agitated, the governor wiped his forehead

with a linen handkerchief. A leaden silence hung between the two men.

"No, Thomas," Berkeley continued in a calmer voice, "the paper I dispatched declares formally that Nathaniel Bacon is a rebel and an enemy of the king's appointed government. I have called for all persons in the colony to assist the government against him."

Thomas rose from his chair.

"Then I have come for naught," he said grimly. "Your declaration bodes ill for Virginia, Governor Berkeley. I came to reason with you but I find reason has become a stranger at Green Spring." He turned toward the door. "I will take my leave of you now, sir."

"You will take your leave with my permission, sirrah!" the governor sputtered as he pushed himself up from his chair. Thomas stopped and faced the raging man but said nothing.

"You come not with reason but with insults, Mr. Arrington. Has the entire colony gone mad? The wild beast multitude rages without sense beyond these walls, and I'll have none of it. Do you hear me, Thomas? None of it!" He paced like a caged wolf behind his desk, his face having turned crimson.

Thomas remained silent.

"You, too, have joined the renegades, I see." The governor spat his words. "And you dare to speak of reason! A pox on reason! A pox on Bacon and his unwashed followers! A pox on the lot of you!" A rush of tears flowed from the governor's rheumy eyes.

"Goddamn your rebel blood, Nathaniel Bacon!" he wailed. "And to think I loved you like a son!"

The governor crumpled into his chair and covered his face with his hands.

Thomas had not moved. He stood erect, his clenched fists at his sides the only sign he had heard the outpouring of venom.

The man is truly sick, Thomas realized with a despair that washed over his anger, submerging it beneath a colder reality. He's sick in mind as well as in body and is incapable of governing. He must be removed from power.

Thomas knew too well the wheels of decision-making from England were cumbersome and slow. Unlikely it was that the king would replace the governor before bloodshed bathed the colony.

His heart heavy, he turned his back on the weeping man and left the library. He walked into the foyer and lifted his baldric and sword from the rack. Forgetting Lawrence's ostrich-plumed hat, he went through the open front doors and out into the steamy night.

The late May moon, near round again, hung high over the Virginia woods, lighting Thomas's way as he led his horse through dense stands of oak and pine. His thoughts were far darker than the heavens, his pace purposely slow. He saw no need for haste with the news he bore.

Like the broad sparkling river below and to his right, he was heading south toward Jamestown. Behind him, at Green Spring, the Chickahominy had met the James and the two had become one in an uneven marriage—the smaller, more peaceful Chickahominy losing its name and identity to the turbulent, powerful James.

Thomas paused. Turbulence and power, he mused. Must they ever prevail? The river rolled onward. Having devoured a weaker one, it rushed by swollen with victory, mindless that in a few miles hence it, too, would be swallowed up by a stronger force.

Thomas shook his head. We are like the waters, he thought. Mindless, greedy and power hungry. Like them we move forward toward dissolution.

Was this to be the end to Virginia and to his own dreams for this beautiful land and all he'd ever known? So rich and full of promise, it is. Its fertile earth yields its fruits, asking naught in return but sweat of the brow and enlightened husbandry.

Deep in thought, Thomas took his horse down to the river and let him drink. No need for haste, he reminded himself. Bad news should journey slow.

A twig snapped in the woods behind him. Thomas reached for his sword and ducked into the shadows of a large rock.

Something was moving up on the bank, back among the trees. He heard footsteps on the soft earth—a man and a horse, by the sound of it. The animal was being led, as he had been leading his own, only with more speed and in the opposite direction toward Green Spring.

Thomasina Ring

Thomas's sharp eyes followed the sounds, waiting for a break in the trees so he might see who was passing.

"C'mon, ye laggard horse! We must meet the lady at midnight, or I'll have your stubborn hide!"

Jeremy!

Thomas was stunned. What in the name of good heaven might the lad be up to?

His initial surprise at hearing the boy's familiar voice turned to puzzled concern. The night woods were filled with perils for an unseasoned youth. And whose horse would he be leading? And to what place? A lady he's meeting? Who, by God?

A peculiar sense of foreboding stopped him from calling out to the boy.

Without knowing fully why he was doing so, he waited until the footsteps had passed from his hearing. He mounted his horse and rode up the moonlit embankment into the dark woods.

Quietly, holding his horse to a slow walk, he headed back toward Green Spring.

Astrid held the hooded black cloak tightly around her as she waited behind a tree near the stable. Damn moon! It had to be nearly full tonight of all nights, bathing its white light recklessly into every nook and cranny. She had prayed for darkness at midnight. Instead, the crazy world seemed to think it was high noon.

At least she'd had the good sense to wear the cloak. By covering her pink dress and light hair, it provided a touch of camouflage.

She was still winded after her run from the large house. She had darted from tree to tree to fence to outbuilding to yet another tree, pausing in the few merciful shadows to be sure she hadn't been spotted.

Music and laughter rang from the house, an odd counterpoint to her shallow breaths and wildly beating heart. So far so good, she thought. She'd been right that the party would be at fever pitch, and she'd slipped away without anyone noticing. Fortunately, the grounds had been empty of servants or guests.

Now, crouching behind the tree, she closed her eyes and begged Jeremy to come soon. She didn't know how long her luck would hold.

Sounds of raucous merriment including some girlish giggles floated from the nearby stable. A second party evidently was under way at Green Spring.

Good. That meant servants not busy in the house were also happily preoccupied. The coast was clear. Come on, Jeremy, she pleaded under her breath.

"Psssst!"

Astrid pressed against the tree and jerked her head toward the dilapidated barn behind her. Someone was in there!

"Countess, 'tis me. Jeremy. Over here!"

Astrid smiled. After a fast glance around to be sure no one would see, she scurried from the tree's shadow, across the moon-washed field, and through the open door of the dark barn.

The air inside was heavy with the dusky, pungent smells of tobacco, old hay and rotted vegetation. Her eyes stung and she blinked, trying to adjust to the thick blackness around her. She couldn't see a blasted thing.

"I be right here, Countess, and I have your horse and gear." Jeremy's whisper, barely suppressing his excitement, was right in front of her.

Astrid reached out her hand.

"I can't see you, Jeremy," she said, "but thank God you're here. We must hurry. Do you have a candle?"

"No. We dare not, milady. Your eyes will grow accustomed to the dark. I can see you a mite." His rough hand circled hers. "Here I be, Countess." He guided her over a few feet. "And here's your horse. A fine steed I found for thee."

He placed her hand on the animal. She touched it gingerly, not sure what part of its anatomy was beneath her fingers. A flank, maybe. It was firm and sinewy. A good sign.

Slowly she was able to make out shapes and outlines of her surroundings. Jeremy was close beside her and held a large bundle. The horse was restless, but stayed obedient and didn't make a sound.

"These be your hiding clothing, Countess. Fit for a working lad and not the likes of you, I fear," he said apologetically as he thrust the bundle into her hands. "'Tis coarse stuff, but sturdy and dark like you wanted."

"Thank you, Jeremy. I'll don them immediately." She placed the bundle on the dirt floor of the barn and hurriedly opened it. Throwing off her cloak, she reached back to begin unhooking her bodice. Her fingers were trembling.

Jeremy cleared his throat and moved away from her side. "I'll stand over by the door and keep the watch for thee," he said.

Astrid couldn't resist smiling as she watched the boy hasten to the door, keeping his back turned toward her.

Poor sweet Jeremy, she thought, bowing to my modesty when it's help I need with these tiny clasps. Impatiently, she ripped the hooks apart and removed her dress. Dropping it in a pile of pink fluff at her feet, she loosened her petticoats and stepped away from them.

Hurry, damn it! She fumbled through the sack, found baggy pants and pulled them on, tying them quickly around her waist. The loose jacket covered her camisole. She knew she'd possibly been foolish to do so, but earlier she'd stuck her crumpled journal between her breasts, and the camisole held it secure. The journal was the only thing she felt a need to carry away from Green Spring.

She buttoned the jacket up to her neck. The pair of leather boots was genius on Jeremy's part. After shedding her useless silk slippers, she yanked the boots up over her cotton stockings. Only a trifle large, they'd do, thank God.

In the bottom of the bag lay a knitted cap—a monmouth cap, it was called. She'd seen them on workers at the wharf. Another stroke of genius! It would cover her light hair.

"I'm ready, Jeremy," she whispered. Suddenly, she was cold with fear. Her heart thumped. So far everything had been a piece of cake.

Almost too easy, maybe. She knew the hard, uncertain part was ahead.

But there was no turning back. She had to escape!

Jeremy returned to her side.

"I sold your diamond, Countess, and did well for thee," he said. "The merchant Woodward was slobbering for it, and I drove a mighty bargain. After purchasing the horse, clothing and a bit of hardtack for your journey, there be close to twenty pounds sterling in this purse. It will perchance help thee betimes."

Astrid took the purse and a small cloth sack from the boy's outstretched hand. "How much is twenty pounds, Jeremy? I know not the worth of money in your land."

"Worth nigh four men's tobacco crop in one year," he answered. "It be a king's ransom, I wager, and shall put thee in good stead."

"So much for one diamond ring?" Astrid was astounded but pleased. She hung the purse around her neck and shoved it beneath her jacket.

"Aye. Even the niggardly Woodward saw its rare value."

"Woodward, you say?" Astrid almost laughed out loud. Derek's ancestor? A weird sort of recycling, if that's the case.

But there was no time for amusement. She knew she should hurry before they were discovered. It was now or never!

She took a deep breath to steady herself and reached for the horse's bridle.

"I go now, Jeremy," she said. There was a

tremor in her voice despite her determination to sound brave and sure of herself.

"Can you ride, Countess? Ladies in the colony sit sidewards behind on a pillion. I've ne'er seen one astride a horse."

"Give me a lift up, and you'll see one now," she said. "Yes, Jeremy, I can ride as well as your men."

She placed her boot in the stirrup and with a boost from Jeremy slid up easily onto the saddle. She leaned forward and patted the horse's strong neck.

"A fine steed, lad," she said. Mounted, she felt a little calmer. The horse's powerful energy, though under restraint now, pulsed solidly against her thighs.

Jeremy sighed. "I fear for thee, Countess, and beg again to accompany thee. The dangers are too great for thee to journey alone."

Astrid looked down at the boy's open, worried face. For a moment she wavered. She knew he would be a help.

But no, this was her own battle, and she wouldn't risk his life. She'd do it alone.

She shook her head. "You've done enough, dear friend. Give me your prayers and naught else. And God willing, we'll meet again."

Bowing his head, Jeremy looked down at the earthen floor. He wiped his nose with his sleeve and raised his eyes to meet hers.

"I owe thee my life, Countess," he sniffed. "And I love thee dearly. I plead with thee . . ."

"No," she said firmly, urging the horse forward.

Jeremy stepped aside. Frustrated, he kicked up a puff of dirt from the floor.

"Godspeed," he said sadly.

Astrid lowered her head, preparing to pass through the door.

And then she saw him.

"Master Thomas!" Jeremy gasped.

Astrid froze.

Chapter Eleven

"Jeremy? What in Satan's name . . . ?"

Thomas ducked through the barn door, squinted into the darkness and placed his hand on his sword.

"I . . . I mustn't tell, Master Thomas," the boy stammered. "Only 'tis a good deed I do, sir."

Jeremy was standing to his right. Even in the gloom Thomas could recognize the lanky shape and the thatch of sandy hair.

"A good deed? Explain yourself, lad!"

He sensed others were in the barn. How many? Who? He tightened his grip on the sword's haft.

A horse whickered. Soundlessly, Thomas pulled the blade from its sheath. A shaft of moonlight through the door caught the metal with a sharp stab of silver.

"Who's there?" he asked, moving deeper into the shadows. He now could see the horse and its rider, but a lad, by the looks of him.

"Peter, is that you?" Thomas questioned as he edged closer. "What mischief are you lads . . ."

Faster than thought, the boy lunged forward, dug his heels into the horse's ribs and slapped the reins. With a leap, Thomas grabbed the bridle to turn the animal's head.

"No you don't," he said through clenched teeth, taking control of the confused horse. He dropped his sword and used both hands to keep the animal from rearing and throwing its slender rider.

The horse snorted and pawed the dirt but obeyed the man's signals.

"Now get thee down, rogue!" Thomas ordered the mounted lad. "And Jeremy, hie yourself over here. This foolishness cries for honesty."

Jeremy ran over as he was told.

"There is danger here, Master Thomas, and there be no time for explaining now." Jeremy's words stumbled, but Thomas heard the pleading urgency behind them.

Whoever this boy was on horseback, he was in deep trouble and Jeremy was trying to help him. Thomas looked up at the young stranger. The lad's face was in the shadows, but Thomas saw how his fingers trembled.

His decision was quick. He trusted Jeremy. Explanations could come later.

"So be it," Thomas said. After sheathing his sword, he jumped astride the horse behind the boy and lifted the reins.

"My steed is tied to the oak yon, Jeremy. Mount it and let's be away from here!"

As they raced through the dark woods, Astrid pressed her face into the horse's mane and clutched it tightly. Thomas had told her to keep her head low; the loud crackle of branches around them told her why.

She couldn't think because her senses were flooded. Sounds encompassed her—stacatto hooves, speeding wind, the tearing swish of leaves. Her body reverberated to the nonstop beating against her thighs, the moist horse flesh pulsing wildly beneath her, the dark heated pressure of the man leaning over her. Electric bolts of moonlight struck the passing trees.

Astrid closed her eyes. Her whole world was a mad rhythm of sound, motion and pressure, blending into one. Night, forest, horse, man, woman had become one speeding world.

The world stopped.

Stunned, she raised her head. All was silence. She saw a river. A man stood beside her, raising his arms toward her.

"Come," he said.

Astrid blinked. Still dazed, she stared down at him.

"Come, lad," he repeated. "We must rest, and the horses need water."

Thomas Arrington! Her head cleared at once. She averted her face, thankful that the moon was behind a cloud. He hadn't recognized her, and she desperately needed time to gather her thoughts.

No denying that he *would* recognize her and probably in a matter of moments. God knows what his reaction will be.

Astrid felt glued to the horse, reluctant to face the inevitable, but the voice beside her was insistent.

Not even a whisper of strategy formed in her mind. Resigned, she started the painful process of unwrapping herself from the animal, only to find that her muscles too were reluctant to dismount. She was stiff and sore.

"I'll help thee," the voice persisted. The arms circling her waist were as determined as his words. He pulled her down, and she wasn't sure, considering the agony it caused her, if it had been gently or not. Thomas held her firmly against him while she steadied herself. He was behind her and still hadn't seen her face. She knew her cap was askew though, and she feared her hair was sticking out here and there.

Maybe he hadn't noticed. She reached up to stuff the telltale strands back under the wool at the exact moment that the moon popped out from behind its cloud.

Thomas stopped her arms in midair.

"What the devil . . . ?" He twirled her around.

"So 'tis you, is it?" He yanked the cap from her head and her unruly hair tumbled out.

Thomas gripped the Hollander's shoulders and stared down at her moon-bathed face. Neither crazed rabbit nor assured coquette did he see now. She looked back into his eyes with the resigned gaze of a trapped deer.

Thomas's heart skipped a beat.

"God's blood," he said, lowering his hands and turning away from her. "What manner of diabolical fate drops you down before me at every turn?"

Astrid had no answer.

She watched him walk toward the river's edge. Jeremy was standing there with Thomas's horse. What's next? she wondered as the man and boy began talking. She hoped she hadn't gotten Jeremy into too much trouble.

Her horse whinnied, reminding her he needed to drink. For a brief instant, eyeing the strong back of the chestnut steed, she considered the possibility of making a break, but she knew she'd never bring it off. The horse was lathered and tired, and she was in even worse shape. Her bones ached along with every one of her muscles. She'd have a hell of a time getting back astride him, let alone outdistancing a hotly pursuing Thomas.

Assuming, of course, that Thomas pursued her. He simply might let her disappear through the woods. She realized with a pang she found that scenario downright depressing, but felt it was highly possible under the circumstances. She had the definite impression he viewed her as a big nuisance.

Astrid took the horse's reins and led him down to the river, choosing a spot well away from Thomas and Jeremy. The horse drank eagerly. She knelt beside him on the sandy soil and cupped up water in her hands to quench her own thirst.

She would have liked to plunge into the river,

clothes and all, to rid herself of the dust and grime she'd accumulated on the wild journey. Thomas would undoubtedly disapprove though, and Lord knows she didn't want to irritate him further. She compromised by splashing some water on her face.

Partially refreshed, Astrid sat back on the damp earth and stretched out her booted legs. She looked over at her distant companions. They had stopped talking and Jeremy was leading Thomas's horse up the rise toward the trees. Thomas himself stood tall and unmoving, looking out at the river.

Glowering, she bet, his number one favorite expression. Frustrated, she picked up a handful of sandy pebbles and tossed them into the water. A fat lot she could do about this foolish situation. She'd have to wait until he informed her of their next move.

She was banking on Thomas though. Whatever else, she believed he wouldn't return her to Green Spring. He might not be one of the rebels, but she sensed he had little love for Governor Berkeley.

But what if that's what he did decide to do? She and Jeremy could talk him out of it, she assured herself. If need be, she'd tell him about Lord Percy's attack. That should turn the trick with a bred-in-the-bones Virginia gentleman.

Thomas frowned out at the James. He'd heard Jeremy's foolhardy story about selling the diamond, buying provisions, and risking life and limb to help the Hollander escape from Green Spring.

The missing pieces were what bothered him. The woman he had seen at the ball earlier this night was a countess in her element, as feathery as the fan she fluttered. Why would she be so desperate to get away? Jeremy couldn't tell him, only trusting blindly that her need was great.

Thomas's trust was less blind.

The Hollander had been a puzzle from the beginning. She was a strange mixture of helplessness and strength, defenseless and frightened one moment, fiery and hotheaded the next. At times, demure; at others, a clever sorceress.

Thomas could not grasp the peculiar pattern. She was unlike any woman he had ever known.

He shook his head. The times were unusual ones. The colony was rife with rebellion, and already he had been swept up in the rotten business. His ordered world had turned upside down with the future itself in doubt.

This mysterious woman claiming to be without memory added naught but further confusion and trouble for him. I must keep my guard, he warned himself, for she's likely royalty and cannot be trusted in these uncertain times.

He looked over at her. She sat with her legs pulled up to her chin, no longer a grand lady in that rough clothing of a servant lad. She turned her head toward him. The moon-kissed gold of her flowing hair compounded his confusion.

Thomas closed his eyes for a moment and took a deep breath. Curse it, woman! Pray cease the sorcery until I know how I can help thee.

With jaws set, he walked toward the Hollander. He would talk with her and find why she had fled Green Spring.

After that, he had no idea what he would do.

Astrid watched Thomas approach. He was hatless, and his black dress clothes were wrinkled and dusty. There was, nevertheless, a resolute dignity about him. She drew her knees up closer and girded herself for the inquisition.

"I must speak with thee, milady," he said as he sat down beside her.

She nodded and waited for his first question.

"I must know the reasons behind your actions this night." It wasn't a question, but it served the same purpose. His expression told her nothing as he kept his eyes on the river.

Her words came out in a rush. She recounted the sordid Lord Dunwoody episode in full and told about the man's bitter hostility toward her and her fears for her life should she venture on a sea voyage with him.

Though she tried to phrase everything in the vocabulary of the time, she slipped occasionally. Thomas would look puzzled, and she'd correct herself or quickly continue her story, hoping he understood most of it.

When she finished, she heaved a sigh.

"And that's why I had to get away," she said.

Thomas was silent. He bent forward, picked up a small stick and began drawing lines in the sand. Wondering if he had grown mute, Astrid looked to see if he was writing her a message.

Except for a few X's, the lines had no decipherable pattern.

At last, he tossed the stick aside, straightened up and faced her for the first time since he had joined her.

"And where, milady, did you plan to run?" he asked.

"I know not," she said honestly. "I only knew I could not sail to England."

Thomas stood. Astrid drew her knees back up to her chest and waited his verdict.

"I shall not return thee to Green Spring," he said, and Astrid breathed a sigh of relief.

"'Twas a blessing, however, that I stopped your foolhardy attempt to escape alone," he continued with a distinct tone of criticism. "The night woods are fraught with dangers, even for the seasoned."

"I thank thee, Thomas," she said with a touch of sarcasm. She knew he was right, but she resented his superior tones. She decided to stand. Seated that way could give him the impression she was cowering, and that was the last impression she wanted to give any man—even a fine one like Thomas, she added in deference to his help so far.

"And may I hope you'll take me back to your mother's house?" she asked. She'd love to see Mrs. Arrington, Lizzie and Ann again. After all she'd been through, it would feel like a home of sorts for her. Besides, she thought with heady anticipation, the point and the mossy spot would be nearby, and surely she could sneak over and try to find her way back to her real home.

"Never!" Thomas's vehemence shocked her. "You have important enemies now, milady, and they will be hunting thee, mark my words. Your presence at their home would endanger my family. I must hide thee at Eagle's Crest until the search is off or they have forgotten thee. And no one must know where you are."

Astrid sat back down. Eagle's Crest? Thomas's home. She was suddenly very tired.

"How far is Eagle's Crest?" she asked.

"Too far to continue this night," he said. "We shall sleep for a few hours and ride in daylight."

Thomas turned toward Jeremy who still stood by the horse on the rise. "Come down, lad!" he shouted.

Jeremy ran to them, his face full of questions.

"It's all right, Jeremy," Astrid said with a smile, ruffling his sandy hair. Thomas glowered disapprovingly, but she didn't care. Jeremy had suffered enough for one evening. "Mr. Arrington will shelter me, and we leave for Eagle's Crest on the morrow."

The boy beamed until he noticed Thomas's expression. Embarrassed, he sidled away from Astrid's ruffling hand.

"Fetch the pack from my steed and both saddles and blankets, lad. We need rest a mite, and dawn is nigh," Thomas said.

Looking relieved to have duties to perform, Jeremy led Astrid's horse up the riverbank and tied him to a tree near Thomas's handsome sorrel. In a few minutes he returned, loaded down with the equipment that Astrid assumed would be their sleeping accommodations.

She was weary enough to sleep on the bare ground, but a saddle blanket would be some protection against insects. She decided not to let herself think about the possibility of snakes or worse.

Thomas spread the blankets close together on the rocky sand and placed the saddles like pillows atop them. Room for two, Astrid noted, too exhausted to care, but wondering nevertheless how the three of them were going to manage this situation.

His next words answered her quandary.

"You and the lad will sleep here, milady, whilst I keep watch," he said.

"But when will you sleep, Thomas?" she asked.

"On the morrow at Eagle's Crest," he said.

Not in the mood to quibble, she sat down on the nearest blanket and took off her boots. Jeremy protested that he wanted to take the watch, but to no avail. Thomas was adamant.

A good thing, Astrid thought, as she watched a dejected Jeremy lie down beside her on the other blanket. The boy was asleep within seconds.

Despite her own exhaustion, Astrid found sleep impossible. Her sore body wouldn't adjust to the uneven hardness of the ground, but she tried to keep her wiggling to a minimum because she wanted Thomas to think she was sleeping peacefully. The saddle felt like a stone beneath her head, and the steamy horsy smell emanating from both saddle and blanket added to her discomfort.

With nothing better to do, she watched her newfound protector. He had built a small fire nearby—she couldn't imagine how and with what—and was standing beside it. He was highlighted in the orange glow, a tall stark figure dusted with gold. His usually stern face was softened by the light of the flames. She wondered what he was thinking. There was a distant, contemplative look in his gray eyes and a special warmth, as if he were seeing something particularly lovely—a tender memory, perhaps, of his wife and child.

The cleft in his chin shadowed deeper in the flickering glow, and she watched his perfect lips curl in a small, secret smile.

Astrid closed her eyes, feeling like an invader in the man's private world. He's entitled to his moments alone, she chided herself, but for a long while the image of the man played across her eyelids until the darkness of sleep enveloped her.

Sometime near dawn, Jeremy groaned and thrashed about. Astrid, only partly awakened, knew instinctively the boy was having a nightmare. She reached for him and comforted him with "shhh" and "there, there." Jeremy quieted and snuggled close to her. She cradled his head against her breast and the two were soon deeply asleep.

Thomas, who had rushed to Jeremy's side, looked down at the woman and lad. Like mother and child, he thought, touched by their angelic faces. He loved Jeremy like a son and felt gratitude to the Hollander for her tenderness.

He watched the two for a while, pondering the near future. He would harbor her at Eagle's Crest, though he had difficulty envisioning her disruptive presence there. It had become a house of men since Sarah, Betty and the female servants had departed for Stafford.

The Hollander's wild hair fell softly against her peaceful face. A scattering of pink rosettes still clung to the golden strands. Her long lashes lay like thick, dark whispers against the high curve of her cheeks.

In this first light of day, she looked like pure innocence.

Thomas turned and walked back to the fire. No, he reminded himself, the woman's not an innocent.

But what is she?

He sighed. Whatever she is, for the nonce she has become my responsibility.

He reached into his pack for his pipe. Lighting it with the flames of a stick he pulled from the fire, he sat on a piece of driftwood and continued his vigil.

The sun was well over the horizon when Astrid opened her eyes. Jeremy was kneeling in front of the fire slowly rotating a small skewered carcass of some kind. The aroma of sizzling meat mingled with the smell of strong coffee. She realized she was starving.

"Ho, Countess!" Jeremy shouted when he saw

she was awake. "Master Thomas found us a rabbit for breakfast, and there be coffee brewed for thee."

As she struggled up from her hard bed, Astrid moaned. Her body felt as though it had stiffened into a permanent state of knotted pain.

"Good grief!" She winced, unraveling herself to her knees and then with even greater difficulty to her feet. She pressed her hands against her lower back and arched her shoulders. "Whew, I feel like a twice-baked pretzel."

"That be Hollander talk, I wager," Jeremy said with a timid laugh. "I understand naught what you say."

"I understand very little myself, lad," Astrid said with a deeper truth than the boy could know. She rubbed her elbow and yawned. Shading her eyes from the bright sun, she looked around for Thomas.

He was standing out in the shallow water. His back was toward her and he was shirtless, his dusty black pants rolled to mid-calf. As he raised his right arm, she saw he held a long stick with a knife tied to its end.

"What's he doing?" she asked Jeremy in a loud whisper. Other than looking downright heroic, she could have added as she watched the firm muscles ride up his fine back.

"Trying to spear a fish," the boy answered. "He relishes fresh fish for breakfast."

Astrid shrugged. Tenuously, she began a few stretching exercises to work out her kinks.

Thomas jabbed the stick into the water and let out a whoop as he pulled out his flapping trophy.

"'Tis a grand one, Jeremy!" he shouted. "Now we can feast, lad." He turned with a look of victory on his face and ran barefooted out of the river and onto the bank.

He paused when he saw the woman. She was performing some manner of peculiar dance, a strange to-and-fro gyration with her arms outstretched. Was it a morning ritual for Hollanders or a witch's pagan response to the rising sun? Her eyes were closed, and her face was lifted toward the light.

Pagan, he decided, and continued up the bank.

As he started cleaning the fish, Thomas eyed the Hollander warily. She had seated herself, spread her legs before her and was bowing low with her face buried first in one knee and then in the other.

There's no comprehending the woman, he grumbled. His knife slit the fish sharply down the middle, and he began gutting it with diminished enthusiasm.

Chapter Twelve

By the time they reached Eagle's Crest, Astrid was a nervous wreck and irritable, to boot.

It was all Thomas's fault. The man was absolutely unreasonable.

He'd insisted she ride sidesaddle on his sleek sorrel, while he sat behind and handled the reins. It was awkward as all get out. The stretched reins chafed against odd places on her anatomy, and she had to squirm to avoid them, only to have them move to another spot even more annoying.

If she could have sat on the horse like she wanted, she'd be a hell of a lot more comfortable, but that tyrant Arrington wouldn't hear of it. "Ladies do not ride in that manner," he had said, and there was no changing his stubborn mind. Hadn't he noticed she'd been astride the horse last night? That should have shown him she knew how to ride.

He'd sent Jeremy ahead on her horse "to warn Joseph about our unexpected visitor and have him prepare the upper chamber for her."

Astrid had resented the word "warn," and she knew only his stilted manners prevented his calling her "unwanted" instead of "unexpected." That "upper chamber," meanwhile, sounded cramped.

She shifted her bottom on the slippery saddle for what must have been the thousandth time. Oh well, she told herself with exasperation, I'm getting conditioned for being cramped.

On top of everything else, Thomas didn't talk to her during the whole journey. He'd grunt a word or two if she tried to break the monotony with a comment about the hot weather or something equally innocuous, and that would be the sum total of conversation.

She finally gave up and lapsed into complete silence herself. This gave her lots of time to think, which is why she was a nervous wreck when they arrived.

Eagle's Crest might have been a pleasing sight if she hadn't been in such a foul mood. It was as large as Shirley but not nearly as gloomy, and the grounds were ten times neater. All of the outhouses were brick, and the animals were penned as they'd been at Green Spring. The vegetable and flower gardens had a well-tended look.

Somebody works like the devil around here, she thought. Thomas the Tyrant must make his servants put in overtime.

Jeremy greeted them with a shy smile and took the horse back to the barn after she and Thomas dismounted.

Surprised, Astrid didn't see anyone else around. No field hands were visible, and no one came out of the house to welcome them. She'd expected a housekeeper to be on the scene, maybe somebody like Marcy. That had been one of her hopes since she felt badly in need of allies.

As she followed Thomas toward the front stoop, Astrid heard a soft, off-tune whistling from around the corner of the house. Turning and screening her eyes from the sun, she saw a fragile looking old man shuffle into view. His shoulders were stooped. The sun-pinked top of his bald head, fringed with white sprigs, gleamed like a beacon guiding his way. His whistling continued, a slow tune measured to his incredibly slow pace. A basket filled with curled leafy greens hung from his arm.

Astrid realized the man didn't know they were standing there.

"Ho, Joseph, my fellow!" Thomas yelled and ran over to him. Astrid watched as he took the old man's basket and patted the stooped back. "We're home at last, good Joseph, after a hot and dusty journey. And you've been out picking green kale for our supper, I see." Thomas was shouting, even though he was right beside the man. "Jeremy told you, I trust, that we have a guest for the nonce. Come, I'll make the proper introductions."

Astrid noted that Thomas suddenly had become garrulous. Obviously, his willingness to converse depended on who was around.

She felt lonelier than ever as she watched the two men approach. Joseph had twisted his head to see Thomas and was talking nonstop, using his gnarled hands to punctuate his words. Astrid couldn't hear what the man was saying, but Thomas looked attentive and happily engrossed.

Feeling like a nonentity, Astrid wondered if they were going to walk right through her and go on into the house.

But they stopped a few feet away and Thomas began his introductions, again speaking loudly. She assumed the old man didn't hear too well.

"Lady Van Fleet, this fine gentleman is Joseph Whiteside, a friend of my father's who has become through the long years like a father to me. Joseph, Lady Van Fleet, a lost Hollander noblewoman without memory who will live protected in our home until we find more satisfactory refuge for her anon."

Astrid stared at Thomas through most of his long-winded introduction, then smiled sweetly at the older man and offered her hand.

Joseph Whiteside cocked his head and squinted up at her with an odd little sparkle in his yellowish eyes. Astrid quickly put down her hand. Ladies don't shake hands here, she reminded herself.

"A Hollander noblewoman you say, Thomas?" he wheezed. "In the clothes of a 'dentured boy?" A dry chuckle gurgled from his throat. "A story this be worth hearing, methinks."

"Suffice it to say, Joseph, that—"

"I'll explain it myself, Mr. Whiteside." Astrid interrupted Thomas, an edge of testiness in her voice. She'd be damned if she'd stand there like a stone and let them talk about her in the third person. "At length and at your leisure, sir, after I've had an opportunity to bathe away this dust and grime and if possible have found more suitable clothing."

She was becoming garrulous herself and likely too forward, but she was at the end of her rope.

"I like your spirit, little lady," Joseph said with a nod. "We welcome you to Eagle's Crest, which too long has been absent of spirit. I await your story with patient expectancy, but it will be at your leisure, not mine."

Astrid warmed to the ancient fellow. He was as withered and contorted as a dried catalpa bean and probably weighed about as much, but that sparkle in his eyes gave her hope. There was liveliness there as well as a sense of humor. Maybe even a tender heart.

She believed she'd found her ally at Eagle's Crest. Glancing at Thomas's stern face, she sensed she needed one.

Joseph hobbled off into the house, telling Thomas, "The upper chamber is prepared for the lady."

Thomas led her in and up a staircase. What little she saw of the downstairs impressed her as relatively spacious, open, bright and clean. It was still the Spartan architecture and furnishings of the times and not nearly as grandiose as Green Spring. Though it was far bigger than

Edward's house, it shared the same primitive freshness. Its scale was nearer Shirley's, without the overstuffed dreariness of that awful house.

The upper chamber delighted her. It was white and lightly furnished, with opened half-casements on three sides. The bed was smallish, making her wonder if this had been his child's room, but she kept this thought to herself.

"'Tis beautiful, Thomas," she said with enthusiasm. "I shall be comfortable here, and I thank thee."

A near-smile brushed across his lips. Maybe it was the bright room, but Astrid thought his face even radiated a bit. It was hard to stay mad at him when he looked like that.

"I have only Joseph here to help in the house, milady," he said. "A bath for thee this afternoon will be impossible, for he will be tending to the cooking."

Astrid's heart sank. If she didn't bathe soon, she'd go crazy. Besides, what did Joseph have to do with it? Surely Thomas didn't expect the old codger to carry up a heavy tub and bathe her.

She saw the river through the window and made up her mind. Maybe ladies don't swim these days either, but she wasn't going to let that stop her. She'd better establish some independence quickly or she'd go crazy.

She looked at Thomas and smiled coyly. "Have you some large napkins I may borrow, perchance?"

"Napkins, milady?" His eyes looked puzzled.

"Linens. For the table. I know not what you call the things," she said.

"Aye, we have linens," he said. "Why would you have need for linens?" He looked uncomfortable.

"Uh, for a personal and necessary cause, Thomas." She felt like giggling. He probably thought she was having her period, for God's sake, and needed those nasty clouts the women used, but she had another necessity in mind. She was going to assemble a bathing suit.

"I'll bring thee linens," he said, turning on his heels and leaving the room in a hurry. Astrid laughed to herself and plopped down into a chair by the window. She took off her boots and wiggled her toes. She knew she smelled to high heaven and couldn't wait to undress, but she'd have to wait until after Thomas had brought her supplies.

She wondered what she was going to do about clothes. She'd hate to put these things on again, but after her swim maybe even they would feel better. Eventually, she was going to have to make herself something to wear. She eyed the windows, but there were no curtains.

Hell, even Scarlett had it easier.

Thomas watched the woman run down to the river. Perplexed, he followed her, keeping back a distance. He had taken her the linens, and she also had asked for toweling. He supposed she had done whatever the women do with the linens when their sickness comes upon them, and the toweling she carried now in her hand.

He stopped behind a tree, observing her with suspicion. When he saw she was rapidly removing the mean clothing she wore, he grew uneasy. He started to avert his eyes but was relieved to see she wasn't totally uncovered. She had tied a piece of linen over her breasts and another was wrapped around her nether parts. While he was trying to figure out what in Satan's name the woman was planning, she slid into the water and floated away from the shore.

He watched with wonder. She was a golden streak in the silver river, gliding like a fish through the shallow waves. Her arms raised and lowered in a slow, smooth rhythmic pattern that propelled her forward swiftly against the current.

Never had he seen a woman swim, nor had he seen any man move in such an efficient fashion through the water. Once again the Hollander was performing magic, and he stood enchanted on the shore.

A stab of apprehension cut the spell when he realized she was venturing far out into the river—too far, he told himself. The water of the James is deep and can be treacherous. 'Tis time she turn back.

Thomas ran to the edge of the river, cupped his hands to his mouth and shouted to the woman.

"Milady, go no farther! Return to shore!"

Astrid heard the voice, paused and looked back.

Busybody's at it again, she thought, her dander rising. Easily treading in the warm water, she felt exasperated at his undue concern. She was far from tired, and this swim was the very tonic she needed. That man's got to learn I have to have some freedom!

She waved her arm to assure him she was safe, then dived under the water to get away, at least for a minute or so, from his restricting scrutiny.

Thomas saw the maddening woman wave, then watched with horror as she turned downward, a small rounded piece of white the final glimpse of her before she disappeared beneath the surface. He tore off his boots, threw his coat aside and plunged into the river.

God's blood, he thought as he pulled himself through the water, wishing he knew the faster, magical strokes he had witnessed. He must depend on his greater strength alone to find the woman in time.

Within moments, though it seemed hours to him, he reached the area where she had vanished. Fighting time and current, he swam in circles, desperately searching for a sight of her beneath the water. Less than a cubit's length was clear, the farther depths being murky.

As hope began to fade, he saw the shadow below. Though wavy and distorted by the water, the figure, he knew, was that of the woman. Her hair floated strangely around her head and her arms and legs moved slowly, as though willed only by the current.

Quickly, Thomas dived after her, praying he was not too late.

Astrid, surrounded by the buoyant water, reveled in its satiny caress and the encompassing silence. She wished she could grow gills and stay down for hours. After remaining submerged as long as she dared, she headed upward.

With sickening suddenness, she was encircled by a hard, tight grip. She gulped in a flood of water that threatened to strangle her. Filled with terror, she flailed against the creature that held her captive. An octopus? Confused and sensing impending doom, she frantically bit deeply into a hunk of rigid flesh and the choking hold relaxed. She beat away the grasping tentacles, escaping from their slippery reach.

With a wild spluttering she surfaced, took in a lung full of blessed air and began swimming rapidly toward shore.

Behind her, she heard splashes. My God, is it following me? Horrified, she glanced back and saw Thomas's head pop out of the water. He looked angry as the devil.

Astrid immediately understood what had happened. She'd interrupted a heroic rescue. Her heart still pounding from their encounter in the deep, she stopped, turned around and swam back toward him. She'd bitten the hell out of something, and she'd better see if he needed help. At the very least she owed him an apology.

"I'm sorry, Thomas," she said as she neared him. "I thought you were an octopus." She saw the stream of blood flowing from his hand. Alarmed, she reached for him. "Are you all right?" she asked.

He nodded his head and moved away from her outstretched hand.

"I have maneuvered in these waters with far greater injuries, milady," he said. His eyes studied her face. "I thought you were drowning."

She laughed. "Then we were both in error, kind sir. I swim like a fish."

"So I have witnessed." He raised his hand. "And you also have the bite of a damnable shark."

Astrid was sorry about the bite, but pushed back another apology. He deserved it, swooping down on her that way. Besides, he still looked more angry than anything else. They seemed destined to be permanently at loggerheads.

She knew she needed his protection, but at the same time she had to establish her own identity or she'd really drown in this mysterious world.

"Would you deign to race me to shore?" She challenged him with a toss of her sopping hair.

His eyes narrowed. "The match is an unfair one, milady. My length and strength will outdistance thee."

"Then we'll wager," she said with a confident smile. "If I win, you will let me swim unattended in the future."

"And if I win?" he asked, raising his dark brows.

"I will attempt to mold myself into a more docile woman who will anger you less."

He looked interested. Contemplating her offer, he pushed his black hair back from his face with the fingers of his injured hand. She was glad to see the bleeding had stopped.

"There appears no docility in thee, milady, but an attempt from thee to find a mite appeals to me. I accept your challenge."

Astrid thought she saw a whisper of a smile cross his dark face as she swam over to him.

"We will start from here," she said. "On the count of three. One . . ." She eyed the shore, gauging the distance and mapping her strategy. "Two . . . Three!"

Her crawl stroke was strong, and she moved ahead of him with ease. His dog-paddle side-stroke combination can't compete, she thought triumphantly. But she couldn't let herself take anything for granted, because he'd been right about his advantages. Despite her sleeker racing style, the distance between them remained only a frustrating foot or so.

Seeing her goal getting nearer, she added a finisher's burst of steam.

And then the piece of linen began to slip away from her breasts.

Damn! She interrupted her strokes long enough to grab the cloth in her hands, then pressed furiously ahead.

But the lost seconds had taken their toll. Astrid and Thomas reached the shore in a dead heat.

Breathing heavily, she plastered the linen back over her breasts and sat in the shallow water that was lapping against the sand.

"No fair!" she shouted up to him. He was standing over her, his hands on his hips. His shirt clung wetly to his torso, and his pants dribbled puddles around his bare feet. "I had a handicap!"

Thomas looked down at the woman. Her soaked, barely covered body was an arousing distraction that he wanted to ignore, but he couldn't tear his eyes away from her.

When she raised her face, their eyes locked, and Astrid felt a shiver of electricity.

"We tied," she said in a weak voice.

Thomas nodded.

"What do we do now?" she asked. The way he was looking, she wondered if he was going to fall across her and take her right there on the spot. She knew damn well she was wishing he would do that very thing.

But he backed away and turned his head. "If we both have won, then I believe we are committed to each of the wagers," he said with a quiet huskiness. He cleared his throat. "You may swim unattended henceforth, milady, and I may expect to see increased docility from thee."

He picked up his boots and coat. "Get thee clothed, Lady Van Fleet. Meanwhile, I will search through my wife's trunks for more suitable wear for thee," he said with a cool formality.

As he walked back to the house, Astrid sighed and reached for the towel she had left beside her small pile of clothes.

She had to watch this attraction business, she warned herself. First of all, it was dreadfully one-sided. She had read things that simply weren't there. That mention of his wife had reminded her forcefully about his recent tragedy.

Second, she was indebted to him and didn't want to hurt him. A relationship between them could be disastrous—especially for him, because he was trapped in the stricter moral code of his time.

My time now, too, she hastened to add.

Frowning, she stepped back into her soiled clothes.

She was going to have to tone down her ways. For starters, she'd try to stop flaunting her 20th century body before his 17th century eyes. Maybe libido hasn't been labeled yet, but it's bound to be strongly present.

She remembered, somewhat wistfully, that look in his eyes. Yes, libido was present all right. She kicked back the thought with a vengeance. So what if the attraction wasn't one-sided? The bottom line was still the same.

She pledged to herself that she'd work on her end of the bargain. She'd become the model of docility.

At least she had achieved one small victory. She could swim now without his hovering. He'd better stick to that, because she'd be damned if she was going to start swimming in stomachers and modesty pieces.

When Thomas found a few of Sarah's dresses for the woman, he ached at the sight of them. After placing them on the bed in the Hollander's chamber, he walked across to his own chamber —his and Sarah's—so empty now. Their bed, too, was woefully empty.

He removed his wet clothing and lay back exhausted on the dimity coverlet. The slant of the late afternoon sun fell across his damp nakedness.

I am weary, he told himself, thinking of the unnumbered hours since he last slept. Too weary and dead within to remember thee, dear Sarah. He frowned at the ceiling, trying to conjure up his dead wife's face, her dark red hair, the freckles on her small pale arms, the way her body had felt as she lay in his arms.

Cease torturing yourself, Thomas! Sarah is gone from thee forever.

He closed his eyes, accepting the darkness. So weary, he thought, as his taut body began to relax.

Unbeckoned, a silvery mermaid floated into his memory. Her golden hair streamed behind her and wafted across his face. He swept aside the silken strands with his hand and rolled over on his stomach. But she was there, beneath him, her radiant countenance vibrating with life.

Bewitching me, he thought fuzzily as he buried his face in the soft bolster. Haunting me and reminding me too well that I am not yet dead.

Accompanied by a deep stirring in his groin, Thomas allowed himself to drift away with the mermaid through the undulating warmth of gentle waves and into the rapture of forgetful sleep.

Chapter Thirteen

Things could be worse Astrid told herself. After two weeks at Eagle's Crest her days were forming a comfortable pattern of sorts. Though she longed still to be whisked back to her former life, she found she was free of stress for the first time since she'd arrived in the 17th century.

First of all, only a few people were around—a handful of men who worked the fields, old Joseph, Jeremy, who shuttled back and forth between his duties at Bermuda Hundred and his preferred chores at Eagle's Crest, and, of course, Thomas.

The men stayed busy most of the time with this and that, basically leaving her alone. She was grateful, because this gave her the space she needed to adjust.

Then, too, she felt relatively safe. The secret of

her presence had been well-kept. At Thomas's insistence, Jeremy and the others had sworn an oath "to impart to no man nor woman that the Hollander be among us." When a rare visitor arrived on the scene, she stayed out of sight.

Astrid was unclear what she was being sheltered from. Lord Dunwoody should be well on his way to England by now, she figured. Who else could be planning to do her in? The rebellion was heating up, but she didn't have a role in that. She listened in on conversations when she had a chance, but nothing she heard gave her much information about what was going on.

Occasionally she had felt penned in, but she got over it quickly. True, she couldn't wander beyond Thomas's property, but she could roam at will within its boundaries, an exhaustingly large area.

And she was swimming daily. Thomas had kept his end of their bargain.

Astrid knew she hadn't done as well with her own end. Docility didn't fit her any better than the clothes of the era.

Clothing, in fact, had been the cause of her first big scrap with Thomas.

She had appreciated the dresses he'd placed in her room, but hating their bulk and needless froufrous, she had altered them.

Thomas had hit the roof.

"What manner of dress is this, milady?" he asked when she came down for supper that first evening. Disapproval was written all over his face.

Astrid thought she'd done a fine job with her

alterations, considering her lack of sewing ability.

The dress was too short, but she was resigned to that. Astrid was obviously taller than Thomas's wife, and every one of the dresses fell way above her ankles. But no one could fault her for that little imperfection, she decided.

Whacking off the sleeves, however, was apparently a different matter. She'd felt clever as anything when she'd done it, and she considered little cap sleeves most fitting and becoming.

She'd forgotten about the taboo on elbows.

Thomas's thumbs-down attitude caught her off guard.

"What manner of dress, Thomas?" she repeated, at a loss to think of anything else to say.

"'Tis improper for ladies to display their arms," he admonished. "Go find thyself covering."

Astrid exploded. "It's one hundred fifty degrees in the shade, Thomas! Why in hell should anyone object to a woman's arms? Long sleeves are out of the question!"

Thomas looked as if she'd slapped him. She realized he probably hadn't understood most of what she'd said, but she was furious enough not to give a damn.

Joseph Whiteside had come to her rescue. He shuffled into the room with a chuckle and a bowl full of stew.

"Our guest should be allowed to feel at home, Thomas," he said. "Mayhap the ladies in her country dress thus, and we must honor her customs as she honors us with her presence."

Well said, Astrid thought as she frowned at Thomas and stubbornly stood her ground.

So much for docility, she thought.

"You are correct, Joseph, as always," Thomas said, but his expression didn't show he was convinced. "I offer an apology for my manners, milady."

"I offer an apology also, Thomas," she said, deciding she could be gracious now that she'd won. "I mean not to offend thee, but I know not all the proper ways in this strange land."

Thomas nodded, but she sensed he was far from placated.

"I'll fetch the rest of the supper, Joseph," Thomas had said, leaving the room in what she'd describe as a huff.

Episode number two was another victory for Astrid, or kind of a victory, as she qualified it. She'd asked Thomas for a quill.

"And why would a lady want a quill?" he inquired.

She didn't dare mention her journal. "I . . . I wish to teach Jeremy his letters," she said.

"And how do you intend to teach him the king's English when you know it not?" he scoffed.

Astrid should have expected a remark like that, but she heard herself exploding again.

"The letters are the same, Thomas Arrington! Maybe I don't pronounce them to your highfalutin standards, but by God I can outwrite the lot of you. And it's criminal that nobody's bothered to teach the boy."

She felt like biting her tongue. She hadn't

thought of Jeremy's deficiency herself until a moment ago.

"The lad should learn his letters," Thomas had said with a heavy sigh. "I'll give thee a quill and paper also. 'Tis kind of thee to wish to teach him."

Astrid got her quill, along with a silent respect for Thomas and a new responsibility.

Eagle's Crest—June 15, 1676

I may have flunked Education 101, but I'm a helluva teacher! Jeremy's starving for learning, and since I'm starving for companionship, we're a great pair.

He's as quick as a fox. He learned his alphabet and was ready for meatier things before I knew what was happening. After "See Jeremy run" and "Ho! The horse can jump," I was running dry until I remembered the dialogue from *Midsummer.*

Now the lad's spouting things like "Ay me! for aught that ever I could read, Could ever hear by tale or history, The course of true love never did run smooth."

Thank God I know something written before 1676.

And, may I add, thank God for Joseph Whiteside! It's uncanny how he understands me. He stands up for me in my inevitable battles with Thomas, and he senses when I'm at loose ends. He invites me into the kitchen, lets me help and manages to calm me down, just when I'm ready to start screaming.

Sometimes I think I'm somewhat lucky, despite the God-awful circumstances that brought me to this retarded century.

I had Lizzie and Mrs. Arrington to help me right off the bat. Then there was Marcy. Jeremy is still around, and now there's good ol' Joseph.

Bless them all!

And bless Thomas the Gloomy, too, though he drives me nuts most of the time.

Astrid sat snapping beans while Joseph stood over by the fire stirring the kettle. She was perspiring and wishing for a tall glass of Gatorade. The old man looked as cool as a cucumber.

"'Tis hot, Joseph," she complained. "Shouldn't we be cooking outside today?"

"My blood be thinner than yours, little lady," he said. "You might take the beans out under the shade of a tree if you wish."

Astrid sighed. "The gnats pester me. Anyway, I like your company."

"And I yours," he said with a soft laugh.

They were silent for a while. She had never realized beans snapping and a stirring spoon could make so much noise.

"He's fond of you, you know," Joseph said, interrupting her reverie.

Astrid looked up and smiled. "Jeremy? He's a dear lad, that one."

"I was speaking of Thomas."

She frowned.

"I think not, Joseph. I'm but a nettle to that gentleman." She popped a bean with her fingers. "And he wishes me elsewhere, though I have no other place for the nonce."

She suddenly felt sorry for herself and tears sprang to her eyes.

"Feel like a prisoner some days?" the old man queried.

"Uh huh." She stared down at the basket on her lap and tried to get a hold on herself.

"I know, I know," Joseph said gently. He turned around and looked at her. His eyes twinkled. "Methinks you be from somewhere far more foreign than Holland, little lady."

Astrid turned pale and was afraid to say anything.

Joseph put down his spoon and sat down on a stool across from her. "Could I talk with thee a spell?"

Astrid's hands gripped the basket. "Of course, Joseph. What's on your mind?" Her voice quavered.

Joseph, too, looked uncomfortable. He rubbed his knees and sighed. "First, I must tell thee something I ne'er have told another soul. I feel that I can trust thee, however, little lady, and I feel also that you need a special kind of understanding that I might be able to offer thee."

She stared at him. Her palms were damp against the wicker basket.

"When I was but a lad I was struck by lightning," he began. "For two years afterwards, I was dumb. I couldn't speak. What nobody knew, tho', was that I could see things and hear things beyond my ken."

"Things, Joseph?" Her voice was a whisper.

"I thought I'd become a lunatic and was sore afraid. Locked in my silent world I struggled to understand why I knew people's thoughts before they uttered their words and knew with uncanny certainty when the words were true or false."

"You can read thoughts?" Astrid's head was whirling.

He tilted his face toward her and looked searchingly into her eyes. "Aye. 'Tis called second sight. 'Til now I've breathed this not, little lady. By the time my tongue returned to life I'd learned the virtue of silence about many things." A dry chuckle rattled from his throat.

"Why are you telling me this, Joseph?" She felt her world was falling off its axis.

"I believe you know why. So that I can help thee."

"Help me?" He simply couldn't be aware of her truth. He couldn't comprehend.

"I perceive thoughts in thee that bewilder me, little lady. Pictures come into my mind like no others I've seen nor dreamed of. 'Tis enough for me to know that you're not from this world. Why be you here?"

Tears rolled down Astrid's pale cheeks. She shook her head. "I know not why, Joseph."

He shuffled over to her and placed his withered hands on her shoulders. "Have no fear, little lady. I know you speak the truth, and your secret be safe with me. You have memories of a wondrous place that I but wish I could see meself."

"They're useless memories," she sobbed.

"Useless. Oh, Joseph, what can I do?"

He patted the top of her head. "Learn to know that you were brought here for a purpose, my dear one. God works in miraculous ways, and his plans are filled with mystery and wonder. I promise not to pry into your past, for I think 'tis made of stuff my old tired brain could not cope with. You must believe, tho', that I stand ready to help thee."

Astrid wrapped her arms around the old man's stooped back and pressed her wet face into his shirt. Relief poured over her like a balm. Now *this* was an ally! God, she hadn't realized how scared she'd been, how alone. She took a deep breath to calm herself and looked up into his wise eyes.

"I thank thee, my friend," she whispered.

Joseph's face crinkled into a warm smile. "And I thank thee, little lady, for brightening our world." He gave her a squeeze and returned to the kettle. Resuming his stirring, he began to whistle softly.

Astrid's fingers trembled as she picked up a bean. "What do the others think of me?" she asked.

"That you be a Hollander countess with peculiar ways," he said with a small cackle. "Tell me, little lady, are all the women in your world so strong-willed?"

"Much more," she said, suddenly feeling feisty enough to needle him. "They have powers and freedom beyond even your imaginings. They vote; some go into the army and navy; some even govern."

Joseph frowned and shook his head. "Not a fit world for me nor any man."

She tossed a bean at him, and they both laughed.

Thomas walked into the kitchen.

Astrid blushed and began tending to her beans. She wiped her face with the back of her hand, hoping the tear streaks didn't show.

"I heard laughter," he said. "'Tis good to hear laughter again within these walls."

"Aye, Thomas, and we owe gratitude to the little lady here for bringing it to us," Joseph said.

Thomas ignored the remark and leaned over Joseph's shoulder.

"There's stew enough in that kettle to feed an army, my good man," he said.

"Mayhap we expect an army, Thomas," Joseph said in a teasing singsong. "Whose army, we know not, nor does it matter if it be Colonel Bacon's or Governor Berkeley's. This house is prepared for war. We can feed any of 'em, what e'er the side."

Thomas patted the curved back. "You'd provide the whole of Virginia, Joseph, and without complaint, given the need and two or three more kettles." He glanced up at Astrid.

The Hollander looks near tame today, he thought. With the basket on her lap and the wee drops of perspiration on her upper lip she appears as compliant as a parson's wife. Though it was certain no parson's wife he'd ever known would sit barefoot and bare-armed in her host's kitchen.

"I saw today that you have been teaching

Jeremy the art of swimming as well as his letters," he said to her.

Astrid detected a hint of criticism. "And is that a sin?" she asked, too exhausted emotionally to guard her words. "The lad almost drowned last month." She tried to keep the bristles out of her voice but didn't succeed too well.

Thomas raised an eyebrow. "No argument, milady. You did right to do so," he said. He crossed his arms over his chest. "Fact is, I intended to inquire if perchance you might teach me your method of swimming. The lad outswam me today, and his cockiness is unbearable."

Astrid couldn't believe her ears. Thomas Arrington actually had stepped down from his haughty perch and was asking her to do him a favor!

She'd won another round. She was too drained to crow, but she couldn't resist teasing him a bit.

"Jeremy was an excellent student," she said with a too-sweet smile. "His young limbs are flexible and easily taught. Your older and more rigid body may find the moves too difficult." She turned her attention to the basket on her lap and daintily popped apart a few beans, fully aware of the sparks flying from his eyes.

"I am willing to take that risk, Lady Van Fleet." She could tell by his forced steadiness that she'd struck a nerve. "Perchance we should start the lessons at once before I grow even older."

"Joseph needs me here to help with supper,

Thomas," she said in her most docile, ladylike tones, hiding the smile that wanted to bubble forth. She'd love to get out into the water, even with Thomas, but she loved even more being in control of this situation.

"Go on with him, little lady," Joseph said. "No army will come today, and you've readied enough beans for the ones of us who be here."

Astrid threw the old man a withering glance, but he tossed back a wicked gleam that made her feel like giggling. Instead, she rose from the stool and placed the basket on the wooden table in the center of the kitchen.

"Very well, then," she said, staging a resigned sigh. She turned around to face Thomas. "I will meet thee down on the river bank in a few minutes, Thomas."

Joseph was chuckling and nodding over his kettle. Astrid wanted to kick him, but she loved him too much. When Thomas left the room, she went over to the old man and whispered loudly into his ear. "The women in my homeland refuse to take vows to obey their men."

Joseph shook his head. "Not a fit place, not a fit place," he said.

It was Astrid's turn to chuckle. Giving Joseph a big hug, she ran to her room to get ready for the swimming lesson.

Astrid had made herself a bathing suit. It was ugly as sin, but it served the purpose. She'd found a bolt of blue-striped dimity and had whipped up a one-piece thing—she didn't know what else to call it—that covered her from neck to mid-thigh. She'd been stubborn enough to leave it sleeveless, but otherwise she figured it wouldn't shock the bejesus out of anybody.

As she neared the river, with a big towel wrapped around her to hide her outfit as much as to display prim modesty, she wondered what Thomas would be wearing. Nobody had thought of recreational swimming, so bathing suits like almost everything else were yet to be invented.

Thomas was waiting for her, sitting under a tree and smoking a pipe. He was fully clothed, complete with boots, exactly the way he'd been in the kitchen.

This should be interesting, she thought. He'll probably remove his boots and pipe and expect to learn the Australian crawl garbed in 20 pounds of clothes.

But she was wrong. When she arrived, he laid down his pipe, stood up, and without saying a word took off his boots, vest, shirt and knickers. The knickers coming off were a surprise, but she saw immediately that he hadn't thrown caution to the wind. His long underdrawers were heavier than Doctor Dentons.

"Shall we begin my lesson, Lady Van Fleet?" he asked, wading into the water. God, Astrid thought, the man looks beautiful even in that ridiculous underwear. Trying to ignore her thoughts, she tossed aside the towel and joined him.

Thomas avoided looking at her, and she couldn't say she blamed him. They stood side by side for a moment, both of them staring at the river. Feeling uncomfortable as the devil, Astrid didn't quite know how to begin.

To hell with it, she thought and waded out until the water lapped about her waist.

"Come on," she said, "I'll give thee basic instructions here, and then we'll try it farther out."

When Thomas came up beside her, she knew at once she'd miscalculated. Waist deep for her was not waist deep on him. In fact, the water rippled tantalizingly right in the middle of the well-defined bulge in the front of his Doctor Dentons.

Astrid forced herself not to notice and looked up into his eyes instead. That wasn't a safe haven either, she realized, and she focused on one of his ears.

"Now it's really very simple," she said, wishing her body beneath the water would stop reminding her what a gorgeous hunk of a man Thomas Arrington was. "You keep your legs straight and kick in a scissorlike movement. Here, I'll show you."

She floated forward and demonstrated. She was glad to have something to do to help get rid of the physical yearnings that had come over her.

"Now you try it," she yelled, keeping her distance. He complied, making big splashes but moving quickly to her.

"Good," she said, relieved the water now was up to her shoulders and his chest. She wished her voice would act right. She sounded downright squeaky. "But you're doing it too hard and fast. Try to keep your feet below the surface and use this rhythm." She stuck her hands up out of the water and flapped them up and down. "One, two, one, two, one, two."

Thomas smiled, and Astrid gulped. This was going to be tougher than she'd expected.

"Now try again," she said, pursing her lips like a schoolmarm.

Thomas floated off, accidentally brushing across her before he started his kicking routine.

He's good, she thought as she watched him. She could see his legs moving properly now, propelling him forward without a splash. If he catches on as quickly to the arm strokes, we can finish this silliness in a hurry. She longed to be back in the lonely security of her room.

Thomas turned and kicked his way back to where she was standing.

"Methinks I'm ready for lesson number two," he said. Drops of water clung to his thick lashes and became tear-shaped rainbows in the bright sun. Astrid was dazzled but managed to keep herself under control.

She explained the arm movements, the breathing pattern, and how to synchronize the kicks with the strokes. She'd taught dozens of children how to swim at the Richmond Y, and she'd even done a creditable job with Jeremy, but with this grown man she felt strangely self-conscious. She was convinced she was botching the whole thing miserably since she kept forgetting to use the vocabulary he knew.

Nevertheless, Thomas learned the crawl quicker than any of her former students. Before she knew what was happening, he was stroking through the water as if he'd been swimming that way for years.

He's a natural, she thought as she followed him out into the river. He turned and waited for her to catch up. His face radiated with delight.

"I thank thee, milady," he said. "That stroke will put me in good stead henceforth."

She stopped a few feet before she reached him. His enthusiasm was so contagious that she relaxed, treading water and feeling her confidence return.

"Ho!" she shouted. "Are you willing to test your new knowledge with another race to shore?"

"Aye! And woulds't you dare wager this time?"

This was a new Thomas. It was as if the swim had washed away all his sternness and stiff-necked propriety. He was as playful as a boy.

Astrid smiled. "And have you a wager in mind?" she asked.

Thomas floated closer. "If I win, you shall put long sleeves back into all of your clothing."

Astrid didn't like the sound of that proposition. The Australian crawl seemed to instill cockiness in all males.

She pondered her chances of winning and considered them nil unless she could think of something clever. She decided to buy time by playing along with him.

"And if I should win, Thomas? What do you suggest for that wager?"

He laughed, and Astrid felt her irritation rising. "Well, milady, should you outdistance me, I pledge to complain never more about your manner of dress."

"Never more?" Astrid contemplated the luxury of bikinis and sun dresses. "You promise I may wear what I will if I should win the race?"

"Aye," he said with another laugh. Astrid thought he sounded damnably sure of himself, and her adrenalin began to flow.

"You have advantages of length and strength, Thomas. And now with the knowledge I've given thee, you have a further advantage," she said. "Mayhap a race between us is not equal."

"I agree, milady. Move forward twenty strokes before we begin." His offer seemed fair enough to Astrid. She'd been hoping for a ten stroke advantage.

"It's a wager," she said confidently. She made her strokes strong and after 20 was far ahead. She congratulated herself, redesigning in her head her meager wardrobe.

"Count of three," she yelled back to him. "One . . . two . . . three!"

She knew she could beat him. With her skill and the lead he'd given her, it was hardly a race, but she swam furiously anyway. She'd show him, goddamn it.

When she saw him pulling alongside her and effortlessly moving ahead, she struggled to go faster, but it was no use.

He was standing on shore, full of cheer and pulling on his knickers when she landed.

Frustrated, Astrid lay panting on the rocky beach and dug her fingernails into the sand.

Thomas sat down beside her. She put her cheek on her arm and looked up warily at him. He wasn't even breathing hard and was entirely too self-satisfied for her taste. For a brief moment, Astrid contemplated murder.

"Oh no," she groaned. "Must I add long sleeves to everything?"

"Everything but that swimming costume you're wearing, milady."

Astrid sat up and brushed the wet sand off her arms and knees.

"Then I'll wear this damnable costume all the time," she said in a determined voice. "All day—at breakfast, midday, supper, and even to bed. 'Tis comfortable, and I'll wear it 'til it rots on me!"

"No, you won't, milady!" he said with a laugh. His good humor was undiminished by her bad temper. "While you are my guest at Eagle's Crest you will dress as I say, and I say sleeves on dresses."

Astrid stood up and stomped over to a big rock. Now she was the one who was glowering. She sat down on the rock, straightened out her legs and planted her heels in the sand.

"Be reasonable, Thomas," she pleaded. Then she exploded. "Just because you're suddenly some kind of superman Olympic swimmer, don't get it into your head that you're lord and master of the whole universe!"

Thomas stared at her. "Your speech is pocked with Hollander words, and I understand naught but the sense of them. That sense tells me you are unduly angry and as stubborn as my mule Bessie." He reached for his shirt and thrust his arms through the sleeves.

Astrid felt lousy. She'd messed up everything

over a lost race and a stupid wager, and Thomas was glowering again. She couldn't act right if her life depended on it. She'd never learn.

"Oh pooh!" she exclaimed. "Hollander, shmollander! Can't you see I'm only a foolheaded woman who doesn't know which end's up? I'm sorry, Thomas." She burst into tears.

Thomas was confounded. He'd never understood women, but this one was more confusing than any of them. Her strong will was one thing, but these damnable spouting tears were something else. He walked over to her.

"Cease your weeping, milady." He pulled her up from the rock, grabbed her wet shoulders and shook her gently. "I understand you not, but I know I do not wish to see you unhappy in this manner. If I have said aught to bring these tears, tell me and I will slay the words."

Astrid inhaled a sob, trying to get control of herself. "It's not y-you," she blubbered. "It's me, damn it." She clutched the sleeves of his open shirt and buried the top of her head on his bare chest. "You're a kind gentleman and I'm . . . I'm . . . I don't know what I am any more!" Through her tears she looked down at their sandy bare feet. His longer toes nearly touched hers. For some reason, this view of their feet made her cry even harder. For a wild moment she wondered if her hormones had gone completely haywire. Feet! What's so blasted heartrending about four silly feet? This isn't like me at all.

At the same time, her raging emotions made

perfect sense to her. And the gushing eyes and running nose and wracking sobs were a welcome release—from what, she didn't know—but she succumbed, with a topsy-turvy pleasure, to whatever had taken possession of her.

Thomas tried to soothe the woman. He held her, gingerly at first, then tighter against him in an attempt to quell her tremulous outburst. "Shhh, milady. Find quiet and peace within thyself. I know not how to help thee when you are thus distraught."

I know not either what words to use, he told himself, feeling woefully inadequate and finding himself praying that in some magical way comfort and assurance could find a means to flow from his body into hers.

Her face burned into his chest, while her tears soaked through his skin and were flooding his heart. He ached for her, longing for her to turn again into the strong, freedom-loving, sharp-tongued damsel he had learned to expect and to accept, if not to understand.

His arms wrapped her firmly against him. The heat of her body radiated through the cold, damp dimity, and his senses absorbed her soft essence, the fresh scent of flowers and river water wafting from her hair and skin.

Time came to an abrupt halt. He closed his eyes, willing the sun to continue its journey, but pressing his face down into the warm small head that was now, in this frozen moment, his earth's center.

He opened his eyes. "Hush, my sweeting," he

murmured, pushing back the thick wet strands of burnished gold from her cheeks. He cradled her flushed face in his hands and with his thumbs wiped away the tears. His lips grazed her lashes.

"Shhh," he whispered, as her lids trembled and lifted, unveiling the blue of a deep sea. The sun jolted back into motion, but Thomas knew it was too late to save him. He sank into the azure depths beneath him and covered her parted lips with his own.

Astrid accepted his kiss, returning the dark, sweet warmth. A fluid tremor replaced her wrenching sobs with a deeper, more profound pleasure.

She circled her arms around his neck and drew him closer, savoring the heated pressure of his mouth.

"Thomas," she muttered against his lips, as the words slid apart and evaporated into a crimson fog.

His mouth lifted from hers. Holding her face close, he looked down into her eyes. Astrid felt the whisper of his lashes mingling with her own, his hot, sweet breath against her lips. She saw only the rich patina of treasured silver.

"We must part, milady." The gentle huskiness of his voice echoed in her ears like the distant rumble of thunder before a summer storm.

"Why?" Nothing made sense any longer. Her body was smoldering, his was aflame. She felt the throbbing furnace of his groin, begging against her for release, her swollen breasts and the moistness between her thighs pleading for the fullness of him. Why must we part? Why must we ever part?

For long moments they didn't move, their lashes enmeshed, their eyes merging into a single silvery blue ocean, their rapid breaths blending and enveloping them in an ethereal cloud.

The tension mounted. Astrid felt it reverberate through his hands and arms.

We must part. She knew it but didn't know what to do about it. She was under a spell, mesmerized in a dreamlike trance and unable to move. He obviously was in a similar state.

Everything was slow motion. A blink of his eyes seemed to take minutes, a tear in one corner swelling slowly, reaching for a lash, clinging on and riding upward, lingering a long while before losing its hold and gradually dropping downward, out of her sight.

We must part. Like a sleepwalker, Astrid slid her hands from his neck, over his shoulders. She squeezed his arms.

"You speak wisely, Thomas," she whispered, surprised that the words, weak as they were, got past her constricted throat. "We must part."

Thomas released his hold and stepped back. He shook his head as if he had awakened from a disturbing dream.

Astrid sat down on the rock and tried to get her bearings. The sun was still high in the sky, the river glistened as it had earlier, and the birds trilled their same busy songs.

But she knew her world had changed, altered

beyond measure. Her mind pleaded not to let this happen to her, but her heart had a stronger message.

Thomas walked over to her, his shadow engulfing her.

"I have no words," he said. "I beg thy pardon, milady, for my untoward actions this day and wish mightily I could roll back the sun to its morning horizon."

Astrid listened attentively, searching his dark face for an appropriate response but found none. The glare of the sun behind him hid his features from her, though they were engraved deeply in her memory, but his voice told her he was suffering. And she had to do something about that.

"No apologies are necessary, Thomas. I am as much at fault as you." She clenched her hands together and took a deep breath. This was no time to collapse again into tears, she warned herself. "I shall go back into the house and sew on sleeves in an effort to please thee," she said.

"Forget our wager, milady. Sleeves are of little importance."

Astrid looked down at her clasped hands, studying the jagged white circles of her knuckles. She wondered what this afternoon would do to her future at Eagle's Crest. She no longer knew how to act, not that she ever did, she reminded herself. But certainly her feelings for Thomas were going to color everything from now on.

And what were his feelings for her?

As she pondered, he walked back to the tree,

pulled on his boots, picked up his pipe and vest and her towel and returned to her, buttoning his shirt.

When he gave her the towel, she wrapped it around her shoulders.

Thomas reached out his hand. "Come, milady, I will accompany thee to the house."

As Astrid took his hand, the sharp crackle of twigs back in the woods riveted their attention. They turned and saw two rough-looking men on horseback approaching at a slow walk.

Trailing behind, encircled by a rope attached to one of the horses, were three scrawny, frightened Indians—a man, woman and child.

Chapter Fourteen

Run back into the house, milady!" Thomas said under his breath. "I will see to this."

Astrid hesitated. They've seen me, she thought. Why should I hide? Besides, Thomas may need me.

"Hide!" he ordered. The look in his eyes told her he meant business. Frustrated and confused, she scurried up the hill.

Who are those men? What in the world are they doing with those poor Indians? Why are they here? What the hell is going on?

Out of breath, she dashed around to the back of the house and into the kitchen.

Joseph looked up, startled. "Good lord, little lady! What . . .?"

Astrid grabbed him, almost knocking him off his spindly legs. "Joseph!" she sputtered. "There are men here . . . Indians! Thomas made me run . . ."

"Indians?" Joseph asked, a catch in his throat. "Indians here?" He shoved her aside and reached up for the long rifle strapped to the wall.

"No, Joseph," she cried, "don't shoot them! They're tied up . . . pitiful! There's a little boy and a woman."

Joseph pulled down the gun and stared at her. "Tell me who's here, woman!" He opened a pouch of gunpowder and began loading the weapon.

"I don't know." She sat down, trembling. "There are two men on horses, and they're dragging along three scared Indians. It's a family, I think." She squeezed her eyes shut. "It's awful."

"What's awful?" He looked at her with concern.

"All of it." Astrid shuddered. "They came out of the woods—the men, those poor souls tied up. Thomas wouldn't let me stay." She covered her face with her hands.

Joseph set down the rifle and walked over to her. He pulled away her hands and looked down into her eyes.

"Go to your room, little lady," he said softly. "Thomas wants you hidden when guests arrive."

"Guests?" She couldn't believe her ears. "Are you telling me those disgusting men could be guests? Bringing gifts of three human beings, maybe? What do you people do with gifts like that? Eat them, for God's sake?" Her anger surprised her.

"Hush, woman!" Joseph said, shaking his head at her. "I don't know who the men are any more than you do at the moment, but I do know you're supposed to be in hiding."

Astrid stood and frowned at the old man. "What will happen to the Indians?" she asked.

Joseph shrugged. "I don't know, little lady. It depends."

Her face reddened. "Depends on who? On what? God, Joseph, they're harmless!"

"Indians are Indians," he said and picked up the gun.

Astrid stomped out of the kitchen and ran upstairs.

She sat in her room, fuming, her arms across her chest. It was already dark, and she had lit a single candle. Earlier, she had listened through her window, heard the men's gruff voices as they talked with Thomas and heard him invite them in for supper.

Astrid was appalled. Those two ruffians were no gentlemen, and Thomas had invited them into his home.

What's more, they were treating the Indians abominably. She'd watched as the men had removed the rope from the horse and tied its end to a tree below her. The man, woman and child, still lassoed, sat huddled together on the ground.

Thomas hadn't helped the men, but he'd stood by and let this inhumanity happen. And along with them he'd entered the house and abandoned the poor creatures without food or water.

Astrid was heartsick. Thomas was no better than the others. He, too, was uncivilized.

She sat chilled, thinking. She knew she had to do something for that family down there. To hell with Thomas and the rest! She'd take the Indians food and set them free.

As she forced herself to straighten out her thoughts and begin to lay plans, there was a soft knock on her door.

Astrid stared at the white panels and held her breath.

"Little lady, open please."

She walked to the door, opened it and let Joseph in, closing it quickly behind him.

He was carrying a tray of food.

"Your supper," he said. "I brought it as soon as I could slip away without notice."

The smell of the pungent stew nauseated her. Unable to speak, she nodded, then walked back to her chair by the window.

Joseph placed the tray on the table near her and sat down on the bed.

"You look terrible," he said.

Astrid screwed up her face. "Who cares?" she said coldly.

"I do, for one," he said. "And I 'spect Thomas for another."

"That barbarian!" she snarled.

"Oh?" Joseph looked surprised. He tried to catch her eyes, but she kept them fastened on the wall above his head.

"The men are Berkeley's," he said.

What does that have to do with anything? she asked herself. Her face remained expressionless.

Joseph sighed. "We could cut the tension in this room with a knife, little lady. What's bothering you?"

"Everything!" she yelled. Joseph frowned, looked at the door and put a warning finger to his lips.

Astrid continued, lowering her voice but edging it with acid.

"Everything," she repeated. "The great Thomas is down there wining and dining and making merry with a couple of fellow ruffians, while a helpless family is dying on his doorstep."

Joseph put his hands on his knees and stood up.

"You don't understand," he said, looking troubled. "Thomas is doing what he must, and he's bending over backwards to protect you."

"Ha!" Astrid scoffed. "And what about those poor souls outside?"

"Indians killed his family," Joseph said in a low voice.

"Not *those* Indians," she said, spitting out the words.

"Mayhap not. But they be not our concern for the nonce. Your safety is," he said.

"My safety? Good grief, Joseph, the men saw me big as life down at the river. They know I'm here." She felt a twinge of fear.

"Thomas has them convinced you're his sister and in mourning so you can't come down to meet them. They're drunk enough now to believe him."

"His sis . . ." she interrupted, feeling confused.

"If you'll be quiet but a moment I'll explain,' Joseph said.

Astrid quieted down but kept her face frozen

"They're scoundrels, you be right about that. And they plan to take their redskin trophies to the governor to show him Bacon's not the only hero in Virginia." Looking tired, he sat back on the bed. "They saw thee, true, and thought they had found an even better trophy. They'd heard about the yellow-haired Hollander who escaped from Green Spring."

Joseph looked up at Astrid and squinted his eyes. "You're a wanted woman, little lady, and Berkeley has soldiers out searching for you. Lord Dunwoody convinced him before he left for England that you be a spy for the Bacon group."

Astrid shivered. "What does that mean, Joseph?" she asked with a tremor in her voice.

"It means you could be shot on sight, and Thomas could be drawn and quartered for helping thee."

"Drawn and quartered?" She felt weak.

"It's not a pretty thing, little lady. You must develop some patience and trust those who are trying to protect you."

"And . . . ?" Astrid sensed he wasn't finished.

"I recommend that you cease these senseless outbursts. This world moves slower than the one you're used to, I can see that. Be quiet occasionally, and accept the fact that you're here." He pushed himself back up and shuffled over to her.

"I know it requires strength, but I sense you have strength enough and more to draw upon."

Astrid was silent, her face clouded with thought. Joseph ruffled her hair.

"You need Thomas, little lady," he said, "and I be damnably sure he needs thee."

Astrid looked up at the old man. He sees it all, she thought. She shook her head sadly. "I don't know, Joseph. There's a wide gulf between us."

"And you're a mighty swimmer, so I hear," Joseph said with a chuckle, walking over to the door. She couldn't help but smile.

Astrid couldn't sleep. She lay on the feather mattress and stared at the beams over her head. Joseph's words of advice raced through her brain. *Wanted woman . . . develop some patience . . . shot on sight . . . Thomas needs you . . . drawn and quartered . . .*

She sat up, her eyes wide.

She clenched her fists, trying to get a hold on herself.

What else had he said? *This world moves slower . . .*

God, she wished it would start slowing down for her. She'd barely had a moment to think since she had arrived. She lay back and heaved a sigh.

She reached for the quilt and bunched it close to her. What in hell am I going to do about Thomas? Her heart quickened as the afternoon's events flooded through her memory. She buried her face in the pillow. I want him so, she whispered into the plump softness, forgetting her earlier anger and misgivings, forgetting the terror and the dangers, remembering only the overwhelming passion she'd felt in his arms.

A quivering hum drifted up from beneath her window. Astrid's eyes flew open. The Indians! She'd forgotten all about them!

She ran to the window and looked down. They sat close together. The man had his arm around the woman. She was holding the child, soothing its whimpers with a low, mournful tune.

Astrid stiffened. She had to help them! Joseph had told her to stay out of it, but he couldn't expect her to stand by and let those people be carted away as trophies.

She tightened her lips. I do what I must, Joseph, she said silently. Tossing a cloak over her thin nightgown, she picked up the tray of untouched food and quietly left the room.

The house was dark, and Thomas's door was closed. She tiptoed down the stairs. Drunken snores from the front parlor told her the visitors were asleep. Joseph, she knew, chose to sleep behind in the servants' building. The coast was clear.

She ran back to the kitchen and started for the rear door when she heard a man's voice in the yard. She stopped and pressed against the wall. Her heart jumped into her throat.

Carefully, she laid down the tray and sidled over to the open window.

Thomas was out there. He was kneeling over the Indians, talking softly and handing them bowls of food.

Tears of happiness blurred Astrid's eyes. Why had she doubted him?

Thomas straightened up and went over to the tree. He untied the rope, walked back to the Indians and removed the harness that held them. He was speaking their language evidently, because she couldn't understand a word, but she understood what he was doing. She thought she might burst with joy and pride.

"A plague on you, Mishter Arrin'ton!" The rough voice tore through the soft night.

With horror, Astrid saw that one of the men had stumbled out into the yard.

Thomas leaped on him and with one fierce punch to the chin knocked him to the ground. Astrid cheered Thomas on silently, beating her fists against the window sill.

The man was definitely down. Thomas rubbed his hands on his pants and walked back to the Indians.

Busy quieting them, he didn't see the second man lurch from the shadows. He stealthily moved toward Thomas. The man's sword was drawn!

Before Astrid could think, she had grabbed an iron pot from a hook on the wall and was running out the door.

Thomas saw her coming, a look of surprise on his face. At that moment the man lunged into his back.

Thomas fell forward.

Blind with rage, Astrid attacked the man, banging his head again and again with the pot.

"Stop it! Stop it!" she yelled. The man dropped his sword, folded in agony and crumpled to the ground.

Astrid threw down the pot. "Thomas!" she screamed, running to him. He was lying face down in front of the frightened Indians. There was blood on the back of his shirt.

"Thomas!" She fell on him, sobbing. "My God, have they killed you? Please, Thomas, don't be dead!"

Astrid pushed back his hair and laid her face against his cheek. "Be alive," she pleaded. "God, Thomas, be alive!" She bathed him with her hot tears, praying for him to move.

She'd seen blood! Horrified, she pulled herself up and examined his back. A dark stain was spreading on the shoulder of his white shirt. She gasped, tearing away the cloth in a frenzy. The skin lay open, the deep red blood streaming.

Frantically, Astrid placed her hands over the wound, trying to hold it closed. "I'll stop it, Thomas," she sobbed. "Hang in there!" She felt the blood seeping up through her fingers, and she pressed tighter. "Stop, damnit!" she ordered, as if her words and will could stem the crimson flow. Feeling helpless, she fell across him.

"Don't die, Thomas," she pleaded again into his ear. "I love you, goddamn it. Don't die."

He raised his head. "I'm not planning to die, milady, but I cannot move when you hold me down this way," he said.

In a wild mixture of relief and joy, Astrid pushed herself back on her knees. Thomas sat up. His torn shirt fell from his shoulder. He grimaced, holding his hand to his wound.

"'Tis but a scratch," he said, smiling at her.

"A scratch?" She was alarmed and didn't believe him. "You're bleeding to death." She raised her bloody hands to convince him. "We've got to stop it."

Thomas shooed her away. "Nonsense, milady." His eyes, for a brief moment, clung to hers. A reassuring sparkle of vitality there, along with the warm glow of respect and appreciation, calmed Astrid down.

She knew he'd suffered way more than a superficial scratch, but she knew, too, that he was far from dying.

Thank you, God, she whispered.

With surprising agility, Thomas rose to his feet and looked behind him. "Where are Jarvis and Williams?" he asked.

"Who?"

"The governor's two men. Where are they?"

Astrid had difficulty understanding what he was talking about, then it all came back in a rush.

She jumped up. The one she'd downed was lying in a heap and hadn't moved a muscle, the iron pot having rolled into the crook of his arm. He's dead, she told herself. I've killed him. She wondered at her lack of emotion, but she was too confused and exhausted to care one way or the other. Later, she knew she'd have to face that reality.

She picked up the dead man's sword and held it in her trembling fingers.

"This one's dead I think," she said quietly. She stared down at the sword, shuddering with repugnance at its sharp, bloody tip. "Where's the other?"

She looked up at Thomas, but he was walking away from her, cautiously approaching the spot where he had knocked down the first intruder. She saw he was unarmed and ran toward him, intending to give him the sword, when she saw a dark shadow moving behind Thomas.

"He's behind you, Thomas!" she screamed.

Thomas twirled. Astrid held her breath. The two figures grappled for an instant, then rolled to the ground. Astrid heard grunts and the sound of flesh pounding flesh. She winced and ran over to them.

The men were locked together, tumbling in a grotesque tangle of arms and legs. Astrid struggled to see who was who, feeling helpless as she watched the whirl of heads, backs and limbs, able only to discern a flapping white shirt here, a boot there.

Her heart racing, her fiery eyes searching for an opening, she saw that Thomas, the lean, taller one, was holding his own against the heavy, bulkier man.

Astrid was frantic. How long could his strength hold out? He was badly wounded, for God's sake! She knew she couldn't separate them, but she was desperate. She had to help Thomas, but how?

With an outburst of hatred, she kicked one of the stranger's fat legs as it rolled on top of the pile, but her bare toes didn't make a dent.

Cursing her weakness, she stood powerless, her heart pounding, waiting for another opening, a pause in the battle, anything to give her a chance to stop this craziness and have Thomas safe.

Her moment came. The soldier came back on top and for a frozen second the rolling ceased. Thomas was pinned beneath. Astrid stuck the tip of the sword at the back of the man's neck.

"Get off him," she screamed, "or this goes through you."

She was shaking uncontrollably. With gritty determination, she gripped the sword with both hands to quiet it. "Get off *now*," she commanded, nicking a piece of flesh to add emphasis to her words.

The startled man released his hold on Thomas's neck. Thomas reacted immediately by arching his body and kicking him away from him.

Astrid stepped back but kept the trembling sword aimed at the man.

"I thank thee, milady," Thomas said, as he slowly unfolded himself off the ground and stood beside her. He took the sword from her hands and held it over the soldier.

"I request that you depart from Eagle's Crest at once, Jarvis," he said. He nodded toward the stable, not taking his eyes off the man. "Bring their horses, milady."

Without questioning Thomas about the wisdom of letting the man go free, Astrid ran to the stable, threw saddles across the backs of the two horses and led them out.

"Your friend lies unconscious yon," Thomas

said to the man. "Hoist him over his horse, and begone with you both."

Numb, Astrid watched the beaten soldier stumble ahead of Thomas, lift the limp body of the one she'd killed and toss him across a horse, then climb up on his own horse.

His swollen eyes were filled with hatred, the angry glint he threw at Thomas visible even where she stood. An icy chill ran down her spine.

"God rot you, Thomas Arrington!" The man spat the words. "*And* your Hollander countess."

Thomas didn't move, but stood erect, the sword held firmly in his hand.

"Begone!" he said through clamped teeth.

Astrid ran up beside him. "Should you let him go, Thomas? He's a danger to us. We can hold him prisoner," she pleaded.

"No, they must go," Thomas said. "Williams needs a physician. Methinks these two will do us no further harm. Aye, Jarvis?"

The man on the horse didn't respond.

"Horse thieves receive heavy punishment still, Jarvis," Thomas said. "These animals belong to my neighbor James Crews, and I doubt you bought them from him since I know he's in Jamestown."

"His wife loaned them. We lost ours in the Indian skirmish," Jarvis said, his darting eyes showing his discomfort.

"I doubt that," Thomas said, his voice as unrelenting as the set of his jaw. "I shall check at the Crews' place on the morrow. If harm has come to any of that family, there will be a price on your heinous heads."

Thomas's anger was palpable. Astrid held her breath.

"What's more," he continued, "these Indians are Pamunkey. They're without guile and a friendly tribe. Any skirmish was unbeckoned and damnably one-sided and will not be seen with favor, e'en by the governor. Now begone!"

Thomas underscored his order by prodding him with the point of the sword. The man jerked back. With defeat dulling the eyes in his bruised face, he reluctantly urged the horse forward, holding the reins of the trailing horse. As it passed them, Astrid heard the dead man groan.

She hadn't killed him after all, but she almost wished she had—both of them.

"I trust them not, Thomas," she said as they watched the horses and men head for the woods.

"Nor I," he answered with a tired sigh. "But perchance we have bought a little time. Methinks Jarvis will not go too quickly to the governor with news of your presence here." He put his arm around her, and they walked back to the Indians.

The family was standing together under the tree. As they approached the silent trio, Astrid realized she and Thomas were also looking rather pitiful now. Thomas was bruised and filthy, and what was left of his shirt was a tattered remnant. The ugly wound in his shoulder had stopped bleeding, but it was crusted with a poultice of dried blood and grainy dirt.

She had lost her cloak ages ago; her thin gown was stained and stiff with Thomas's blood.

None of it mattered. They were both alive, and he had put his arm around her as if he owned her. In a way he does, she thought.

Seeing the Indians up close, Astrid was fascinated. They were handsome people, their skin a tawny richness, their hair sleek and black as coal. The man was almost as tall as Thomas. He was scantily dressed in a wisp of deerskin brought up between his thighs and tied with a cord below his waist. The woman, who wore long braids, was bare-breasted and colorfully tattooed on her face and body. Her fringed skirt fell below her knees, but it was more apron than skirt, leaving her backside uncovered.

The young boy, who was completely naked, stared up at Astrid and Thomas with wide, black eyes. Tear stains had cleared myriad paths down his dusty cheeks.

"You good man, Thomas Arrington, and you have brave woman," the Indian said. "We remember this night."

Astrid was surprised to hear him speak English.

Thomas answered in the man's own language, and she was reduced to watching gestures to follow the gist of the conversation. Because Thomas still had his arm around her, she was perfectly content.

The Indian woman appeared concerned about Thomas's shoulder. She removed a small pouch that hung between her breasts and offered it to Astrid.

Astrid looked up at Thomas quizzically. He nodded.

"Take it from her. 'Tis powdered root for thee to minister to my wound," he told her.

Wishing for a bottle of strong antiseptic and a powerful antibiotic, Astrid accepted the woman's gift and smiled her gratitude.

In return, Astrid offered the family her horse. Thomas agreed, looking pleased with her.

With a flurry of farewells, the Indians were soon mounted and on their way.

Astrid and Thomas stood side by side and watched them go. "Come into the house, Thomas," Astrid said, her eyes glowing as she took his hand. "I must tend to thee."

Chapter Fifteen

Thomas was not a cooperative patient. More than once Astrid considered tying him down while she worked on his wound.

"Sit thee still!" she commanded impatiently as she bathed his shoulder with the water she'd heated.

None of it had been easy. She'd had to coax the near-dead embers in the hearth into flames, had brought in logs to feed the fire and had lugged big buckets of water from the well.

Thomas protested throughout and caused her no end of problems, insisting he would fetch the wood, carry the buckets, bellow the fire. She pushed him back into his chair and silenced him, her eyes snapping.

"You're only making it more difficult," she

scolded, holding him still as she cleaned the jagged wound.

"And you're a bloody termagant, woman!" he complained, squirming away from the hot cloth. "Making such a fuss over naught."

"Ha! And who is it making the biggest fuss?" She pulled him back and continued soaking and dabbing.

Astrid scrutinized the wound. It looked clean now and wasn't too deep. But it was wide, and she knew it needed stitching or would end up a nasty scar.

She pondered her options, occasionally having to slap his undamaged shoulder to keep him quiet.

Suturing was beyond her talents and first-aid supplies were nonexistent. She was left with the Indian woman's remedy.

Praying it would help, she opened the pouch and poured the powder into the gash. She covered the wound with a fresh wet cloth and fashioned a bandage, wrapping a linen under his arm and over his shoulder, tying it in a bow at top.

"There," she said, not completely satisfied but knowing she'd done all she could under the circumstances. "You may wiggle, squirm and fuss your way upstairs to bed now, Thomas. I'm finished with thee."

She began picking soiled cloths off the kitchen's brick floor.

"Are you truly finished with me, milady?" he asked.

Astrid's heart skipped a beat. The subtle

change in the shading of his voice had caught her off guard. Still bent over, the wet rags dangling from her hands, she looked up. Thomas was watching her, his silver eyes dancing in the firelight, his lips curved in a soft smile.

"For the n-nonce," she stuttered, wondering what the hell she was saying.

Thomas rose from the chair. "Methinks not," he said. She watched, half-flabbergasted, half-dazzled, as he walked toward her. She blinked.

"Nor do methink I shall e'er be finished with thee," he said, taking her into his arms.

A fragment of Thomas's brain advised him to halt at once. You know not this woman, it warned. Cease! A more compelling voice had different orders. There is much you do know, Thomas. She is a shining lodestone drawing thee to her, and 'tis been thus since the moment you cast your eyes upon her. She is good for thee, was meant for thee, is an anodyne for thy emptiness that cries for repletion. There is naught else for thee to know.

Thomas looked deeply into her eyes, the color of periwinkles kissed by the sun, wide now, fully opened, expectant.

But you're injured, Astrid thought about saying, and in no condition to . . .

His eyes were saying something entirely different, and she knew at once she agreed with him wholeheartedly.

As his lips fell on hers with a hunger that denied hurt or exhaustion, Astrid found herself responding with equal hunger. She dropped the cloths and pulled his head closer, thrusting her fingers through the rich dark waves of his hair. Oh God, I've been wanting to do that since Lord knows when.

Thomas gathered her to him, savoring the surprising eagerness of her mouth, the pressure of her swelling breasts, the burning smoothness of her slender back and rounded rump through the thin covering.

My need will overwhelm her, he cautioned himself, as her fingers hushed the warning, tantalizingly circling his ears, entering, shutting away all save his rising desire for her. Thomas held her tight, powerless to resist her zestful responses. Surrender had become a shared, expanding, connecting assent of two, joyously willing to become one.

The fires of this wondrous woman were matching his, fanning his already blazing flames. He buried his face in her silken hair, yearning to lose himself in her—in all of her.

Her lips feverishly kissed his eyes, his cheek, his ear, then pausing. "Thomas," she whispered, sending heated vibrations through the tender channel.

"My sweeting," he moaned before taking possession of her waiting mouth.

Astrid knew there was no turning back, nor did she consider the possibility. Vague problems like wounded shoulder and brick floor flitted through the vapors of her passion but floated away without a trace. There was but one all-encompassing, wonderful thought. Thomas! And she had never so hungered for it as she did this moment.

His hand loosened the ties of her stained nightgown and found her breast, circling it, his delightful fingers testing its hard tip. Good . . . oh God, so good. As the gown slid from her shoulders, she willingly wiggled it down, her motions driving his desire to feverish heights.

He held her face in his hands, the burning silver of his eyes close to hers. "We need go slow for thee, my sweeting," his lips mumbled into her own.

"Oh, please hurry," she contradicted as she pressed her ready, pleading body against him. As her open mouth accepted his, she let her tongue show her need for him. She kicked aside the fallen gown.

"The fur," he whispered.

"Mmmm?" He wasn't making sense, but it didn't matter.

". . . a moment?" She still didn't understand, but his eyes and kisses told her he knew what he was doing.

Through a rosy haze, she saw him pull from the wall a large animal fur and toss it in front of the hearth. Captivated, she nodded her approval.

His eyes fondled her nakedness, devouring her, transforming her into fluid expectancy as he unfastened his knickers and pulled them over his bare feet. Astrid had felt his arousal, had yearned for it, and now, with it palpably visible, her aching desire for him became unbearable. She ran into his arms.

She knew only Thomas, his nearness and their pulsing desire. They sank together on the furry softness, and she opened to him, receiving at last the glorious thrusting fullness she craved.

Their joined release was sudden, a lustrous bursting convulsion followed by slowly diminishing throbbing tremors.

They lay wrapped, bathed in a glow of sweet moisture, their ecstasy sealed in a warm cocoon of shared breaths.

"I love thee, my sweeting," he said.

She heard his lovely words and held on to him tightly.

"I love thee, Thomas," she breathed earnestly. She squeezed him to her. "I love *thee*."

Thomas raised his head, a look of concern on his face.

"Did I hurt thee, milady?"

She reached up and kissed him. "*Au contraire*," she said with a reassuring smile. "*Au contraire*."

He lifted a damnably beautiful bushy brow. "Hollander words, again?" he questioned.

"Aye," she said with a laugh, hugging him close. "And please call me Astrid, though sweeting will do."

It was a long, long time before they went upstairs to his room.

Astrid's heart sang. She smiled, listening to the birds and relishing the sunlight. She was alone in Thomas's rumpled bed, but she was surrounded still with his splendid scent. Even stronger were her memories of his resonant presence.

My God, she thought, remembering his nonstop ardor. What a man! Her zeal had matched his, she knew, but his strength and happy explorations had delighted her, giving her satisfactions she hadn't dreamed possible.

He had left her reluctantly after dawn, kissing her sweetly and apologizing for having to leave her to see to the men.

She had clung to him sleepily, mumbling heartfelt nonsense. He had nibbled her nose, called her his "precious rabbit" and had torn himself away. She knew he would have preferred never to leave, and that felt especially wonderful.

She was humming a lilting melody when she went down to the kitchen. Joseph looked up with a silly grin on his face. He was chopping onions at the table and had tears in his eyes.

"'Twas a busy night, I wager," he teased, wickedly eyeing the fur on the floor. "And Thomas was whistling this morning for the first time since he was a wee lad."

"Oh?" Astrid asked, feigning nonchalance. "Wonder what got into the man?" She poured herself a mug of coffee.

Joseph chuckled. "Farewell, wide gulf. I told thee I'd heard you be a mighty swimmer."

"Joseph!" she admonished, but she blushed and couldn't resist smiling. The coffee burned her lip.

"Look at me, little lady," he said happily. "I be jubilant for thee both."

Astrid put down the mug and hugged him. "It's a beautiful morning, Joseph." She kissed his dried cheeks.

She hung the large fur on the wall, noticing

for the first time that it was as authentic as they come, complete with the beady-eyed, tooth-filled head and giant paws of a black bear. She smiled at it, tickling it fondly behind an ear.

The old man was curious about the night's events. While she cooked herself an egg, she filled him in on the battles with Berkeley's men and the happy ending for the Indians. Her own happy ending she glossed over, figuring his second sight and vivid imagination could take care of that.

"Well, well," he said at last. "This world, too, can be an interesting one, I vow."

She nodded, gobbling down the egg and biting into a piece of heavy bread. Her appetite was enormous.

"Much more interesting now," she agreed, winking at him.

Later that morning, she walked with Joseph to the vegetable garden to help him pick the greens for supper. His snail-paced walk forcing her to slow down, she took the opportunity to look more leisurely at Eagle's Crest. It had become considerably more important to her, and she bombarded the old man with questions about the place and about Thomas.

Eagle's Crest *was* different. She had sensed it, and now Joseph verified it for her. A lot of it was due to Joseph himself. He'd known through some guided instinct, as he put it, about the virtues of feeding land and rotating crops.

"Thomas's father listened well to me," he told her, "but Thomas be the smart one. He's attempted to teach the other planters, but they're either too dense or too indolent to do what he does so successfully. Tobacco can kill land, but all they see is land, land and more land, and they keep on destroying it, paying him no heed."

"A shame," Astrid said, wondering if she, Joseph and Thomas could form an early environmental organization.

But she was brought back to reality by Joseph's next remark.

"Henrico County's gone and elected Nathaniel Bacon and James Crews to the assembly, have you heard?"

Astrid shook her head. Thomas had mentioned Crews to that dastardly man Jarvis last night, but she had been too upset at the time to pay any attention.

"Threw it right in the face of the guv'ner, the people did," he said, frowning. "Word has it that matters are heating up down in Jamestown. First, Guv'ner Berkeley fired cannon and wouldn't allow Bacon to enter the town to take his seat. Then he relented and made him a councilor again and promised him an army of a thousand men. And now he's gone and backed down on that pledge. Bacon's returned to his Curles Neck place nearby and is recruiting people right and left."

"Good grief," Astrid said, troubled at the reminder that this was such an unrestful era. "And you say things move slower around here." She prayed Thomas wasn't recruitable.

"In some ways," Joseph said. "Only in some ways."

Astrid saw a row of black-draped boxes ahead

and asked Joseph about them.

"Beehives," he said. "'Tis way past time to uncover them. I'll do it now." When he began lifting the cloths, Astrid ran to help him.

"'Tis an old superstition," Joseph explained. "When a death occurs in the family, folks believe the bees will go away unless they're covered with a black drape. And every day for a month someone has to raise the cloth and speak the name of the deceased. 'Tis called 'telling the bees.'"

Astrid felt sick. "What was his sister's name?" she asked softly.

"Margaret."

Astrid lifted a cloth. "Margaret," she whispered, feeling miserable. "Oh Joseph, Thomas has lost so many."

Joseph took the cloth from her hands. "The bees will stay, little lady, and Eagle's Crest will continue to produce the sweetest honey in Virginia." He squinted up at her. "Thomas's losses have indeed been great. Perchance that be the explanation for your wondrous presence among us, for God in His wisdom bestows gifts e'en as He taketh away. Life is for the living, my dear one, and each of our days is precious. You and Thomas have much living ahead for thee both. Remember that."

Thomas had misgivings. His spirits had fallen during the day, sinking faster now than the late afternoon sun, already low in the west; his spirits had sunk beneath the horizon.

He was returning from Turkey Creek, the house of James Crews, where he had found the family well. They had verified his suspicions that the horses had been stolen three nights before.

But his mind throughout the long journey had been elsewhere, centered on one woman— Astrid. He spoke her name into the sultry air— the first syllable a sigh from his heart; the second, a sweet whisper of his tongue. Astrid— star. Star-bright she was, shining and radiant, scintillating him yet e'en through the growing gloom of his dilemma.

God's blood, he told himself with a sigh, my dilemma is a heavy one.

My brashness last night has heaped new complications on an already towering pile. Willingly would I have died in defense of her before. A gentleman could do naught else. But now I would die a hundred times over lest harm come to her.

His forehead knitted with an inner pain. And I perchance have done her the greatest harm of all by allowing my unreigned actions to sweep her into my heart this way.

Thomas shook his head, trying to rid it of the demon thoughts that had begun their torment. He frowned. She knows not her past. Dear God! She may be another man's wife! This realization tortured Thomas. What if e'en today she regains her memory and finds she has betrayed sacred vows, her true devotion, her true love.

God in heaven, he prayed, I know I have wronged her with my deeds, but let it not be that she should love another, for 'tis certain my own painful death could ne'er make the amends I would owe to her.

By the time he walked up the path toward the door of Eagle's Crest, he was sorely troubled, ready to beg her forgiveness and to pledge his eternal vigilance against further encroachments upon her honor.

When Astrid ran out to meet him, Thomas's heart constricted at the sight of her. He stopped, his boots held fast to the dusty path, as he watched her speeding toward him—a translucent vision in the golden light, her white dress a gay ripple of gossamer, her flaxen hair flowing over her shoulders.

Thomas closed his eyes and swallowed deeply. Her beauty alone will slay me, he warned himself, searching inside for the strength he knew he must garner, even as he opened his eyes again to look upon her.

She stood before him, her eyes sparkling with joy, her flushed cheeks dimpling her happy welcome.

He stared down at her, his stern resolves melting.

"Hello, Thomas," she said brightly. "Too long the day has been without you. Welcome home."

"Milady, I must beg your . . ."

"And what's this?" she interrupted him, too excited at seeing him to be alarmed by his solemn expression. "A gloomy face on such a day? And when I've gone to such great lengths to please you?" She twirled, flapping her arms that were covered now with wispy sleeves.

Thomas desperately reached for the last whiff of his resolve as it trailed away, as gauzy as those sleeves this treasure of a woman had tacked upon her dress.

Forgive me, God, he prayed again. Your weak servant can do naught but love her. Only Thee knows why she has been brought to me, but if 'tis a test from Thee I have failed.

With tears in his eyes, he embraced her. "My precious rabbit," he breathed into her hair. "'Tis good to be home."

Their supper was interrupted by the sound of a horse's hooves.

Thomas jumped to his feet and grabbed Astrid. "Get thee to thy chamber!" he ordered.

She obeyed from instinct. Thomas and Joseph were opening the door as she topped the stairs, and she pressed up against the wall, listening.

"Welcome, Nathaniel," Thomas said. "'Tis good to see you."

Bacon! Nathaniel Bacon himself was downstairs. Astrid peeked around the corner but could see only a pair of dusty black boots.

"I've interrupted your meal, Thomas," a thin, timid voice said. Astrid was disappointed. She'd expected a historical hero to boom authoritatively.

Thomas, who sounded a thousand times more like a hero, invited him in, and the boots walked into the dining room.

Damn. She sat on the top step, planting elbows on knees and chin in the cup of her hands. Back to coventry, she sighed, rising to go to her room, when Thomas came to the bottom of the stairs.

"Lady Van Fleet, please join us. I wish thee to meet our neighbor," he called up to her.

My, aren't we formal? she thought but was too delighted to quibble. She almost tripped in her excitement as she ran down the stairs.

The introductions were quick, and Astrid sensed a tenseness in the room.

"'Tis a pleasure to meet the Hollander countess whose bravery is praised by the lips of the legions who fight for freedom in our colony," Nathaniel Bacon said with a sweeping bow as flowery as his words.

"Bravery?" she protested. "But I have done naught . . ." She felt a little silly and looked to Thomas for support. A mistake, she knew at once. His face was darkly troubled, terrifying her.

"What is it?" she asked, her voice trembling.

"You are safe for the nonce, milady," Thomas said quietly. It was the sober solemnity in his eyes that told Astrid he had more to say.

"Jarvis and Williams are dead," he continued. "Nathaniel and his men found them this morning, Pamunkey arrows in their backs."

"They deserved it," she said coldly. "The bastards raided the Pamunkeys."

Bacon raised a brow at her language but smiled. "We know that, my lovely countess," he said. "But their queen has told us they killed them not for revenge but to protect the woman with hair like the tassels of maize."

Astrid took a sharp breath. "My God," she

said, sitting limply in her chair at the table.

"Jarvis and Williams will bear no tales now," Bacon said. "You will be safe at Eagle's Crest."

That was a relief at least. She had no intention of leaving.

Joseph brought in an extra plate, and Thomas invited Bacon to sup with them. The dark young man accepted the invitation, tossing his plumed hat into the corner, and he, Thomas and Joseph took their places at the table, joining Astrid.

Her stomach was in knots, and she picked at her food. She had the distinct feeling she was waiting for a second shoe to drop. Something more than the death of two villains had caused that concerned look on Thomas's face.

The men talked about the governor's vacillation, his broken promise to arm Bacon with a thousand men, Bacon's retreat to Curles "to enlist volunteers to display to the man the injustices he foists on our freedom."

Astrid studied the man she'd been forced to read about in her history classes, the one who'd punctuated so many conversations since she'd arrived. Nathaniel Bacon had a glint in his eye that some might call charismatic, but she saw something else—a glimmer of madness. His wan complexion gave her reservations about his stamina. His handsome, pockmarked face had a noble set, but the smallness of his features and stature signaled a weakness that disturbed her.

I wish the hell I could remember what happened to him, she fussed at herself, knowing full well that wouldn't make a bit of difference.

But she couldn't shrug off her concern for

Thomas. She turned her attention to him, reveling in his strength and yes, oh yes, his perfection.

"You will come with me, Thomas, will you not?" Bacon was saying.

The other shoe had dropped.

Thomas, for God's sake, don't follow him! But she knew she couldn't say anything. His decision was out of her control, and she loved him too much to pressure him. He would do what he must, but she crossed her fingers.

Thomas pushed himself away from the table and walked over to the sideboard to pour brandy in four rounded goblets. Astrid held her breath, watching him intently. His serious face gave her no hint what his decision would be.

He placed a glass in front of each of them, sat down and raised his own.

"To freedom from tyranny, Nathaniel," he said. Astrid's heart sank.

Thomas looked across at her, his eyes warmer than the candle's dancing flame. "Though I cannot accompany thee to Jamestown on the morrow, my good friend Nathaniel, my prayers are with thee and with thy men. I must stay here for the nonce for the safety of the countess."

Astrid sedately lifted her glass, wishing she could turn cartwheels and set off firecrackers.

As Bacon was leaving, she expressed her concern about the Pamunkeys.

"Are they endangered because they slayed the governor's soldiers, sir?" she asked.

"Not by my men, Countess," he said, placing his feathered hat on his head. "In fact, their queen has given ten of their best warriors to join with me for the cause of freedom, for they, too, love Virginia.''

"No one loves Virginia more than I," Thomas said with conviction.

"And that I know, Thomas," Nathaniel Bacon said with a warm smile. "Know I also that I may count on you anon when my need may be greater. For the nonce, there is greater need for you at Eagle's Crest." He tipped his hat at Astrid and went out into the night.

Joseph shuffled around the table, stacking the dishes.

"We will help thee, Joseph," Thomas offered.

The old man shook his head. "There's but little to do, and I prefer tending to it in solitude," he said. "The two of you are wearier than I. To bed with thee both."

Astrid saw him wink at her behind Thomas's back. She wanted to chastise and hug him at the same time.

Instead, she took Thomas's hand, and they climbed the stairs.

Chapter Sixteen

Astrid lay curled in Thomas's arms. She'd never been more comfortable in her life nor more content, she thought with a smile, nuzzling into his neck. Something deeper and sweeter had entered their love tonight—a warmth beyond fire.

He slept now. Dreamily, she watched the even rise and fall of his magnificent chest and felt his feathery breaths waft across her face.

Lovely, she thought, so lovely. She laced her fingers into his hair. For you, Thomas Arrington, I would gladly travel through more than time.

Astrid nestled her face in the curve of his shoulder and followed him into a blissful sleep.

She felt the deep rumble before she heard it, a subtle vibration like muffled drums. She shifted her position, reaching for Thomas.

And then, in a blinding flash, Astrid's world shattered.

A sharp blast jolted her awake. She sat up, startled. A stab of white light tore through the windows, piercing her eyes.

She recoiled in pain. Her scream caught in her throat.

What's happening? "Thomas, help me," she whimpered, her hands groping wildly for him. Another shaft of light shredded the darkness. She stared at the empty sheet beside her, struck numb by a far more unmerciful fright.

Thomas is gone!

A crescendo of roars reverberated through the room, deafening her. Holding her ears, she jumped from the bed and ran to the window, her face contorted in terror.

Frantic searchlights crisscrossed the black sky, illuminating a row of tall brick buildings across the street. Throbbing pulses of sound blasted her ears.

Astrid cringed and fell to her knees. As she struggled to crawl away, her fingers snagged on the knotted weave of shag carpet.

Carpet? Buildings? Confused and terrified, Astrid looked back toward the window. It was dark now, quiet. A cool breeze rippled the sheer curtains. A weak flicker of light played across the walls, and she saw the familiar design of faded cornflowers on the wallpaper.

Astrid gasped. She was in her Richmond apartment!

No, I don't want to be back here!

Her eyes darted around the room. Each object taunted her—the television set's cold blank stare, the VCR blinking a green, eternal midnight, the yawning, silent speakers of her stereo, the whimsical geometry of the Miró poster.

My God, she sobbed, crumpling, her face deep in the carpet. Was it all a dream? She raked her hands through the thick loops, hating their synthetic plushness.

Was Thomas only a dream? An icy despair gripped her. She felt hollow and empty.

Life without Thomas? There could be no life without Thomas.

"Astrid?"

A man's voice. Astrid raised her head. He was coming toward her.

Derek! She shook her head wildly, lifting herself back to her knees.

"Go away!" she screamed. "Leave me alone. For God's sake, leave me alone!" Distress twisted her words into a plaintive cry, blinding tears streaming down her face.

"Derek," she pleaded, "let me go back where I belong."

His hands grabbed her trembling shoulders. She tensed, pounding her fists against his arms.

"No, Derek, no!" she sobbed hysterically.

"My sweeting . . ."

Astrid caught her breath. That voice! The room jarred, and the blurred face above her came into clear focus.

"Thomas?" she whispered, not trusting her nebulous conclusion. "Did you come back here, too?"

"Come where, my rabbit?" He gathered her into his arms. "You've but had a troubled nightmare. The storm has disturbed thee."

"The storm?"

Dazed and shaken, Astrid clung to him. "It was awful, Thomas," she cried.

The apartment, the fear—all of it was sharply lucid, torturing her. She had to be rid of it.

She heard her voice, out of control. "You were gone, Thomas," she babbled, "and there were searchlights and tall buildings and noise and then I was back there in my Fan District apartment with its stupid TV and stereo and I knew I'd never see you a . . ."

"Shhh," he whispered, tilting her face toward his. "You're speaking strange Hollander words, and I make no sense of them. The nightmare is finished, my love. You are here with me and all is well."

Astrid was afraid to move. She clutched him closer, trembling. Don't disappear, she prayed. Be here, Thomas. Wherever we are, please be here. Please be real.

He felt real, his heart beating against her ear, his large, warm hand holding her head against his strong chest. He sounded real, his deep voice a soothing resonance. She wouldn't look at him, fearing he would vanish. She closed her eyes, testing her desperate hopes with more reliable senses.

"Peace, my sweeting," she heard. His lips brushed her forehead, his hands combing her hair back from her cheeks. "I am with thee, and nothing can harm thee."

She felt his soft lips cover hers. Only Thomas feels like this, she told herself, but she still kept her eyes closed, afraid to break the spell.

Slowly, her trembling lessened.

He gently cradled her head and laid her back on the pillows. As she sank into the plump feathers, she became aware of the wonderful aromas of Eagle's Crest—the lavender, bayberry, beeswax and pine mingled with Thomas's special, magical woodsy-wildflower scent.

Astrid knew, finally, that she was at home. She opened her eyes.

Thomas was above her, a raven lock spilling over his forehead. The vertical line by his left brow was deep with concern. She studied each detail of his beautiful face, indelibly etching them into her brain, determined she would never lose him again.

Astrid reached up to him. "Come, my love," she whispered. "I need thee now. I need thee with me."

Thomas came to her with a convincing reality. She surrounded herself with him, welcoming his pulsing pressure. He is tangible, hard and perfectly tangible, present now, here, filling me. The other was phantom, the stuff of shadows. This . . . this is . . .

"Yes, oh, yes!" she cried into the burning darkness, rising toward his palpable thrusts, clenching her teeth into the firm flesh of his shoulder as Thomas, propulsive and solid, pervaded her, erasing all doubt that it really was he, Thomas, now!

Far from vanishing, he lay over her pressing

her into the feathers. Astrid held him inside her, reluctant to let him go.

"Stay forever," she moaned, clinging to him.

He smiled down at her. "There's no place else I could rather remain."

Thomas lovingly sprinkled her face with kisses, found her mouth and lingered there, his hands slowly caressing her thighs, her hips, sliding tantalizingly up to her breasts, his fingers flicking across the soft tips until they responded to his splendid touch, swelling, upright. His lips left hers, feathering kisses down her cheek, under her chin, over her shoulder, reaching at last the rising, pillowy curve and circling his sensitive target, closing in and capturing it.

Astrid succumbed to the sensuous pleasures he offered. She writhed beneath him, acutely aware of a tremulous fullness stirring deep within her. She felt her own moist warmness swelling to meet his surging power and tenderly envelop it, then give way gladly to the stronger force, welcoming its overwhelming mastery, happily accepting the inevitable fulfilling conquest.

A contented silence embraced them.

Astrid sighed and smiled up into his eyes. "I thank thee for bringing me back to thee," she said with a whisper.

Thomas's face darkened. He rolled away from her and propped his head with his hand, his elbow deep in the mattress.

"We must talk about your nightmare, sweeting," he said. He fingered her damp hair, gently pushing it away from her forehead.

"Why talk about it? It's over. Past," she said, not wanting to let its awful memory intrude on these perfect moments.

This was her home, she knew intuitively. This plain 17th century room, its walls and windows bare, its wide plank flooring devoid of shaggy covering was her home. It was her former life that was removed from reality, all plastic and synthetic.

Here everything is natural, solid and genuine. Astrid looked up at him.

Most of all, there's Thomas. She smiled. He is my real home.

"Is the nightmare truly over?" Thomas asked, sounding troubled.

Astrid nodded, locking her eyes on his, trying to read his thoughts.

"Who is Derek?" he asked.

Her heart skipped a beat. She knitted her brows, trying to remember what she might have said in her hysteria. "Wh-who?"

"You called to Derek, Astrid, and begged him to let thee go where you belong." Thomas lowered his arm, lay back on the pillow and stared up at the ceiling.

"Astrid," he said, his voice low, filled with pain. "Your past has been shut off from thee. Derek may be your husband."

"No, Thomas," she blurted, "I have no husband. Derek is . . . Derek's a nobody."

His face drawn, Thomas looked up at her. "How can you be so sure? Are you not without memory?"

"No . . . yes!" She sat up, covering her face

with her hands. "I have some memory, Thomas," she said quietly. "It's of no importance."

He pulled up beside her and put his arm around her. "'Tis of great importance to me, dear rabbit," he said. "I should die if you were another's."

Astrid leaned into his chest, wishing she could tell him the unvarnished truth. "I can belong to no other man but you, Thomas, that I know," was all she said.

Thomas was silent. She raised her face to his, searching his silver eyes. "Trust me," she pleaded. "I am yours. That much I do know with certainty."

"God help us," he said, hugging her to him. "I must believe thee," he breathed into her hair. "I must."

"You're a damnable woman," Thomas smilingly chastized her the next morning. "Seems my every encounter with thee results in fresh bruises."

"Poor baby," Astrid cooed, kissing his formerly well shoulder which now bore the small bluish imprints of her teeth.

"God's blood!" he exclaimed, stretching back to look. "'Twas my battered arms I spoke of. I hadn't e'en noticed this freshest wound. 'Tis good I heal hastily." He kissed her nose.

"I'm sorry," she said with a pout. "I was only checking to see if you were real."

"And what did you discover?"

She laughed. "You're real and you taste good."

Thomas hugged her. "I shall beware if e'er I see thee bring the salt cellar to our bed. Mayhap sorceress Hollanders feast on their mates for breakfast," he said with a big grin.

"We prefer them for supper," she teased.

He gave her a final squeeze and got out of bed to begin dressing. She felt lethargic and watched him, her eyes dancing with love.

"There's much we need discuss, rabbit," he said, buttoning his knickers. He was looking serious again. She tried to duplicate his expression but found her facial muscles uncooperative. They only wanted to smile.

"Discuss what?" she asked lightly.

He shoved his arms into the sleeves of his shirt and sat to pull on his boots.

"A plan to provide thee sure protection from the governor's men for one," he said. "'Tis only a matter of time before others come looking for thee at Eagle's Crest."

He stood, buttoning his shirt and looking over at her. His eyes struck her as the most beautiful eyes she'd ever seen—clear and deeply earnest. She only wished she could wipe away their worried concern.

"Then, too, I must find a way to wed thee," he said.

Astrid was taken by surprise, but knew at the same time she should have expected it, given the propriety of the times and all. A satisfied flipping of her heart told her it sounded like an incredibly wonderful idea.

"Are you proposing, Thomas?" she asked, barely breathing.

"Aye, of course I'm proposing," he said, as if it were an obvious conclusion. His eyes clouded, putting her on alert.

"'Tis only there are obstacles for us," he added.

"Obstacles?" Her mind raced, hooking unhappily on the most likely obstacle. Thomas was so recently widowed. There must be a required waiting period for remarriage. She hated to think about his terrible losses, let alone talk about them, but she blundered on, hoping to get it out in the open and let him know she didn't mind waiting however long it may be.

"Is it because 'tis been too brief a time since the death of . . ." she started.

"No, rabbit." He stopped her, shaking his head. "'Tis thee. You have no records, no papers. The courts require same."

"Oh." That's one hell of an obstacle, she had to agree, and there was not much she could think of to do about it, either. Her birth records, even if she could get them, would upset a lot of people, including Thomas.

"Then we may never be able to wed," she said, now thoroughly depressed.

Thomas came over to the bed and pulled the quilt up over her, tucking it under her chin and stroking her face.

"I shall find a way, my sweeting," he said with a reassuring determination. "Though I know not how, I shall find a way."

He bent and kissed her lightly on the forehead. "'Tis only dawn," he whispered. "Sleep, little rabbit. I shall return from the fields before supper."

"That was quite a performance last night," Joseph exclaimed when Astrid came down for breakfast. "Full of sound and fury, signifying nothing."

"What on earth are you talking about, Joseph?" she asked with a frown.

"Don't tell me you slept through it," the old man said. "Some of the worst lightning and thunder I've e'er experienced." He chuckled. "Perchance you were distracted by a more pleasurable storm."

Astrid ignored Joseph's naughty comment and sat down with a sigh.

"We needed the rain," she said.

"That be the devilish part," he said. "Not a drop fell. After all that fiery introduction, I expected a deluge." He squinted at her. "Do you wish to tell me what's bothering thee, little lady?"

"Dammit, Joseph. I almost messed up things to a fare-thee-well." She held up her thumb and pinched it against her forefinger. "I came that close to telling Thomas everything about me."

Joseph frowned. "Why, in the name of God? Know you well that e'en I want not to know your truth, tho' I have glimmers at times what it may be."

"I had a stupid nightmare during the storm, I guess." She turned pale, remembering the horror, and told Joseph the substance of her bad

271

dream. She sensed he already knew.

"I was hysterical," she continued, "and said heaven only knows what. Thomas now thinks words like stereo and television are Hollander talk."

"Stereo? Television?" Joseph interjected. "Peculiar words, little lady."

Astrid nodded but was too preoccupied to fill Joseph in on electronic wonders.

"I thought a nitwit I used to know was there and called his name, and Thomas is worried about my past, of course," she said. "He's concerned I'm married or something, and I tried to convince him I'm not. But it's damn hard to be convincing when you're not supposed to be able to remember anything."

"True," Joseph agreed. "Makes things difficult I vow. 'Twould be good if you could find an acceptable past now, wouldn't it?"

Astrid looked at him with interest. An inspired idea lit up her face.

"That's it, Joseph!" she squealed. "That's exactly what I'll do."

She bounced up and down, ecstatic with her brilliant decision.

"Joseph, I'm going to get my memory back."

Chapter Seventeen

Astrid and Joseph spent most of the day concocting, revising and rehearsing. By the time Thomas returned to the house, she had her new biography down pat. She almost had herself believing it.

"I've wonderful news," she shouted excitedly as he walked into the kitchen. "I was just telling Joseph. I remember everything!" She threw her arms around his neck.

"Everything?" Thomas's eyes held surprise and a trace of fear.

"Well . . . not absolutely everything," she admitted. "The last part, before you found me, remains unclear, but the important things, the really important things, I do remember." Astrid was glowing.

"This occasion deserves a celebration," Joseph said. "We shall have the prized Malaga this eve." Humming merrily, he brought out a dusty bottle and began pouring the sweet wine into three glasses. "Supper can wait. Let us three sit, lift the wine and listen to the little lady's history. I, for one, am filled with eagerness."

"As am I," Thomas said. He looked more apprehensive than eager as he led Astrid to the table.

They tapped glasses and sipped. Thomas's eyes studied her face. Astrid, noting that her sprightly happiness alone wasn't setting his mind at ease, quickly reorganized her planned presentation. She couldn't bear to see him uncomfortable, even for a minute.

"To begin, Thomas, I have ne'er married, and there was no man important to my life." She tilted her head and smiled. "Does that allow thee to relax so that you can hear my story?"

Thomas nodded and exhaled a sigh of relief. "Aye, milady," he said, returning her smile. He sat back in his chair and raised a brow, waiting. His gray eyes twinkled silver. "Now, dear rabbit," he said, "please tell us the less significant portions of your history."

Astrid let her rehearsed words tumble out, taking care to construct them properly for him. She wasn't a countess, she told him. Indeed, she wasn't even a genuine Hollander, though it was true she had been born in that faraway land, on the eighth of April, 1649. Her family had moved to the colony of New York when she was but a child. Her mother, Denise, was French; her father, Johann, Dutch. He was a wealthy merchant. As the Van Fleet's only child, Astrid had been highly pampered. The diamond had been a birthday gift this past April.

New York customs were far different from Virginia, she said. There were more towns, a gayer social life.

She'd lived in a town called Richmond. Since Astrid remembered she had told Thomas on the day of her arrival that she was from Richmond, she threw that in now in case he remembered their first conversation. She figured there was little chance he'd be able to check it out. For all she knew, there might be a Richmond somewhere in New York.

The Van Fleets and most of the townspeople spoke Dutch, but she'd also learned some English. She'd had a tutor, she said, and an education equal to that of a boy's. As a child she had learned to ride and swim and was taught an Oriental art of self-defense.

Thomas nodded, a wry expression on his face, at this last revelation. Astrid was amused but pretended not to notice and continued.

There had been a terrible fire at their home. Set by villainous enemies of her father, she believed. Mayhap it had been the unscrupulous fur traders her father, a principled, honest man, had exposed and refused to deal with. Astrid had been sheltered from her father's business affairs, so she didn't know for sure what the circumstances were.

When Joseph refilled the glasses, she took a couple of swallows, checking Thomas's reaction to her saga up to this point. He appeared absorbed. Encouraged, she went on.

She had been to a ball and was returning home in a carriage when she saw the house ablaze. It burned to the ground, her parents and all of the servants dying in the inferno.

Astrid's eyes filled with tears. Thomas moved to comfort her, but she shook her head and gestured for him to remain seated.

"I wish to tell thee all, Thomas," she said, feeling very brave as she blinked back the tears, bit her bottom lip and continued.

She had been horribly distraught, bewildered and stunned, she told them. A crowd of people had stood around staring at her. Her escort for the evening was an old friend, Derek Rembrandt. Astrid had been strapped to think of Dutch names, so she'd picked one she knew was authentic and safe, she hoped, under the circumstances. Derek was like a brother, she added, just in case Thomas had any disturbing thoughts on that matter.

For terrible moments, she said, as the twisted rubble of her home smoldered before them, no one moved to assist her. She was incapable of doing aught for herself.

Two well-dressed gentlemen had emerged from the crowd. They were barristers, they told her, and in her father's hire. She was to come with them, for they were authorized by Mr. Van Fleet to handle his affairs and to care for her upon his death.

Astrid shuddered, thoroughly involved in her story.

The men had been lying, she said. 'Tis likely

they themselves had lit the fire. She didn't know. But once away from other eyes, they had thrown her into a waiting carriage, had bound her with ropes, and had taken her to an isolated cove where they had traded her for a chest of stolen gems to pirates in a brigantine with black sails.

Astrid had liked that ominous touch of black sails. It sounds damn convincing, she thought. Thomas's jaw was clenched, and his hands were balled into fists. He was with her so far, and she prayed she could carry off the rest.

The pirates had treated her surprisingly well at first. They had been respectful and hadn't compromised her, though she was sorely frightened of them. They were fierce in appearance, with most of them wearing a black patch over one eye.

Several days into the voyage, however, they had run into gales and high seas. A mighty storm tore at the ship, and her fear had been great. She described the beating wind, the torrents of rain, the deck near vertical as she hung to the rails lest she be swept away into the cauldron of the violent seas.

Astrid resurrected every storm-tossed scene she could remember from late-night movies to add color to her drama. It was working. Thomas was transfixed. Even Joseph appeared mesmerized, and he'd been contributing to the invention all day.

After the night of horror, she told them, the dawn had brought calm and clear skies. But the crew cast suspicious glances her way, and she heard angry grumblings. A woman on a ship was bad luck, they said. They wanted her gone.

Their captain, who had protected her heretofore, though he had ne'er come close to her, she hastened to add, feared mutiny from his restless crew and agreed, after hours of argument, to be rid of her.

The crew had requested she be thrown overboard at once, but the captain, who she suspected once had hoped to make her his bride, ordered otherwise. He had two of his most trusted men row her away in a small boat to "leave her bound on land near settlement."

"My memory begins to fade from that time," Astrid said. "The men treated me not well when the brigantine was no longer in sight. They relieved me of my garments and jewels—all but the diamond which I convinced them had a curse upon it—and bound me in the wrapping in which you found me. I was forced to lie huddled in the boat's bottom and knew not where I was. My last memory, before I saw you at the point, was naught but the darkness of terror."

Silence fell in the kitchen. Her story finished, Astrid bowed her head and stared at her half-filled glass of wine. She felt depleted.

Thomas reached out his hand and covered hers. "My sweeting . . ."

Astrid raised her head and looked at him. His eyes were moist with compassion and shining with tender love. Her heart twisted in pain. *Forgive me, Thomas, for deceiving thee*, her mind cried out. *'Tis only for thee and thy peace that I have spun this web of falsehoods.*

She loved him so, and yet she was guilty of building a sham foundation for his own love. What else could I do? she rationalized.

Nothing, she told herself. Though she wished she didn't feel so utterly ashamed.

Eagle's Crest—July 16, 1676

It's a lovely world!

The sunlit days find me moving through the house and out into the gardens performing tasks I'd never dreamed to do, and learning, learning, learning. I've found joy in a myriad of chores from weaving to weeding. Such pleasures as tending a crop of vegetables from sprouts to leafy fullness were woefully hidden from the earlier Astrid.

Indeed, I look back at the beginning pages of this journal and wonder at the changes wrought in me.

The nights bring differing pleasures, of course —ever-changing, ever-increasing delights that fill me with awe, with gratitude, and with a deep, fulfilling happiness beyond belief.

There's one beautiful, consistent and recurring theme through the glorious music of my days and nights.

Thomas, Thomas, Thomas.

Have two others ever loved as we now love?

I think not.

Blessed I am, for I've found a perfect world.

See, dear diary, how I'm moved to poetry these days? And little wonder. 'Tis the midsummer of my heart and I live in the stuff of dreams.

Thomasina Ring

With my presumed past out in the open at last, Thomas's step is lighter, his smiles more radiant. He would wed me tomorrow, but there is still the problem of proper documents for me. This state of affairs weighs more heavily on him than on me. It's a barrier, I know, but a minor one I feel, considering the more formidable ones we've crossed.

Thomas and I were meant for each other. I've accepted that truth and no longer concern myself with useless questions such as "How did I come?" or "Why am I here?" It's obvious why, and the how doesn't matter.

I am convinced now that my invented past has fully as much substance as what I once thought of as my real past. None of it is material. There is only today and, I pray, a coming parade of even lovelier tomorrows.

Joseph, who sees so deeply, tells me I've made a full adjustment, and he's set to rest my anxieties that I may be swept back. "The universe is filled with mysteries," he said to me, "and your coming here is but a small one compared to many of the others. You are here because you should be. You fit. I believe strongly that God has brought thee here to right some terrible wrongs bestowed on our beloved Thomas. You won't be returned to your old world, my dear. Something far wiser than you and I knows you are meant to be here."

And so, as you see, I need you no longer, my crinkled, faded, hidden friend. I thank you for the support you provided me in those early days when I was confused and frightened. Even later, as my life gradually began to adjust to the rhythms of a different age, it has been a solace to know you were close and willing to receive my thoughts, observations and dreams.

I will keep you for a while, not to use you further, but because I cannot yet bring myself to destroy you. Someday I must; possibly, even now I should. But you are safe, as am I.

Farewell, my friend, and thank you.

"Word has come from my brother Robert," Thomas told Astrid and Joseph at supper toward the end of July. "The colony is embarking on full war."

Governor Berkeley had withdrawn to Gloucester, he said, to raise troops, but the majority of the militia, including Robert, had refused, showing loyalty instead to Nathaniel Bacon. Bacon himself is said to be at the Falls with near a thousand men, preparing for Indian raids, but messengers from the south have warned them that the governor and his men are marching up to confront and quell the Bacon forces.

"I received the disturbing news when I visited Edward and Mother today," Thomas explained. "Robert had sent a messenger with the information from Gloucester. Henry Isham visited and imparted the remainder."

Joseph sadly shook his head. "The guv'ner has gone mad," he said. "Why in the name of God doesn't he leave the popular hero alone to fight the Indians?"

"Because he fears that very popularity will unseat him," Thomas said. "The man is indeed mad. He has become too accustomed to power and appears willing to destroy Virginia rather than lose even a portion of that same power."

Astrid frowned. The rotten world was intruding again.

"What will Bacon do now?" she asked. Thomas had said "full war," and a new worry stabbed her. Would Thomas feel obligated to join him?

"Isham believes, as do I, that he will turn away from his Indian forays and march with his stronger forces to battle the governor."

Astrid wasn't comforted by these words.

Thomas changed the subject. "The rabbit pie is e'en better than before, my Astrid," he complimented her with a smile. "If your cooking continues such improvement, we may make you full-time cook in the kitchen and give our Joseph a needed rest."

She had made her second 17th century quiche. It was a labor of love and, like the first one, an improvisation. Thomas had looked at that first one with skepticism, but after reluctantly taking a bite he had glowed with approval. She'd told him it was common food among the Hollanders. Thomas felt that "keesh" was too harsh-sounding a name for such a delicacy and dubbed it "rabbit pie" in honor of its creator.

But today, even his obvious satisfaction with her cooking couldn't dispel her growing apprehension.

She listened half-heartedly as Thomas and Joseph talked about the added troubles of the continuing drought and the endangered tobacco crops.

"I have worries for Edward and his family," Thomas said. "Today he told me he fears he will not reap enough this year to pay his taxes. I must find a way to help them," he said.

Astrid looked up. "I have silver, Thomas, from the sale of my diamond," she said. "You and your family shall have it."

Thomas expressed surprise at the silver, but there was no accusation in his voice as he asked her about it. Astrid had almost forgotten it herself. She had hidden the small bag, along with her journal, under a loose floorboard in her chamber on that first afternoon at Eagle's Crest.

With my journal! Astrid jumped up from the table. "I'll fetch the silver now, while you and Joseph finish your supper," she said, trying to keep the panic out of her words.

"You shall not!" Thomas said adamantly. "The silver is yours, dear rabbit, and our need is not so great that we should share in it. Now seat thyself and attempt for once in your life to be a proper lady." The warmth in his eyes imparted pride rather than impatience.

Astrid sat. Her heart was still lodged in her throat, but she managed to stage a huffy retort to his remark.

"For once in my life, you say, Mister Judge of Propriety? I shall be as proper henceforth as *I* wish and not a dollop more."

Thomas and Joseph laughed affectionately, both of them nodding exaggerated resignation at having such an impossible woman in their midst.

Still shaken by her close call, she pledged to

herself that she'd burn the incriminating journal the moment Thomas left the house the next day.

But the next day was Saturday, and Thomas didn't leave the house. At least, he never left her side. Ordinarily, Astrid would have been ecstatic having him close like that.

A growing uneasiness about the journal, however, kept her from total bliss.

There were a couple of notable exceptions. In the afternoon they had gone for a swim. As had become their custom over the past joyous weeks, they swam without the dubious benefits of their earlier coverings.

After a strenuous race and a series of playful romps in the water, they lay side by side on the sandy shore, letting the sun's bright fingers pluck the drops off their bare bodies.

"'Tis good," Thomas said with a contented sigh.

"Mmmm," Astrid agreed, feeling drowsy.

"But we need now make it e'en better," he said, sounding lusty as the devil as he rolled toward her.

Astrid's drowsiness departed the moment his lips touched hers.

And for a lovely period of time she forgot the journal and let Thomas completely erase her uneasiness, replacing it with far stronger and more satisfying emotions.

Nor could her meddling nerves outmatch the excited happiness she felt when Thomas made his surprising announcement before supper.

"Joseph and I have found a way to get thee papers," he said, gleaming. "We shall be wed within days, my dear rabbit!"

Joseph knew a man who could devise counterfeit documents "that deceive the most careful eyes," according to Thomas. Though he would prefer to obtain the genuine papers, he said, the long journey to New York was out of the question given the uncertainty of the times. Thomas had at last agreed to Joseph's plan.

"My love for thee is too great to accept further postponements," he said. "In God's eyes you are already my wife. With but minor trickery we can seal that covenant under the inferior laws of man."

Astrid's eyes brightened with tears. She hugged them both and listened to their plan.

The old man would sail with Jeremy the following day to Varina Parish, ostensibly to go to church. Instead he would go to the cabin of his old acquaintance who would draft her documents.

"They will look as authentic as the original," Joseph promised. "I know this man's work. They will look properly aged and will be stamped with New York colony insignia and signatures."

Astrid suspected Joseph had firsthand experience with the man's forgeries. Whatever, she was bursting with gratitude for his connections.

She happily supplied Joseph with her biographical data and wished him a safe journey.

"'Tis not a long one, little lady, e'en for someone as old as I," he said with a twinkle. "I shall be back at Eagle's Crest with proof of your birth before sundown.''

With Joseph and the other men gone on Sunday, Astrid and Thomas spent a blissful morning alone together, rising hours later than Thomas's habit, though not from sleep.

She fixed a Western omelet for their breakfast, causing him to comment on the endless varieties of Hollander cookery.

It was during their second cup of coffee when Thomas dropped the bombshell.

"As soon as we are wed, my love, I must leave thee for a time," he said, his serious eyes scaring her as much as his terrible words.

"For God's sake, why, Thomas?" Astrid felt as if she'd been struck in the solar plexus. She was afraid she already knew the answer.

"I shall ride with Bacon," he said, verifying her fears. "Long enough I have shunned my duties to Virginia. You are strong enough to withstand a period without me, and you will not be alone and unprotected, I have seen to that."

"*You* have seen . . . *you* have decided . . . Thomas! Will you never learn that *I* have a brain? That *I* may have something to say about . . ." She was sputtering, beside herself with anxiety for him.

"It's a stupid war, Thomas," Astrid continued. "A mere footnote in history, I suspect." She caught herself in time to add the "suspect," but couldn't stop her protests. "It's not worthy of your participation, not important enough to risk even one of your perfect eyelashes."

Thomas stood, walked over to the window and looked out at the grounds of Eagle's Crest.

Astrid watched him, tears of frustration running down her face.

He spoke at last, his voice calm but heavy with feeling. "I am this land, Astrid. I shall fight to preserve it."

Dear God, she thought, he will go. He must, and I must let him go. Somewhere within me I shall find the courage and grace to equal his.

She wasn't sure she could, but she wiped away her tears and joined him by the window.

"You are right, my Thomas," she said softly, lifting her chin. "Forgive my outburst. I believe I understand better now and want not to add to your already burdened mind. Our love is strong enough to withstand far more than a needed separation."

He looked down into her eyes. "I thank thee, precious rabbit," he whispered, wrapping his arms around her and holding her close. "I thank thee."

"You'll miss me," she teased naughtily an hour or two later. "Bacon and his cohorts will have no such pleasing antics on their agenda, I vow."

"Too true," he said with a broad grin before nuzzling his face between her breasts.

They were still in the kitchen, on the well-remembered bearskin. The breakfast dishes sat on the table, unwashed and forgotten.

"And if this continues," he said without a trace of worry in his voice, "I will be sorely weak and of little use on the battlefield."

"They will find thee the fiercest warrior in all of Virginia," she contradicted with a giggle. "I shall stuff credentials into your satchel with my sworn testimonies to same."

"How can I love such a wicked woman?" he mumbled, nibbling her neck.

"Easy," she said, pulling him to her.

"Now would you tell me your plans for what I'm to do while you are out saving Virginia?" she said lightly, pulling a dish out of the soapy bucket and handing it to him to dry.

Thomas explained that Edward, Ann, Lizzie and his mother were coming to Eagle's Crest to be with her.

"I told them you were here," he said, "and that I intended to wed thee soon. They are happy for us, Astrid, and will witness our marriage."

The Arrington's Bermuda Hundred land was withered, he told her, and Edward had consented to bring his men to Eagle's Crest to try to save Thomas's stronger crops while he was away.

"The family will be company for thee," he said with a smile, "and Mother and Ann will be a beneficial influence on my bride. She sorely needs instructions in womanly docility, I vow."

Astrid flipped soapsuds at him. He laughed, tossing the towel over her head.

"And you will be well-protected," he said retrieving the towel and continuing his drying, "though I believe the governor and his men are too occupied to pursue thee."

When they had finished in the kitchen, Thomas told Astrid he had a secret to show her.

"Come upstairs with me, rabbit," he said, taking her hand. "I have been remiss not to show thee this before."

He led her into her chamber. Though she hadn't slept there in weeks, they continued to call it her chamber.

"We have a hidden passageway that leads to a dense stand of trees by the river," he said. "'Tis an added protection should the house come under attack. 'Tis narrow, but e'en Mother will fit through if the need arises."

He walked toward the far wall. Astrid stood back, paralyzed. He was bending to lift her own secret floorboard!

"As you see," he said proudly, "the floor looks unbroken at this spot, but beneath there's a trapdoor . . ."

Thomas stood, the board in his hand, staring down at the small square containing Astrid's bag of silver and crumpled journal.

"No!" Astrid screamed, running to grab the papers.

Thomas looked at her quizzically. "You have already found the entrance, I see," he said.

Astrid held the journal against her breast. "I but found a shallow hole," she said, terror filling her eyes. "I knew nothing of a passageway. I hid my silver there."

"And papers, too?" he interrupted, searching her face. "What are those papers, Astrid?"

"Nothing," she said, trying desperately to shred them. "Naught of importance, Thomas. Only Hollander scribblings I wrought with the quill you gave me. But an idle entertainment in the long afternoons while you were in the fields." She wasn't being coherent and knew her fright was making him suspicious, but she couldn't control herself.

Thomas must never see these papers!

"Why do you tremble thus if they are not important, my love?" he asked. Thomas looked deeply concerned. "What secrets have you hidden with your silver?"

"No secrets, Thomas!" She shook her head frantically. "Believe me," she pleaded, falling to her knees. "You must believe me, Thomas. I have no secrets from thee." Sobs wracked her body, and she fell forward. The papers fluttered from her fingers.

Thomas stooped, picked them up and put them back into her hands.

"I shall not read them, Astrid," he said. She looked up, clutching the papers. His face was dark with worry. "Nor shall I wed thee until you tell me their substance." His suffering eyes grabbed hers, held them and permeated her soul.

"I know love," he said, his voice a choked whisper, torturing her. "Only with thee, perchance, have I touched what I know to be true love, but love can have no secrets. There must be no mystery between us. You must trust me, Astrid. You must trust our love."

Astrid cringed. She had reached the one final, impossible barrier between them—his ability to believe and accept her awful truth.

There's no choice, she told herself, tormented with fear.

She pushed the papers into his hand.

"Please read them, Thomas," she sobbed. "But before you read them, I beg thee to listen to my story."

Chapter Eighteen

They sat on the floor of her chamber until the late afternoon sun threw slats of dull gold across them.

Astrid told him all of her impossible story. Thomas listened attentively, but she sensed a growing distance separating them.

"I cannot accept this tale of madness," he said at last, rising to his feet.

"I knew you could not, and that is why I wished never to tell thee," Astrid said. She stared at her hands, drained of all feeling except loss.

Thomas sat in the chair by the window. "I shall read your papers as you request, milady," he said, folding them and shoving them beneath his shirt. "But I must wait before I look upon them. I think I could not bear to read them now."

He put his head into his hands. "My God," he cried, "you weave far worse than witchery with your revelations, woman! Can you truly expect me to believe thee?"

"No," she said quietly. "Nor have I found it easy to believe. I know only that 'tis true, Thomas, and I pray that you can find it in your heart to accept me." She looked longingly at him, her tears distorting him into liquid, blurring patterns she could no longer distinguish.

Astrid was desperate to reach him in some way, to see him become solid and whole again. "Though I came into your life unwittingly and unwillingly," she said, "I want nothing more than to remain with thee forever. There is no possible understanding of this, Thomas. I ask not understanding but acceptance . . . and love."

Thomas didn't move. He sat back, his eyes closed.

Finding further words eluding her, Astrid said no more and watched him. Her prayers were fervent, but she received no comfort from them.

When a hearty whoop from outside ripped through the room, both Astrid and Thomas jumped up, startled.

He looked out the window.

"The men have arrived," he said. "I shall go down to meet them."

Astrid followed him down the stairs. Her movements were slow and trancelike.

Jeremy bounded into the hall with Joseph, his

steps sprightlier than she remembered, close behind. "We have the documents!" they shouted in unison. Joseph leaned against the doorframe, wiped his forehead and waved a paper in the air.

"Let the wedding begin," the old man said with a bright smile.

Astrid held onto the railing.

Without looking back at her, Thomas pushed past Joseph and Jeremy.

"We shall have no wedding," he said and walked out through the door.

Gloom descended on Eagle's Crest. Thomas brought over the Arrington family on the following day and rode away to join Bacon.

He didn't speak to Astrid again before he left.

She wanted to die. The family's arrival stirred the air with noise and confusion. It swirled around her, but she moved within her own thick cloud of desolation and heard none of it.

In a moment of privacy, she told Joseph about Thomas's awful discovery. The old man shook his head. "God help thee both," he said, reaching for her cold hands. "God help thee."

He tried to give her a sliver of hope, but it didn't work. "I'll place the forged documents in safe hiding," he said. "If any man could come to grips with a situation like this, 'tis Thomas. He be strong, and he loves thee deeply. You must have faith, little lady."

Astrid pulled away her hands. "No, Joseph, it's over." She walked out of the kitchen.

That night it began to rain.

Astrid lay on the small bed in the room that

was hers once again. She now hated the room. It was filled with the ghosts of bitter memories.

The windblown rain beat against the closed casements. She covered her head, struggling to shut out the relentless, slapping torture.

Take that and that and THAT! the rain pounded over and over, bombarding her with its spite. You deserve this, the accusing wind screamed. You, an interloper, dared to dream you could live in harmony with a world not your own.

Astrid absorbed the punishment. The darkness of her mind paid no heed as it watched her once-bright inner fire turn into a heap of sputtering ashes, die, be picked up by the howling wind and scattered away.

A more wrenching thought had captured her attention. Thomas is somewhere out there in this brutal night! She clutched the covers and dug her face into the pillow. Protect him, she prayed into the tear-dampened linen. Please, God, protect him.

The gray rainy days flowed from one into another with little variation. The whole household was subdued. They talked in whispers and may have walked on tiptoes, their footsteps were so soft. It was something more than respect for the deep unexplained sadness of one within their midst. It was as if they themselves had assimilated Astrid's deadened vibrations.

The weather provided a fitting backdrop. It rained almost constantly for three weeks.

Astrid took on few tasks. There was little for her to do anyway. Dorothy and Jenny had come with the Arringtons, and Joseph was annoyed with the women at first, complaining they were underfoot in his kitchen. Finally, in exasperation, he turned over the cooking entirely to them. He sat by a parlor window most of the time staring out at the rain.

Mrs. Arrington and Ann did the spinning and sewing and spoke quietly together in another corner of the parlor.

Lizzie worked on a sampler, sighing a great deal and looking miserably bored.

Edward, Jeremy and the other men worked long hours in the fields despite the weather. Where drought had threatened the crops before, flooding was the current danger.

Astrid roamed aimlessly through the house, finding no solace in any room. One afternoon, she idly looked through the shelves of Thomas's books, hoping to find something to occupy her mind. There was no light reading among the volumes, she noticed with dismay. Even the titles were a mouthful—*The Landlord's Law, The English Expositor*, Heylin's *Cosmography, Purchas Pilgrimes*.

With a tired sigh, she picked out a slim volume of John Donne's poems and went into the parlor. She chose a wooden chair near the hearth where a low fire blazed, breaking the chill of the room.

Astrid opened the book, scanning the pages with little interest. Then, lines and words leapt out at her, stabbing her already broken heart.

Come live with me, and be my love . . . Dear love, for nothing less than thee Would I have broke this happy dream . . . Dear, I die As often as from thee I go . . . The straight Hellespont between The Sestos and Abydos of her breasts . . .

She slammed the book shut and tightly closed her eyes. John Donne was a terrible selection, she realized, clenching her teeth.

"I see that you read, milady," Mrs. Arrington said from across the room.

"Yes," Astrid responded. "But I find I am unable today to engross myself in these words."

"Perchance you may be willing anon to tutor our Lizzie in her letters," the woman said. "She has already learned all that Ann and I can offer."

Frowning slightly, Astrid considered the request. She looked over at Mrs. Arrington who was eyeing her with a compassion that pulled at her heart.

Lizzie straightened up, a sparkle of hope brightening her big green eyes.

Astrid couldn't turn her back on Thomas's dear mother nor the sweet child.

"Aye," she said without enthusiasm. "I would like very much to work with Lizzie."

Beginning the next day, Astrid scheduled two hours each morning and two every afternoon for the girl's instruction. Lizzie was as bright as Jeremy had been, and her progress was quick.

They found a book of Shakespeare's plays on the shelves, and Astrid led her through *Midsummer Night's Dream*, the one she knew best.

Lizzie took delight in the fantasy, giggling over Bottom and his troupe of players. Astrid had the girl memorize lines, and the two of them acted out whole scenes, sometimes forgetting the time and running right into the supper hour.

The lessons brought a small chink of light into Astrid's dark days, and Eagle's Crest gradually began to resound with the normal noises of a busy household.

Joseph went back into the kitchen, and though he fussed constantly at Jenny and Dorothy, the three of them managed to produce an endless succession of hearty meals.

Toward the end of August, Astrid realized she was pregnant.

It hit her like a ton of bricks. She frantically counted the days. According to her calculations, she hadn't had a period since early July.

Maybe the turmoil I've been through has delayed things, she tried to convince herself, but it was no use. She could feel herself changing inside. Her breasts were tender. A strange, atypical calmness had entered her, and she was sleepier than usual.

She was carrying Thomas Arrington's child!

Astrid didn't know what to do about it. An odd mixture of emotions battled within her—anxiety, contentment, despair, peace. Suffusing all of it was the deep satisfaction of knowing that Thomas had left her a part of him. No matter what the future held, she would have that part, growing within her even now, to nurture and to love.

It would be awhile before anyone would surmise, but before then, she'd have a plan. That was a necessity, because none of them must ever know. She would have to leave Eagle's Crest, of course. But she had the silver. She could buy land elsewhere, perhaps in Maryland, and she would have Thomas's child with her and would never be alone again.

Mrs. Arrington became sick the next day. It was a virus, Astrid suspected. Flu, probably. Her fever was high, and she was wracked with chills.

Astrid helped Ann tend to her. They forced liquids and kept wet cloths on her forehead.

On the following day, when Ann came downstairs flushed and trembling, Astrid sent her back upstairs to bed and tended to them both. Lizzie became cranky on the third day, and Astrid had three patients.

She went from bed to bed, offering comfort and broth. She slept fitfully, running to their sides when she thought she heard them cry out.

Edward, who was a pale shadow of his younger brother, cared for Ann during the long nights. The couple slept in Thomas's chamber, and Astrid was thankful she didn't have to go in there at night. It was hard enough to enter the room during the daytime.

It was a stubborn illness, and Astrid grew concerned when none of them showed signs of improvement.

Joseph told her he had seen it before. "It takes longer than you think it should, but most everyone recovers," he said late one afternoon. "There be no name for it. Folks generally call it 'ague.'"

Little comfort, Astrid thought. They're fading before my eyes. She longed for enlightened medical practices.

She barely heard the light tap on the kitchen

door. Joseph indicated she should crouch out of sight and he squinted warily out the window.

"'Tis only the Pamunkeys," he said happily and went to invite them in out of the rain.

It was the Indian family Astrid had met earlier.

"We come to repay thee, Woman with Golden Hair," the man said.

Astrid didn't know what to say. She stared at them in disbelief. They were covered with soaked deerskins and were smiling and nodding at her. The boy's wide black eyes were filled with wonder.

"We bring your horse back to thee and humble gifts from your friends," the man continued. "We do whatever we can do for thee."

Astrid saw her horse through the window. A large skin-covered bundle was on its back.

"Have you medicine?" Astrid asked. "We have fever here."

The man turned and spoke to the woman in words Astrid couldn't understand. The woman bowed her head, stepped forward and handed her a small pouch.

"My wife says you should make a potion of these herbs and give it to your sick ones," the Indian said.

Astrid took the pouch and smiled gratefully at the trio. "I thank thee," she said with a bow. "You are my friends, and I thank thee."

The Indians left soon after. Astrid quickly mixed water with the herbs and stirred it. She poured it into three cups and with-self assurance born from experience started out of the kitchen.

"You're going to try voodoo remedies, little woman?" Joseph asked, a twinkle in his small eyes.

"You bet!" Astrid said with enthusiasm and went to minister to her patients.

Mrs. Arrington, Ann and Lizzie all took turns for the better the next day, but Astrid made them stay in bed.

"Remain quiet through the night," she ordered them, "and I shall allow you to get up on the morrow."

She was bone tired when Edward came in for supper. The two of them, with Joseph, shared the table. She had taken trays to the others.

"If this rain continues, Thomas's crop will be as lost as mine," Edward said, looking dejected.

"How bad was your crop?" Joseph asked, passing him the bowl of stew.

"Ruined," Edward said. "There's naught to pay the taxes I fear."

"When are the taxes due, Edward?" Astrid asked.

"By September eleventh," he answered. "God knows what I'll sell to meet them. I have little of value."

Astrid pressed. "What happens if they are not paid?" she asked.

"I lose my house and land," he answered.

"We must find means," she said determinedly.

"Perchance the war will delay the reckoning," Joseph chimed in, sounding like a grim Pollyanna.

"Little good a delay would be," Edward said

with a dour tone. "There are but few drops of blood in a turnip."

Joseph turned the conversation to Edward's experiences with Bacon in the Occaneechee campaign. Astrid paid little attention, planning instead how she could help the Arringtons.

She enlisted Jeremy.

"It will be too dangerous, Countess," he said. "They are warring, and 'tis hard to know who is on what side."

"You can lead us properly," she insisted. "You were in Jamestown last week and know the safest paths."

"Aye," he agreed, but quickly demurred. "The guv'ner is in the town now, and his men are everywhere, fortifying against an attack by Bacon's troops. You are an accused spy, milady, and orders are to shoot thee on sight."

"They shall not know me," she said confidently.

Jeremy didn't look convinced.

"Look, Jeremy, we must do this." She took him by the shoulders. "You know the Arringtons would never agree to take my silver for their taxes. We two can take it to Jamestown, pay their and Thomas's taxes in full, and be back before they know what we've done."

Jeremy frowned, his young face growing serious. "I could go alone, Countess. 'Tis wrong for thee to take this risk."

Astrid wavered. Maybe she was being reckless to put herself in potential danger this way, but the need was so great. Jeremy was only a boy and too unseasoned for such heavy responsibility. It would be neither fair nor right to send him out alone. Success was much more likely with the two of them. They had been an excellent team so far.

"Haven't we two been lucky in our endeavors thus far, Jeremy?" she asked.

"Aye," he nodded, "but . . ."

"No but's, my lad! We'll sneak out tomorrow evening."

Astrid cut off her hair. Those blonde tresses had gotten her into enough trouble. She would look like a servant boy or die trying.

As she prepared for her journey with Jeremy, she had only one misgiving. After paying the taxes, her silver would be gone, and that was the keystone of her plan for her and her baby.

My baby. Mine and Thomas's. She smiled. It would be a sturdy fellow, she knew, and a boy—she knew that, too—who would be exactly like Thomas.

That was a comfort, though little else was.

I'll find a way for us, she pledged to her child. We may be sacrificing the silver, but we're doing that for your father and his special family. And though you'll never know them, my love, I know you would want me to help them. We shall discover other means for our future. There *will* be a good life for us.

Astrid donned the black clothing and boots she had worn when she escaped from Green Spring and pulled the monmouth cap over her cropped head. When she was sure the family was sleeping, she slipped from the house and met Jeremy in the stable. Behind, she had left a short note telling Joseph and the Arringtons that she and Jeremy had gone on a hunting foray. She knew they'd be troubled when they read it, but that was not her concern at the moment.

The ride to Jamestown went without incident. Though tired from lack of sleep, she and Jeremy entered the town with growing confidence. To the few people on the muddy streets, they were merely two servant boys on horseback running an errand for some colonist up in the wilderness.

The distant hammering indicated Berkeley's forces were busy building their fortifications at the front of the town. No one was likely to pay any notice to two lads.

After Astrid gave Jeremy the bag of silver, he went into the court tax office to complete the transaction. He returned with sealed papers in hand and a smile on his face.

"'Tis done," he said proudly. "Eagle's Crest and Mister Edward's Bermuda Hundred land are safe for another year, and there's silver left over for thee." He handed her the pouch that jingled slightly.

"How much?" she asked, hoping mightily there was enough left for a small piece of land in Maryland.

"Five pounds," Jeremy said, dashing her hopes.

"Then we'll get supplies for the family while we're here," she said, "and blow the rest of it."

"Blow, milady?" Jeremy asked, puzzled.

"Forget it, lad," Astrid said with a chuckle, moving her horse forward.

They were loading the horses with the variety of goods she had bought when she saw a familiar figure swagger down the street.

Astrid grew cold at the sight of Percival Dunwoody. She couldn't believe her eyes. Could he have returned from England so soon? She had no idea how long the voyage took. He had left three months ago. Could he possibly be back? And why in God's name has he returned?

Her heart pounding, she tightened the satchels around the horses and gestured to Jeremy to come quickly.

"Don't look now, but I think that's Lord Dunwoody heading this way," she said in a breathless low voice. "Let's get out of here!"

Without asking any questions, Jeremy jumped up on his horse, and Astrid mounted hers.

"Go slowly until we pass him," she whispered. "We don't want to draw any attention."

They kept their horses to a walk up Back Street.

Lord Percy, nattily dressed as usual, looked at them without interest. "Ugly damned outpost," he mumbled to himself and walked into an open tavern.

When they felt it was safe, Astrid and Jeremy brought their horses to a gallop and sped over the narrow wooden bridge of the isthmus and out of the town. Only when they were a mile or so away did they slow down enough to congratulate themselves that he hadn't recognized her.

A short while later they saw another horseman approaching them. Astrid tensed, checking the side of the road for a possible egress.

"Jeremy! Be that you, you ugly rogue?" the distant voice yelled. Alarmed, Astrid looked at Jeremy.

"'Tis Peter Cook," Jeremy said, grinning. "He's a friend, milady. You need have no fear."

Astrid and Jeremy stopped their horses and waited as Peter drew close.

"Who's the lad with thee?" Peter asked, shading his eyes to inspect Jeremy's companion.

"A new 'denture from England, that's who," Jeremy answered.

"Beware of this road, you two greenhorns," Peter said, pulling up in front of them. "I saw three of the guv'ner's men but five minutes ago heading this way. They may well be hiding behind those trees waiting for thee."

"Stop jesting, Peter," Jeremy scolded.

Peter looked at Astrid closely. "They're bringing soft-looking lads over these days," he said. "The seasoning fever will have this one laid low before Christmas."

"Stop it!" Jeremy shouted angrily.

"So defensive?" Peter asked, looking curious. Then he laughed wickedly and winked. "Have you gone soft yourself on a green lad, Jeremy?"

"This is the countess, Peter," Jeremy blurted. "Watch your words!"

Astrid threw Jeremy a nasty look.

Peter registered surprise and stared at her. "The countess? By God, Jeremy, you speak the truth! I would recognize those sky-blue eyes anywhere." The lad grew sober. "Forgive me, milady," he said, bowing respectfully. "I forget my manners, but you have become a legend among our ranks and 'tis an honor to make your acquaintance."

Astrid didn't smile. "Were you lying about the Berkeley men being on the road, Peter?" she asked, feeling a rising fear.

"No, milady. There were three, heading this way. They . . ." The tall boy stopped in midsentence, his eyes widening, fixed on the road behind Astrid and Jeremy.

"They're behind thee," he gasped, "no more than a furlong away!" Astrid looked back. Three men on horseback were moving slowly toward them. They were talking and laughing and didn't look in pursuit of anyone.

Peter nodded his head backward and began to turn his horse. "Follow me, quickly!" he said. "I will take thee to Green Spring."

Astrid slapped her reins. "Not Green Spring, for God's sake!" she shouted as she, Jeremy and Peter began racing up the road.

"'Tis safe," Peter shouted back to her. "Bacon and his men are camping there."

Chapter Nineteen

The grounds of Green Spring were swarming with people and horses when Astrid and the two boys arrived. Small campfires dotted the once-manicured gardens, trampled now by a thousand heavy boots. The air was thick with the smell of human sweat, burning wood, smoking food and gunpowder. The acrid combination made Astrid's eyes sting as she entered the unruly encampment.

She was acutely aware of far deeper discomforts. Uneasiness, apprehension and sheer fright made her want to turn and run.

Thomas is somewhere in that throng. He must not know I'm here!

Astrid tried to reassure herself. The scene was conducive to a low profile. Three lads could be swallowed up without notice in a crowd like this.

To be on the safe side, she kept her face hidden as they tied their horses to trees on the outskirts of the pandemonium. They unloaded the supplies Astrid had bought for the Arringtons and hid them beneath a clump of straw.

"We need disappear among a group of your kind," she told Jeremy. "We shall rest here overnight and depart at dawn for Eagle's Crest."

Jeremy looked disappointed. The active preparations for battle around him had lit a fire of excitement in his eyes, but he gave Astrid a resigned nod. "Aye, milady," he said. "Follow me. I see a few fellows of my acquaintance yon."

Peter went with them, and they joined a small knot of young men gathered in a far corner around one of the smoking fires. In her loose black clothing and monmouth cap, Astrid felt like one of the crowd.

"Where be your musket, Jeremy?" one of the boys teased. "Do ye plan to fight the loyalists with your pale bare hands?" The boy was holding a rifle that exceeded his own height by a foot or more.

Jeremy ignored him, asking instead what kind of supper was bubbling in the iron pot.

"A tasty stew," another lad said with a raucous laugh. "A veritable feast is brewing there with shanks of the Susquehannocks, prime backsides and limbs of loyalists, and the choicest delicacy of all, the withered scrotum bags of the old guv'ner!"

Knowing the boy was pulling Jeremy's leg, Astrid couldn't resist a small smile, but Jeremy was far from amused, obviously concerned about his lady's tender ears.

"Watch your tongue, rogue!" he bellowed. "There be a la . . ."

Astrid's elbow poked his ribs sharply, nearly knocking away his breath. Though surprised, Jeremy displayed his quickness once again.

"We have an unseasoned lad in our midst, so the lot of you keep your words civil," he commanded.

Horseplay and rolling of eyes greeted Jeremy's statement. "Ha! 'Tis time the lad grow bags of his own!" and similar shouts echoed around the fire. "On the morrow we march to battle, and that'll make men of us all."

Jeremy was exasperated, but said no more.

Astrid began to worry later when a flask of rum started passing around the campfire. She noticed Jeremy took a hefty swig. When it was passed to her, she pretended to do likewise, letting most of it dribble down her chin, to the hearty applause of the entire group.

She knew she could use a little brain numbing, but she thought about her baby and continued her pretense of drinking on the second and third pass of the flask.

The group was growing boisterous, and Jeremy's speech was beginning to slur. Astrid feared he might disclose their secret in an unguarded moment. She decided to remove her possibly triggering presence as unobtrusively as she could.

"I wish to sleep now, Jeremy," she whispered

to him. "I shall find a vacant spot nearby. Continue your merrymaking, but remember we depart at dawn."

Jeremy's rum-bright eyes glistened toward her. He nodded, showing he had comprehended at least some of what she'd said.

It was Peter who bollixed everything. As Astrid wiggled surreptitiously away from the circle, the tall boy saw her and stood up on unstable legs.

He swung the flask around his head. "Three cheers for our countess!" he shouted drunkenly.

Astrid froze. She wanted to strangle him.

The group grew silent as 20 pairs of astounded eyes stared at her. The 21st pair, Jeremy's, was covered with his hand.

"The countess?" . . . "The Hollander be among us?" . . . "The brave woman who outwitted the guv'ner, who has quelled the Indians and who breathes life into the dead" . . . "Let us see the hair of gold . . ."

The buzz became an excited roar. The boys jumped to their feet and bowed in unison toward Astrid, who sat dumbfounded, her mouth open. Jeremy, who still was seated, gave her a worried look and moved to her side.

"To the countess!" the boys shouted again and again. "To the countess!"

Horrified, Astrid saw people from other groups taking note of the hullabaloo, peeling away and coming forward.

So much for anonymity, she thought, hunkering down in an effort to disappear. She felt like crying.

"Let's get out of here," she said to Jeremy out

of the side of her mouth, getting to her feet.

But Astrid saw it was too late. A massive crowd pressed forward, ringing around her. The word "countess" whistled loudly and ominously over the encampment. She grabbed Jeremy's arm and hung on to him. Her frantic eyes darted across the sea of curious, excited faces.

"Move aside!" a deep voice shouted. Her heart leapt to her throat. The people quieted, the sea parted and a tall figure walked through and stood before her.

Thomas! His anger was sharp and tangible, cutting into her. Astrid cringed and pulled closer to Jeremy.

"Why are you here, milady?" Thomas bellowed. She had never seen his face more stern. He was bearded now, a full black beard that added to his authority.

Astrid's lips trembled. Thomas's irate eyes pierced her, striking her mute. She shook her head, unable to answer.

Thomas turned to Jeremy. "Speak, lad!" he shouted. "Tell me why in the name of God you have brought her to this place of danger?"

Jeremy looked stricken and opened his mouth to speak. Astrid saw the boy's pale, frightened face and her protective instincts surged forward.

"Say naught, Jeremy!" she ordered. She straightened her shoulders and walked up to Thomas.

"We are here because I commanded the lad to come with me," she said. "I have heard that Bacon needs recruits."

The crowd cheered while Thomas glowered.

Astrid continued. Her knees were weak, but her voice grew stronger.

"There are other women in this camp. We love Virginia as much as you men, I vow, and are willing to fight and die by your sides for a just cause."

The crowd roared with approval, tossing their hats into the air.

Determination pulsed against Thomas's iron-like jaws. "You shall not fight, and you shall return to Eagle's Crest at once," he said.

Astrid's eyes shot fiery sparks, and she defiantly threw back her head.

"And what of that, my people?" she cried out to the attentive crowd. "Shall I be forbidden to join your march as Mr. Arrington commands?"

"Nay! Nay! The countess shall fight with us!"

Astrid smiled and looked back at Thomas, her face shining with victory.

"The people have spoken," she said.

Thomas clenched his fists and scowled at her. He turned away quickly and pushed his way through the cheering mob.

Jeremy was delighted that he would get a taste of battle, but he expressed concern about Astrid's participation. She attempted to set his mind at ease, but it was hard going, especially when she wasn't too pleased at the prospect herself.

That man brings out the worst in me, she fumed, remembering Thomas's perverse determination to put her in her place.

Now suddenly I'm Joan of Arc.

Astrid had neither the heart nor desire for battle, but she knew she was committed to carry through.

She sighed and shrugged her shoulders. I may as well make the best of it, she told herself as she sat for a long while contemplating her next move. There *were* women in the camp. That's it! Why not? I'll organize The First Virginia Women's Platoon.

Astrid stood up and brushed the dirt off the seat of her pants. Move over, men of Virginia, she said grimly. You're about to see equal rights in action.

She walked through the camp, collecting all the women she could find. It was a motley crew, about 30 when she'd finished her roundup. Most were camp followers, tavern wenches and a few servants, but they all followed Astrid eagerly and the men encouraged them. She had become a folk heroine, whether she'd wanted that role or not. Lord knows, she told herself, I don't deserve it.

They were even saying she'd "quelled Indians," for heaven's sake. She wondered if all legends had been built on such shaky ground.

Astrid looked at her circle of troops. Not a respectable 17th century virgin in the lot, she'd bet, but they were a lively and sturdy bunch.

"Who of you can shoot?" she asked.

Nine or ten raised their hands.

"Good! I'll get muskets for thee. Now, can any of you handle a sword?"

A surprising number responded affirmatively. One brazen frump said she had "more experience with the short blade," creating an outburst of bawdy laughter.

Astrid quieted them. "We'll arm thee with swords," she promised, having no idea where she'd find enough weapons.

"Do some of you ride?" she asked. When no hands went up, Astrid looked thoughtful.

"I ride," she said, "and have a horse with me. I'll be mounted and lead thee." The women applauded and cheered at this news.

That was, as far as it went, the totality of her battle plan. She knew nothing about war strategies in any era, let alone this one, but she was gaining respect for her troops. Their enthusiasm was catching.

Astrid told them to get some sleep, suspecting many of them had different plans for the night, but she wasn't going to let that worry her. She had enough on her mind.

Gathering sufficient arms was her next order of business, and Jeremy helped her. He needed some for himself.

She was amazed at her success and in wonder at the graciousness of the people in the camp. Most of those she asked had "brought more than one man can use at one time, Countess," and happily handed her muskets, gunpowder and swords until she had an arsenal large enough to supply twice her need.

Astrid looked at the pile of ugly weapons and shuddered. "What will we do with all this?" she asked Jeremy.

"Fight for Virginia!" Jeremy answered, thoroughly swept up in the surrounding madness.

"I mean, what is all of it?" She reached down and pulled out a long shaft with a steel spike and an axlike blade. It was horrible looking, and she hated to think what its uses might be. "This, for example. What does one do with it?"

Jeremy chuckled. "That's a halberd, milady. What you do with that is throw it in a ditch. That was for the old days when they wore armor and had different wars."

"Oh," Astrid said and tossed it aside. She wished she knew what kind of wars they had now. It was hard to visualize what was ahead for them.

Jeremy instructed her on the differences between the matchlocks, the flintlocks and the less complicated fowling pieces in her armory. The forked handspikes for loading the guns were easy enough to comprehend. Astrid wryly noted, however, that they had forks for their weapons but hadn't thought of them for their tables yet.

Progress, she was finding out, began in the battlefields.

Fed up with the subject of war, Astrid finally called it a day. She'd sleep on it, she decided, bidding Jeremy goodnight.

Some of the people had provided her blankets, and one of her admirers had placed a bunch of wildflowers on her bedding.

But tired as she was, she didn't find sleep easy. In the quiet, the image of Thomas haunted her. He was so near and yet a universe away. He won't accept me, a wailing voice inside her cried. I love him, her deepest spirit replied.

Astrid shed numerous tears that night before

her exhaustion overcame her and pulled her into sleep.

Thomas sat on the steps of Green Spring looking out at the huddled throngs on the grounds.

Astrid is among them, he thought. He had struggled to put her out of his mind. The rain, the mud, the swamps, the turmoil of the past few weeks, all of them he had welcomed, praying for them to wash her from his thoughts.

She is a sprite from the underworld, he told himself, sent to wrench me from my senses. An immigrant from the future, she claims.

Nonsense! There must be a divine order, and God in his wisdom would not allow such happenings.

Thomas's brows drew together, and he closed his eyes. God in heaven, his mind cried out, give me strength to withstand her unworldly temptations. They have ensnared me, I admit. But let them not draw me away from all I have known and understood.

He felt no better when he opened his eyes. She was yet present in his mind's eye, tormenting him beyond reason.

I cannot believe her, he told himself. I cannot!

She had been irritatingly wondrous this night. She was strong and filled with fighting fire, resisting his will but clamping into his heart as no woman he had known could e'er affect him.

His hand pulled out the crumpled papers he had kept by his chest, and he unfolded them. The script was strangely wrought, the ink smeared from weeks of rain and tears. Unnumbered hours he had pored over them, trying to decipher the sense, the reason for which he was searching.

Once again, though they were embedded in his memory, he studied the words.

Astrid assumed they would begin their march at dawn. She woke early and steeled herself for the coming day. She sorted the weapons and waited for her troops to arrive.

When she saw everyone else eating leisurely breakfasts and relaxing in various stages of undress, she realized nothing was going to begin anytime soon.

"What's happening?" she asked Jeremy.

"Word has it we start for Jamestown after midday. General Bacon will speak to us first," he said.

General? She had thought Bacon was a mere colonel. A wartime commission, she figured. Self-imposed was her second guess.

She took it upon herself to spend the idle time familiarizing herself with the mysteries of guns. She had plenty of help, most of it confusing, but after a few hours she at least knew which end got the powder stuffed into it and the differing methods of ignition required for the staggering variety of artillery. Swords were swords, she figured, and armed herself with one. The pointed end was the one you stick into people.

Astrid didn't believe she'd ever use any of these things, but she was determined she was going to look like she might.

If nothing else, she'd show Thomas Arrington that she could take care of herself.

When Nathaniel Bacon came out to give his warm-up speech to the people, she barely recognized him. He stood out in the crowd, she'd have to admit. He looked like one of the Three Musketeers, she thought with dry amusement. From plumed hat to sweeping cape he was a model of the well-dressed hero about to lead his troops to victory.

It was his pasty complexion that drew Astrid's attention as well as the feverish brightness of his eyes. The man was weakened and ill, and she wondered why no one else noticed it.

She found out why when he began to speak. He was a mesmerizing orator who had the masses wrapped around his finger within seconds.

Astrid, too, listened spellbound. He told them of the dangers in the battle to come and the strength of the fortified town. Then he called upon them to follow him for the cause of right. "Come on, my hearts of gold!" he shouted to the rapt assembly. "He that dies in the field lies in the bed of honor!"

The ovations rang to the cloud-speckled heavens. Even Astrid was moved, though she had no intention of dying if she could arrange it. And she prayed Thomas Arrington was of a similar mind. And Jeremy. And Peter. And her own undisciplined troops.

Hell, she thought suddenly, we're not play acting! These men are serious about this thing. She felt genuine fright for the first time since she had stood up to Thomas the night before. She had been out of her mind to get herself into this craziness.

But Astrid went along with them. She was in it all the way. When the women gathered expectantly around her, she found herself distributing weapons, shouting orders and snapping everyone into line as if she knew what she was doing.

Astrid mounted her horse, coming close to stabbing herself with her own sword, and gestured grandly for the First Virginia Women's Platoon to follow her.

An unexpected lift to her spirits came a few moments later. She heard the rich, husky voice first. "Countess!" it was shouting. Astrid turned and saw the unmistakable dark round shape running toward her.

"Marcy!" she screamed. "Marcy, what on earth brings you here?"

"Same as you, Countess." The black woman puffed as she pulled alongside her. "War brings out de best in peoples, and I wanted to be part of it."

"I'm not sure about that," Astrid said with a laugh. "Come on up and ride with me, and we'll talk and catch up with one another on the ride to Jamestown."

Marcy's eyes rounded like big brown saucers. "I'se afraid of horses, Countess," she said. "I'll walk here beside you."

"Nonsense, Marcy," Astrid said, calling over Jeremy to give the woman a boost. It took several husky men in addition to Jeremy to get a reluctant Marcy atop the horse behind Astrid.

"See," Astrid said, smiling back at the startled woman. "'Tis far better to ride, and we can talk much better this way."

Marcy sat sideways on the horse's back and held on to Astrid for dear life. She didn't look convinced at first but gradually her smile broadened when she realized she wasn't going to fall off and wouldn't have to walk the two miles to Jamestown.

The march began. Drummers at the head of the wide line began their steady tattoos. Bacon was up front on a noble steed. With a sinking heart, Astrid noted that Thomas, on his handsome sorrel, was riding beside him.

The rest of the people followed in varying degrees of regularity. Astrid kept her platoon relatively orderly, though roguish comments from the less disciplined male troops occasionally interrupted their rhythm. Generally, the men's respect for Astrid kept these interruptions to a minimum, and she learned to ignore them and chastened the women if they responded in kind. Soon, when all of the women had learned to copy Astrid's regal expression, the comments stopped entirely.

Meanwhile, she and Marcy chatted as much as they could. Astrid learned that ruffians from the Bacon contingent had attacked and plundered Shirley, causing the family to escape for their lives. "And de poor missus heavy with child like dat," Marcy said with a sad shake of her head. Neighbors had sheltered them. With no room or need for the Shirley servants, many of them had been released, including Marcy.

"I wasn't happy with dose Hill peoples no-way," Marcy told Astrid. "With nothin' better to do I decided to come he'p de Bacon soldiers. Dey needed good cooks."

While Astrid listened to Marcy a brilliant idea struck her, giving her renewed courage. This strong, dependable ally was now as homeless as she was!

"Marcy, when this battle or skirmish or whatever is finished, would you consider remaining with me?" she asked. She thought through the possibilities, her heart quickening. They could return to Green Spring to retrieve the supplies she'd hidden. She still had a couple pieces of silver. In some way they could find a small cabin in the frontier, and she could tutor planters' children.

It would work. She knew it would. Most of all, she knew she could never return to Eagle's Crest.

"I'd come with thee with happy heart," Marcy said, giving Astrid a big squeeze.

Feeling worlds better, Astrid brightened and ordered her troops to step more lively.

Astrid had no way of knowing that in the following days she would come face-to-face with hell itself.

Chapter Twenty

At first it was only a private hell.

When the Bacon troops stationed themselves outside Jamestown, the women were relegated to the far rear lines. From her limited observation post, Astrid saw no signs of activity. She was tempted to say the battle had been called off, but she knew better.

Astrid was curious and frustrated. Something is going on up at the front, she told herself, but what? She hated to be in the dark. Besides, she was more than a little frightened.

She was deeply worried about Thomas. She had serious concerns, too, about Jeremy and Marcy and Peter and her shabby troops and all the others, including the heralded General Bacon.

Astrid admitted she also had fears for her own

safety, but only because of her baby. I have to come out of this madness unscathed, she ordered herself, because my baby is depending on my pulling through.

Her baby—Thomas's child—had become more important than anything else she'd ever considered a priority item. She longed for the leisure to contemplate this new wonder, this complete change of direction in her life.

But being part of a force supposedly preparing to invade Jamestown precluded such luxury. Though she was excluded from any preparations that might be under way, she had the distinct feeling something might happen at any minute.

On their second day camped outside of the town, two things happened to increase Astrid's anxieties.

First, one of her women brought a piece of news from the front.

Second, Thomas confronted her.

The woman, Lucille Potts, returned after a night of unexplained absence and asked for Astrid's ear.

Lucille's good friend Willie had sneaked off for "an 'our or two with me charms, but 'is mind weren't 'round, ne'er mind the rest of 'im," she complained. According to Lucille, the men were shoveling earth "in front of the palisade the guv'ner's men 'ave set a'fore us."

Astrid struggled to understand the woman but got the gist of it. Bacon was attempting to dig a protective trench the length of the palisade, a staked fence that Berkeley had installed in front of Jamestown. With only two spades available for their task it was slow going, and the Bacon forces needed a miracle to buy some time. Willie and hundreds of others were doing what they could around the clock to help with the digging, using swords, rifle butts and their bare hands, but it wasn't looking good for them.

When Thomas came to Astrid, it wasn't news he brought but a set of orders. "You and your women need remove from this area, milady," he said. "Go far back. Far, far back, to Green Spring or farther. We know not what shall transpire within the following days, but this is business for men, not for women."

Having Thomas face-to-face again was disconcerting, to say the least. Astrid held Marcy's arm and tried to look defiant and brave. Inside, she was a quivering mess. She wanted to run into his arms, feel him against her once more and hear his deep voice hoarsely cry "dear rabbit." The last thing she wanted was to stand in a muddy wilderness and pretend he meant nothing to her.

But Thomas was better fortified than Berkeley's Jamestown. He stood stiffly in front of her issuing his commands. Astrid, like Bacon's men, attempted to dig in and not give an inch.

"Perchance we can help," she said, disturbed that her words didn't come out as forceful as she wished.

Thomas didn't scoff, but he looked determined as hell. "'Tis men and time we need, not useless women. Now go, milady, and leave us to do what we must. Free us from the concerns of your presence."

Astrid raised her chin but moved closer to Marcy. "Have no concerns for us, Thomas," she said. "My women and I shall not interfere with the work of the men."

"You will leave then?" he asked.

"When I give the orders, the women and I shall move," she said.

Thomas studied her intently, his eyes as sharp and silvery as his sword. Astrid tried to put steel in her own eyes, but she wasn't sure she succeeded.

"Your words give me not the assurance I desire," he said.

"I have said what I am required to say and naught else," she responded, wishing she felt as strong as she hoped she sounded.

"Then I pray you shall obey me with your actions more than with your double-edged words, milady," Thomas said, his voice as taut as his body. He turned and left them.

Marcy looked down at Astrid. "'Tis Master Thomas who has yo' heart, Countess, I knows it," the black woman said, hugging her close. "I've wondered 'dese long days who t'was, but I needs wonder no longer."

Astrid buried her head in the dark warm bosom. "Thomas has no heart," she said, wanting to cry but not allowing herself. "It matters not what I feel for him, Marcy."

Marcy kissed the top of Astrid's woolen cap and watched Thomas walk toward the front. She said no more on the subject. Had Astrid looked up into the woman's wise ebony eyes, she might have seen the reflection of what Marcy had observed.

Thomas Arrington has a big heart, an aching heart, and it beats for but one woman—the Hollander countess.

Lucille Potts came up with the idea.

"The men need time to dig in," she said. "I have a thought 'ow we can 'elp 'em."

Astrid listened. Lucille had been in the service of Major John Page, whose house was up the river nearby at Middle Plantation. Major Page was a loyalist and away, back inside the Jamestown encampment with the governor.

"We bring the mizzus Page here and place her in front of the palisade, and none of the guv'ner's men dars't attack a'fore our men finish their diggin'," Lucille said.

"Mrs. Page would never come," Astrid said.

"Oh, milady!" Lucille laughed. "I ne'er figgered we'd send 'er a proper invitation like!"

Astrid considered Lucille's proposal. Kidnapping a woman and placing her in the line of fire was not only distasteful but was downright uncivilized, she told herself. She decided it was a terrible idea and put it out of her mind.

But before the afternoon was half over Astrid had reconsidered.

A volley of shots at the front numbed her with fear. Her first thought was for Thomas who was up there, unprotected.

Jeremy ran back to report that it was Bacon's

men who had fired through the palisade into Jamestown, a brave attempt to show strength and to thwart an early attack before the trench was dug.

"It appears to have succeeded," Jeremy told her. "The guv'ner's men scattered like a pack of scared deer."

"How long before the trench will be finished?" Astrid asked him.

"Another full day at least." Jeremy looked worried.

Her heart sank. Berkeley would not wait that long to attack. Even now he was probably rallying his men to take advantage of the rebels' vulnerable position.

When Jeremy returned to the front, Astrid pondered the situation and knew something had to be done.

She was deep in thought when Lucille came up to her with Millie Lewis in tow.

"Millie used to serve wit' th' Ballards," Lucille said. The Thomas Ballard family also lived up on river land nearby, she explained. "'Tis like the Pages," Lucille said. "'T'would be e'en better wit' two of th' loyalist wives standing up front."

"Aye," Millie piped in. "An' three be e'en better yet. The mizzus Nathaniel Bacon Senior, wife of our fine gen'ral's old loyalist cousin, is visitin' wit' mizzus Ballard. The ladies be unprotected."

"Oh!" Lucille exclaimed, her sallow complexion almost glowing. "Th' mizzus James Bray would likely be wit' mizzus Page! We'd have four of 'em, Countess. 'T'would hold off th' guv'ner, damn right 't'would!"

Astrid looked at them, her mind running at top speed. "But we couldn't endanger the ladies thus," she protested. "'Tis not a suitable strategy."

Lucille insisted otherwise. "Th' loyalists be wrong'eaded," she said. "But ne'er would they shoot at a laidy. There be no dangers to 'em, Countess."

The women may be right, Astrid mused. Chivalry *is* still alive in these times. Lucille's scheme was beginning to look better and better.

Knowing it was a decision born of desperation, Astrid agreed to give it a try.

"We'll do it," she told the women, mustering her courage. Lucille and Millie clapped their hands excitedly and ran off to round up the other women. Marcy shook her head and put an arm around Astrid.

"How's you gonna bring those ladies here?" she asked.

Astrid's brow crinkled. "I'll think of something," she vowed.

She mapped a game plan that began to look feasible. She needed three more horses and riders for starters. On Astrid's orders, Millie sneaked up to the front and brought Jeremy to the rear where Astrid waited impatiently. They had to get moving in a hurry.

Jeremy listened to her and responded negatively. He doubted General Bacon and Thomas would ever agree to such an ungentlemanly tactic, he said.

"They need not know until we've accomplished it," she remarked. "When they see how well we succeed in holding off the governor's attack they'll sing a different tune," she added.

"Perchance," Jeremy said, his face clouded. He pinched his lips in deep thought and nodded. "I will help thee, milady," he said at last.

"Good! Now here's what we must do . . ."

Jeremy ran back to the front and returned shortly with Peter Cook, another lad they introduced as Harold Nelson, and three horses. The boys came close to backing out when they realized Astrid was going with them, but she prevailed, convincing them that Bacon needed as many hands possible for the trench digging. "Why strip him of another when I ride better than any of you?" she challenged them.

She briefed them on her strategy. They would split up—two of them going to the Page home, the other two going to the Ballards.

Jeremy knew the Page place, he said, and insisted that he would go with Astrid. Harold was familiar with the Ballard home, and he and Peter took that as their assignment.

"The ladies are unguarded, my women tell me. Their men are all in Jamestown," Astrid said. "We will strike this afternoon. Treat them gently, lads, and try to quell their fears. Put them on your steeds and walk them back."

The four armed themselves and mounted their horses. "Return as quickly as you can," she told Peter and Harold. "We shall meet on this spot with our quarry within two hours."

Before they went their separate ways, Astrid had another thought. "Get spades and picks from their sheds if you can, lads," she shouted. "The general needs more tools!"

Astrid and Jeremy dismounted in a copse of trees near the Page house and surveyed the area. It was quiet.

"The shed yon would have some spades," Jeremy said, considering that suggestion of Astrid's far better than the other portion of her plan. "Best I get those now before we stir things up attempting to capture the ladies."

Astrid nodded her agreement. "I'll cover thee," she said, loading her rifle and bracing herself behind a clump of bushes. "Run fast!"

Her heart was thumping as Jeremy dashed across the grounds and entered the shed. She tensed, her finger on the trigger, praying she wouldn't have to pull it. What on earth am I doing here? she asked herself, feeling almost faint with panic. Saving Thomas, she answered. A surprising renewal of courage calmed her down considerably.

Jeremy poked his head from the shed, then ran back toward her with an armful of tools. Astrid jerked to attention when the house's front door opened and two women walked out into the yard. She held the rifle against her cheek and sighted over the quivering barrel.

When Jeremy ducked through the bushes beside her, she breathed a sigh of relief. The women were talking and hadn't seen him.

"That's the ladies Page and Bray," Jeremy said, trying to catch his breath. "They be easy prey if they meander o'er near us," he said.

"I'll watch them," Astrid whispered. "Load the tools on the horses. We'll want to move fast when we've seized them."

The women came no closer but sat on a bench beneath a tall chestnut tree. Astrid eyed the house for signs of others. She felt sure the ladies wouldn't be alone; there would be servants around if no one else.

When Jeremy came back to her side, they decided on the best way to capture the women. Jeremy would run to the house to fend off whoever may be in there, while Astrid would approach the women and keep them covered with her gun. She knew she'd never in a million years actually shoot them, but the inhabitants of the house needn't know that.

Both the element of surprise and their weapons were on their side. Jeremy and Astrid felt sure they'd carry it off, though her heart was in her throat. She had no way of knowing that Jeremy was probably as nervous as she was.

"Let's go!" she ordered. As they scurried out from the thicket, Astrid's cap was pulled from her head by a dangling twig.

The startled women saw them coming and jumped to their feet. Jeremy ran past them toward the house, looking ferocious with his musket aimed at the door. "Come out! You're under attack!" he yelled.

Mrs. Page and Mrs. Bray huddled close to one another and trembled. The other lad was moving nearer, his flintlock directed at them. His short yellow hair was spiked around his head, adding to their terror.

"Come with me!" Astrid ordered.

The women meekly obeyed.

Good, Astrid thought. She was far from ready for any kind of protest from them.

Jeremy concentrated on the house. Two servants had emerged with their hands up, their eyes round with fright. He held them there until Astrid had taken the women back into the copse of trees.

Then he shooed the servants inside the house and ran to join Astrid.

Neither Jeremy nor Astrid knew that a third pair of eyes peered out from a second-story casement. The eyes were pea green and glinted with malice. They had seen the yellow hair of the lad who had taken away the lady of the house and her friend.

The cold eyes withdrew from the window, but not before a calculating look of recognition had swept across them.

Astrid and Jeremy got the women up on the horses and led them toward the Bacon camp. The walk took only a half-hour, and they were well within the time schedule Astrid had established. She hoped Peter and Harold had had the same good luck at the Ballard home.

She tried to comfort the frightened ladies. "No harm will come to thee," she said. "We shall return thee to your home whole and hearty by nighttime tomorrow."

Mrs. Page whimpered and stared down at Astrid.

"You are no lad, I vow," she said. "You have

the voice of a woman."

"'Tis that Hollander we've heard talk of, I wager, Elizabeth," Mrs. Bray said from the other horse. "Tho' it appears she's taken scissors to her hair. The renegade countess had clouds of yellow hair so the talk has been." Mrs. Bray was by far the more confident of the two women. Astrid decided she'd watch her with care.

She was distressed they'd recognized her, but under the circumstances she couldn't imagine any harm it would do. They weren't likely to be able to tell anyone who didn't know already.

Both of the women were clothed in dark dresses with the omnipresent white aprons around their waists. Ruffled caps circled their graying hair. They reminded Astrid with a pang of Mrs. Arrington, which made her feel sadly guilty about putting them through this torment.

But the cause is good, she reminded herself. Nevertheless, she made a private pledge that she'd work overtime to see that her promise would be kept and that no harm would come to them.

Peter and Harold, with a grumpy Mrs. Bacon and an almost hysterical Mrs. Ballard, arrived at the camp soon after Astrid and Jeremy. The two lads also had collected a good supply of digging tools.

Astrid sent the boys to the front immediately with their booty of spades and picks. "The men will cheer thee when you arrive with this help," she said, but cautioned them to say nothing about the four ladies. "General Bacon must know naught of this," she warned. Nor Thomas, she pleaded internally. "I will let the poor ladies rest before I place them before the barricades."

She also had to get her plans jelled, a fact she didn't bother to tell the three lads who were itching to get back to the front.

After requesting her troops to keep an eye on her prisoners, Astrid went over to a quiet hill to think. She was tired and sat back against a tree, stretching out her booted legs. Heaving a big sigh, she closed her eyes and let her mind go blank for a few moments. A gentle breeze ruffled her unevenly cropped hair. She came close to sleep, but the distant sounds of joyful whoops from the front lines snapped her fully awake. The boys had arrived with the tools.

Now, she had to decide how to proceed with part two of her plan.

The sun was setting in a big crimson ball, tossing blood-red streaks in the western sky. It would soon be dark. Should she wait until morning to post the women in front of the palisade? Her body begged her to do so, but her mind was of a different opinion. Berkeley may choose the cover of darkness for his attack, and she had to prevent it at all costs.

At all costs—the words haunted her. Her lips moved in a silent prayer. "Dear God, let this madness soon be over and watch over us, please. No harm must come to these ladies who have done naught to deserve the role I'm forcing on them. Let not a hair of Thomas's head be touched. Protect all of the others, too, who have become so dear to me. And please, dear God, cushion my baby as I expose myself to the dangers that may await me."

Astrid stood up, took a deep breath and headed toward her group of women. She had her plan fixed in her head. It's just a bit of deterrent warfare I'm conducting, she told herself, trying to bolster her courage. A vagrant tear stood in the corner of her eye as she walked within the circle of her troops and began barking orders.

Astrid exchanged clothing with one of the more respectably dressed servant girls. In the black dress, white apron and ruffled cap, Astrid was a slender version of the four captive women. She would not leave them alone, she had decided. She would stand before the palisade with them.

Next, she dictated a letter to Mrs. Page, requiring the woman to write it with her trembling hand. The letter was addressed to Major John Page and would be delivered to her loyalist husband inside fortified Jamestown.

Astrid and her troops sneaked up to a vacant end of the palisade. She called to a startled guard on the other side and pushed the letter through the fence and into his hand. When he saw the number of guns sticking through the posts, all of them aimed at him, he turned and ran lickety-split to deliver the message.

Astrid then rounded up her hostages and took them with her to the center of the front lines where the Bacon men were furiously digging their growing trench. Other men were dragging bushes and felled trees to the area.

She held her breath, girding for the heated

reactions she knew were coming.

"Mrs. Page, Mrs. Bray, Mrs. Ballard, the senior Mrs. Bacon and I have come to help thee," she announced loudly. The men nearest her looked up, their mouths dropping open. Out of the corner of her eye she saw a tall figure marching toward her. She steeled herself and continued. "The ladies and I will stand before the palisade, exposed to any attack from the governor's men, tho' I think they will not attack with wives of four of the prominent loyalists among them protecting thee."

A cold shiver down her spine interrupted her speech. Thomas Arrington was coming closer, and she swallowed hard.

"A message has been delivered inside Jamestown," Astrid continued, her voice wavering only slightly. "The men know their wives are here. I believe you gentlemen have time now to finish digging your protective trench without fear of attack."

"Milady!" Thomas bellowed, standing in front of her, his bearded face red and glowering. "You would have us hide behind the aprons of captured women? Begone with thee this instant!"

Nathaniel Bacon walked up beside Thomas and stared at Astrid. "The brave countess is displaying her mettle once again I see," he said, sweeping into a theatrical bow that made Astrid feel a little better. That Three Musketeer costume and the overdone gestures almost convinced her she was in the scene of a play after all.

Thomas brought her back to reality. "Order

Thomasina Ring

her gone, Nathaniel. This heinous trickery is not worthy of your rank nor of your gentleman army."

Nathaniel stood tall and looked up into Thomas's face. "My proud army consists of more common men than gentlemen, Thomas," he said. He turned to his men. "What say you, men? Shall we allow the countess and other ladies to stand before the palisade?"

"Aye!" they shouted in unison.

Thomas glared at Astrid. Her large eyes pleaded to him to understand, but his strong disapproval was all she received in reply before he turned and pushed through the men.

Astrid was shaken but went about her task of stationing the women along the palisade. She placed herself between Mrs. Page and Mrs. Bray. The five women faced the fortified town, their white aprons as moonlit armor protecting the men behind them. Through the stakes, Astrid could see knots of people moving about in Jamestown. A few men came forward and craned to look at the women, then ran back to the others, gesticulating and pointing.

It was working! There would be no attack while they stood there. Astrid was relieved, feeling strengthened by the encouraging words of Bacon's men as they continued their digging.

Thomas weighed heavily on her thoughts. He is truly gone from me, she told herself with a finality that wrenched her. She had considered her heart thoroughly broken before, but now it had shattered into a billion pieces.

The five women stood before the palisade all

night. Astrid spoke to the others when she saw one of them faltering, assuring them of their safety and their promised return on the morrow.

"It won't be long, Countess," one of the men said near dawn. "Our trench is dug, and we're filling it now."

Filling it? Astrid didn't understand. She heard frantic swishings behind her and glanced back to see them hoisting trees and shrubbery inside the ditch—a protective screen for them and a damnably clever strategy!

Her legs were becoming wobbly from exhaustion when Nathaniel Bacon approached her. "You may have the women returned to their homes, my brave countess," he said. "You have saved us this night, and I shall be eternally grateful to thee."

"I shall need Jeremy Robins, Peter Cook and Harold Nelson and their horses," she said. "We shall return the ladies at once." She hoped her strength would hold out for the short journey. Once back, she planned to go back to that quiet hill and sleep for 24 blessed hours. Everybody else was exhausted, too. Surely they'd postpone the battle until their troops were rested.

Marcy insisted on accompanying her on the trip to the Page home, walking beside the horse. Astrid sat astride in front of Mrs. Page. The black woman kept up a lively chatter "to keep the po' countess from falling asleep in dat saddle."

It was Marcy whose wide dark eyes witnessed the beginnings of Astrid's next and greatest challenge. Forced to stay back in the copse while Astrid and Jeremy walked Mrs. Page and Mrs.

Bray to the door of the house, Marcy watched with horror as a contingent of armed men ran from all directions and surrounded them.

Lord Percival Dunwoody walked through the door and stood laughing, his hands on his hips. "We have thee now, Hollander wench," he crowed. "They are waiting for thee in Jamestown."

Marcy stared from the trees. The two other ladies ran sobbing into the house. Lord Dunwoody swaggered over to the countess and spat in her face. The countess kicked and screamed but was held in the iron grip of the soldiers. "Leave the boy," the lord said, "but leave him dead. The wench is all we want," he ordered.

The soldiers holding Jeremy hit him hard over the head with their rifles and backed away as the boy fell to the ground. Astrid was tied and thrown across a horse, and the group started toward Jamestown.

When the men and their bundled trophy had left, Marcy ran from the copse to Jeremy. His head was bloodied, but the boy groaned. She lifted him and carried him to his horse, carefully placed him over the animal's back and pulled hard on the reins.

Marcy ran with all of her strength toward the Bacon camp.

Chapter Twenty-One

Thomas Arrington paced the length of the completed bulwark, battling with his thoughts.

Astrid is damnably strong-willed, she is, and stubborn beyond measure. Irritating, too, with her unbalancing effect on me. It has been thus since the day I first encountered her.

Different forces marched into his thoughts. Her courage, 'tis greater than most men; her inner strength, 'tis a complement to my own. Indeed, the woman almost single-handedly has made possible these defenses for the Bacon troops.

Thomas stopped and pressed his hands to his temples. Heavier artillery was being pulled into his head.

He heard her laughter, saw her frolic through the sparkling river, felt her delightful body rising to meet his caresses, responding, eager and unbelievably satisfying.

Thomas groaned. Trying to push her from his thoughts he joined in the preparations for war around him. He assisted a group of men who were moving a cannon into place, helped a lad prepare his musket, then checked his own weapons.

She wouldn't go away. Her face was in the blade of his sword, her laughter in the whisper of wind through the trees, her sparkle in the bright noonday sky, her love burning into his heavy heart.

Today I well may die, he thought, but without her I am already dead.

A decisive blast exploded within him. Thomas stood erect as the wrenching reverberations hammered into his soul. He knew with sudden clarity what he must do. I must go to her. I must ask her forgiveness for my foolish, blind obstinance. Astrid must know that my love for her is greater than all else in this mysterious universe. She must know my love for her is stronger than time itself.

With tears brightening his eyes, Thomas walked to the rear lines to find Astrid.

She wasn't with the women. "She 'asn't returned," Lucille Potts said as worried faces surrounded Thomas. "Peter and Harold came back more'n an hour ago," one of the women said, concern heavily weighing her words.

Thomas stiffened. "Did she go to the Page place?" he asked.

"Aye," they responded, their pale, uplifted faces nodding. "Wit' the lad Jeremy and the black woman named Marcy. The countess was sorely tired, Master Thomas, but she was determined to see the ladies safe at 'ome."

Thomas ran for his horse, leapt astride and sped north through the woods, leaving the tight circle of women in a cloud of dust.

His heart galloped faster than the hooves beneath him as he headed toward Middle Plantation. His keen eyes searched frantically through the blurred rush of trees for sight of her. Dear God, he prayed with heated fervor, let her come to no harm. Keep her out of danger, dear God.

When Thomas saw Marcy running toward him, he pulled back on his reins sharply. The wild terror in the woman's eyes struck him numb with fear.

The bloodied lad lay across the animal behind her. Thomas tightened his grip on the reins and narrowed his eyes, looking with desperate hope for another rider behind them.

Marcy's words tumbled out, rolled mercilessly over his tenuous hope and crushed it.

"Master Thomas! De countess has been captured!" she screamed. "Dey's taking her to Jamestown, a full dozen soldiers and 'dat evil Lord Dunwoody with 'em!"

Thomas dismounted and ran to the woman.

"Tell me all quickly," he ordered. He hurried back to Jeremy and cradled the limp head in his arms. The boy was unconscious, his sandy hair soaked with blood. "When did this happen? To Jamestown they're taking her? Are you sure, woman?"

Marcy nodded, great tears running down her quavering cheeks. "'Twas no more than an half-hour ago, Master," she said, trying to catch her breath. "I heard dat lord say to her 'Dey is waiting for thee in Jamestown, Hollander wench.' Dey tied her and flung her across a horse," she cried, "and dey headed south, going de back way toward the town."

Thomas took a linen from his pocket and wrapped the boy's head. "Take him to the general's physician with haste," he said. "I shall hie to follow the rogues."

Marcy's eyes widened with her panicky plea. "Kill 'em all and bring back our brave countess, Master Thomas."

"God willing, I shall, Marcy," he said, his jaws clenched. He mounted his horse. "Now hie, woman! We want Jeremy back with us also."

He dug his heels into the sorrel's side, slapped the reins hard and disappeared through the trees.

Marcy jerked the horse behind her into a fast run and led him strongly in the other direction.

Astrid ached with fear. She huddled in the corner of the one-room Jamestown jail. A dismal twilight permeated the room; two small, barred squares high on the walls were taunting reminders that light and air might exist somewhere in the world. The cold dampness of the dirt floor creeped through her skin, meeting her inner chill and locking her in an icy grip of hatred and terror. Her hands and legs were bound, the sleeves of her dress torn from her shoulders.

She was not alone. Percival Dunwoody stood over her, tormenting her with his arrogant, poisonous words.

"Revenge is sweet, my Hollander trollop," he said with a sneering smile. "E'en now they prepare the noose for your slender neck, and I shall watch with joy as you struggle beneath the coarse thick rope."

Astrid cringed, hating the man above her more than the coming pain of her death.

He chuckled, bending to let his fingers play across her throat. "Such a lovely neck," he crooned. "Made for caresses far gentler than a hangman's cold embrace."

Astrid wrenched away from his slimy touch and glared into his snakelike eyes.

"Unhand me, you bastard," she spat. "I prefer a noose to your loathsome hands!"

"Ah, and e'en yet she's a fiery wench, sparking my desire for the feel of her beneath me." He knelt beside her, running his moist, cold lips up her bare arm. The bristles of his mustache cut into her skin.

Astrid squirmed away from him, grunting her disgust.

"You cannot wiggle far enough from me, I vow," he said with a chilling laugh. "I have thee bound before me and shall toy with thee as I wish before they take thee away to an e'en worse fate."

He moved toward her.

*　*　*

Thomas dismounted outside Jamestown and stood in the shadows of the trees as he surveyed the scene before him. No guards protected the town, and few people were on the streets. There was no purpose in their strides, no visible signs that preparations were underway for battle. It was eerily quiet.

He braced himself and walked out into the sunlight. A lone guard stood outside the small brick jail. Thankful the man was a stranger, Thomas walked past him and tossed a friendly nod. The man looked sleepy and returned Thomas's nod with a vacant stare.

In the distance, Thomas saw a trio of men fastening a rope to a tree. They, too, were unknown to Thomas. New arrivals to the colony, he surmised. As he saw what they were doing, a sharp pang of dread penetrated his chest. He measured his steps, attemping nonchalance as he approached the men.

"And who be the deserving rebel that gets the noose this day?" he asked. The shadow of the rope fell across his face.

"A prize they have brought to us," one of the men responded with a chuckle, looking down from the tree at Thomas. "The Hollander countess was captured this morning, have you not heard? Remain for a while and you shall see us hang the beauty." Thomas tightened his fists.

"T'will be a spectacle fit for the eyes of thousands," a second man shouted from a heavy limb. "Only thousands no longer be here." He shook his head sadly. "A shame that be, when e'en the guv'ner himself won't see the good work we shall do with his final order 'fore leaving."

"The governor's departed?" Thomas asked.

"Aye, and most t'others, too. Slipped away to the Eastern Shore they have and abandoned the town to the fool rebels."

"But the rebels don't know it yet," the first man said. "We have time enough to complete our task."

"And where may the Hollander wench be awaiting your services, kind gentlemen?" Thomas asked, keeping his voice light.

"In the jail, o'course," one of the men said. "She has noble company for her last hours," he added with a crude laugh. "Providin' her with royal comfort, I s'pect."

Thomas felt sick as he eyed the squat brick building. At once he knew that time had suddenly become a serious matter, and it was running out for both Astrid and himself.

He restrained his impulse to storm the jail. He wished the men good day, promising them he would return "for I do not wish to miss your enticing afternoon performance," and walked slowly away. Only his heart raced.

Thomas ambled over to a small hill. Hidden by a clump of maples near the river, he gathered a quantity of red leaves that had fallen to the ground and heaped them into a large dry pile. He emptied a pouch of gunpowder in their midst. Suppressing the haste that surged impatiently within him, he tore a long-dead creeper vine from one of the trees and fashioned a fuse. Keeping low and out of sight of the hangmen, he slowly unwound the vine, pulling it carefully along the ground until he was at the back of the jail.

Taking two small flints from his pocket, he stooped and rubbed them together fiercely, hating his trembling fingers and cursing the endless seconds before the first feeble sparks dropped to the vine.

"I have thee bound before me and shall toy with thee as I wish before you are taken away to an e'en worse fate."

Thomas heard the polished voice ooze through the tiny window above his head. He stiffened, urging the sparks to ignite, praying for the dry vine to grab their fire.

At last, a small finger of flame began to creep forward, climbing painfully slowly up the low hill and back toward the trees. Thomas stood and pressed against the bricks. He held his breath, muttering a deep prayer.

The explosion tore through the warm air, rattling his teeth. Thomas stayed hard against the wall. The three hangmen whooped and jumped from the tree, scattering in panic toward the center of town.

Thomas waited. The guard scurried around the side of the jail, his gun aimed at the hillside where a ball of fire leapt through the trees.

Thomas moved fast. He slammed his rifle against the man's head, and the guard dropped forward, crumpling to the ground. Thomas ripped the ring of keys from the man's baldric and ran to the front of the jail.

As he pulled his sword from his sheath, he flung open the door.

Percival Dunwoody jumped to his feet, his startled eyes straining to focus on the man standing in the bright doorway. He blinked.

"Is that you, guard?" he said with a trembling voice. "What be the nature of the uproar out there?"

Thomas moved silently into the dim cell. Behind Dunwoody he saw Astrid, her face twisted with fear.

The blade of Thomas's sword glinted. "'Tis I, Thomas Arrington," he announced in a strong voice. "I have come for the woman."

Lord Dunwoody stepped back. Thomas heard the near silent whisper of a drawing sword.

He lunged forward, clashing his blade against the man's outstretched rapier.

The clang of steel against steel resounded through the cell.

"God rot thee in hell, Thomas Arrington!" the English lord snarled. His court-practiced fencing maneuvers defied Thomas's stronger thrusts.

Dunwoody's confidence grew. He danced sideways, coming close to laughter as the longer, finer steel of his blade fended away the Virginia man's sword again and again and teased it into false moves.

"Aha!" Dunwoody shouted, "I'll have at thee now, my rough fellow. You shall not have the Hollander strumpet. Instead you shall welcome soon the sharp point of my steel in your coarse heart." He maneuvered swiftly, thrusting the rapier toward Thomas's unguarded chest.

Thomas jumped to one side and snapped his sword across the man's deadly blade, lifting it into the air. Leaping forward, he plunged the sharp metal of his own sword deep between the man's ribs. Lord Dunwoody dropped his rapier. With a look of surprise, he fell to the cold earthen floor and groaned. A weak bubble of blood gurgled from his mouth. With but one spasm of final agony, the English lord lay still.

Astrid cowered in the corner. Bound by chains of terror as fully as by the ropes of the Berkeley men, she had seen everything that had happened but without comprehension. Unlinked thoughts rolled weakly through her paralyzed mind. *Percival Dunwoody is dead. There is light in the cell. Thomas is here.*

Thomas ran to Astrid and gathered her into his arms. "My rabbit," he cried, pressing his bearded face against her tear-stained cheeks. "Have they harmed thee?"

Astrid sobbed. She shook her head, holding it close to him. A soothing balm washed over her, spreading inside and softening the jagged pieces of her splintered heart. *Thomas is here. Thomas is calling me "rabbit."* One by one the scattered splinters began to float and join together. *Nothing again can ever harm me.*

He held her face, looking down into her eyes. "I love thee and ask thee for thy forgiveness," he said. "It matters not from whence you came. It only matters that you ne'er leave me."

She smiled through her streaming tears. "I love thee, Thomas," she whispered, "and I shall never leave thee."

He kissed her, and Astrid's heart, whole at last, sang a full-throated song.

"God's blood!" he exclaimed, staring at her head. "The dastardly rogues have shorn thee!"

"No, I cut it myself before I left Eagle's Crest," she said.

"Why, for God's sake?"

"To look like a lad," she answered, a sparkle in her swollen eyes.

He hugged her. "You were doomed to defeat, my sweeting. I would ne'er mistake thee for a lad."

Astrid longed to hold him, but she was trussed.

"I am bound, my love," she reminded him. "If you will free me from my fetters I shall provide thee with certain proof that I am a woman."

He laughed. "Not here, my hearty rabbit, though I long for thy evidence. We must get thee to safety outside of town." With his knife, he cut her bonds and lifted her into his arms.

"My horse awaits us. Let us return to the camp."

Astrid looked down at the stiff, curved body of the despicable Lord Dunwoody as they left the cell. She shuddered and held her arms tightly around Thomas's neck.

He ran with her through the deserted streets

and placed her with care on the back of the sorrel. Astrid remembered Jeremy with a jolt.

"Thomas, I think they have killed Jeremy," she said with a catch in her throat. "They beat him brutally at the Page place."

"Marcy has taken him to the camp's physician," he said, looking troubled. "We must pray the boy's youth and stamina shall be on his side."

Astrid and Thomas were greeted with cheers when they entered the Bacon encampment. Marcy immediately took her under her care. She was pale and too weak to walk, but her eyes shone with joy.

"Master Thomas has told thee of his love for thee, hasn't he, Countess?" the black woman asked with a smile as she carried Astrid to the quiet hill. Astrid nodded and leaned into Marcy's warmth.

After Thomas checked on Jeremy's condition and received the good tidings that the lad was conscious and asking for food, he ran to the front to tell Bacon that Jamestown was empty of people.

"The governor could not keep his weak troops together when they learned of our greater numbers and strength," he told the general and his officers. "He has lost some of his leaders, too, so the hangmen said. They didn't have the heart to fight against their fellow countrymen. The governor has retreated to the Eastern Shore with but a few of his most fervent loyalist supporters."

"Jamestown is ours!" the men shouted. "Without a shot we shall take it."

Bacon looked melancholy. "I have word that Giles Brent is coming from the north with a thousand men or more to move against us," he said. "We must burn the town and pull back to Gloucester to prepare for battle with them."

"Burn Jamestown, Nathaniel?" Thomas asked, astounded. "What is your purpose?"

"The governor must have no place to return to establish himself, and the great blaze this night will warn others that our force is a strong one. Perchance Brent and his men will be frightened away by the inferno."

William Drummond nodded his head. "'Tis an ideal plan, Nathaniel. I ask only that you allow me to save the town's records before you set the torches."

"Aye," Richard Lawrence said. "Jamestown must be burnt to the ground. I shall light the torch to my own house, for I see the good reason we must do this deed."

Thomas disagreed with vehemence. "You shall destroy the heart of Virginia with thy action, Nathaniel," he said. "The people's support for thee shall waver, for they love thee as a courageous leader and not as a firebrand."

"Jamestown will burn this night," the general said with dark firmness and turned his back on the group.

* * *

Wearily, Thomas walked back to the hill to be with Astrid. She was asleep. The women had covered her with a blanket and sat around her. Marcy stood when she saw Thomas.

"The countess needs us not with de Master Thomas here to watch over her," she said.

The women smiled, nodded and rose in unison. They sauntered down the hill to leave Thomas Arrington alone with his countess.

Thomas sat against the tree and gently moved the sleeping woman toward him, placing her head in his lap. He fingered the soft stubs of her golden hair and studied her streaked but peaceful face.

His lips moved in a soft whisper. "Astrid and I were meant for each other. I've accepted that truth and no longer concern myself with useless questions such as 'how did she come?' or 'why is she here?' 'Tis obvious why. The how doesn't matter. Our pasts are immaterial. There is only today and, I pray, a coming parade of even lovelier tomorrows."

Astrid opened her eyes and looked up into his glorious face. The setting sun glowed its radiance upon him.

"You set my journal to memory, Thomas?" she asked in a low voice.

He bent and kissed her cheek. "No, my rabbit, it was filled with words I could not or would not allow myself to comprehend. I set to memory only the important segments." He smiled into her eyes.

"Have two others ever loved as we now love?"

she asked, returning his smile and sitting up to put her arms around him.

"I think not," he replied.

She gave him a vigorous squeeze, belying her weakened condition. "That was indeed an important segment, my love."

They lay on the ground, savoring the close warmth of each other until they fell into a shared, exhausted sleep.

They woke near midnight, the chill of the early autumn evening drawing them closer to one another. Astrid opened one eye to assure herself her beloved was as real as he felt, hard and strong in her arms. His silver eyes were watching her, his sweet breath caressing her lips.

"I love thee, Thomas Arrington," she whispered nuzzling into his soft beard. Slowly she became aware of distant shouts, the sharp smell of burning timbers, and the ominous crackle of flames. Startled, she sat up and saw the angry red glow over Jamestown.

"Thomas, the town is burning!" she cried.

"I know." He pulled her down beside him. "The Bacon forces are burning the town and 'tis the end of the Arringtons' support of a misbegotten rebellion. We return to Eagle's Crest on the morrow and shall pick up the shattered pieces of our lives. The land shall endure, our love shall endure, and Virginia shall endure." When he held her close, she heard the muffled drums of his heart beating against her ear.

"Thomas," she whispered, "the time is not yet

ripe for rebellion. In a hundred years, in 1776, our great-grandsons will break away from England and will fight for and win their independence, and the country will someday reach to the Pacific Ocean and will be strong and mighty and . . ."

Thomas hushed her with his lips. "Say no more, dear rabbit. 'Tis not right I should know. There is only today . . ."

". . . and a coming parade of even lovelier tomorrows," she said, opening to his kiss.

Astrid and Thomas Arrington were wed at Eagle's Crest on October 3, 1676. The parson of the Varina Parish church officiated. Witnesses included Elizabeth, Ann, Edward and Lizzie Arrington, Joseph Whiteside and Jeremy Robins. Marcy, Jenny and Dorothy watched from the kitchen where they had prepared a feast "worthy of a king and queen."

Joseph Jeremy Arrington, the first of a goodly number of robust children, was born to the couple on April 8, 1677, Astrid Arrington's 28th birthday.

Today, the Curles Neck area of Virginia remains sparsely populated. Tangled forests mingle with open fields of weeds and pasture grass. In the summer, goldenrod and Queen Anne's lace carpet a particular hill overlooking the James River. The wildflowers frolic in the soft warm breezes.

It's said by residents of the area that on sparkling midsummer days chimes of bright laughter can be heard ringing through the air.

The phenomenon is accepted by the people who return again and again to the happy spot to picnic among the wildflowers.

There has never been an explanation.

Epilogue

Nathaniel Bacon died on October 26, 1676, probably of dysentery. He was 29 years old. His burial place is unknown. The rebellion that bears his name continued sporadically for less than three months under divided leadership.

Bacon's Rebellion ended officially on January 16, 1677. Governor William Berkeley, angered and bewildered by the turmoil, once again took over the reins of the Virginia colony. At least 13 rebels, including James Crews and William Drummond, were hanged for their participation in the uprising. More than 30 others were imprisoned.

King Charles II sent a commission to the colony to investigate the rebellion. The commissioners' report, relatively thorough and unbiased, reflected wrongs on both sides.

Thomasina Ring

A broken man, Governor Berkeley sailed for London on May 5, 1677, to plead his case with King Charles. He was never allowed an audience with the king. Berkeley died "of heartbreak" in England on July 9, 1677, at the age of 71. He is buried in Twickenham.

Historians are divided in their appraisal of both Nathaniel Bacon and Governor Berkeley; each man has been designated as hero by some and scoundrel by others. The truth possibly lies somewhere in between.

The "White Aprons" episode during the rebels' attack on Jamestown has been a source of controversy for more than 300 years. This "unchivalrous" use of women has been exhibited by Berkeley supporters as proof of Bacon's villainy. Bacon supporters have rationalized that the women were not harmed in any way, and, after all, the tactic worked.

Bacon's Rebellion, like a number of similar skirmishes in the early colonial days of America, planted seeds in the fertile minds of the people that the governed must have rights against unreasonable tyranny and should have a voice in their government.

Nathanial Bacon may have been the first orator in Virginia to speak of and to the people.

Patrick Henry, in the same colony, uttered ringing words with more lasting effect 100 years later.